TRADING TO THE DEEPS

TRADING TO THE DEEPS

THE MAGIC BELOW PARIS™ BOOK EIGHT

C. M. SIMPSON
MICHAEL ANDERLE

LMBPN

DISRUPTIVE IMAGINATION

Version 1.00, April 2020
ebook ISBN: 978-1-64202-907-9
Print ISBN: 978-1-64202-908-6

TRADING TO THE DEEPS TEAM

Thanks to our JIT Readers

Veronica Stephan-Miller
James Caplan
Diane L. Smith
Dorothy Lloyd
Kerry Mortimer
Larry Omans

Editor

SkyHunter Editing Team

DEDICATION

This is for all those who believed in me enough that, eventually, I had the courage to believe in myself.

Thank you.

—C.M. Simpson

To Family, Friends and
Those Who Love
to Read.
May We All Enjoy Grace
to Live the Life We Are
Called.

— Michael

A MORNING RENDEZVOUS

Marsh stood on the wall above the gate, watching the sunrise. Day came slowly, touching the craggy spires of the long-dead ruins with faint outlines of gold and pink. It was a spectacular sight, but it wasn't what she'd come for.

Somewhere to the south-east, her brother and his wife were already at work, and in the cavern above them, her uncle would be cursing his troops through their morning drill. The patrols from Ariella's Grotto would be securing the surface above their home, and the druids they'd lent would be working double-time to speed the growth of one last crop for Briar's Ridge.

In the fields beneath the castle wall, she could see their druids doing the same. Winter was coming, they said, and she had no reason to doubt it.

Beyond them, Mordan and her cubs were hunting. The kat was inordinately pleased to have her children back, even if they were mostly grown, and the kits were adjusting to having a mother again, which reminded her…

Aisha? Where are you? she asked, sending the thought through the link between them.

Nooowhere? The reply came back full of false innocence and carefully shielded so as not to give a single clue to the girl's whereabouts.

Don't make me come out there to find you! Marsh warned.

Couldn't! came back as fast as light and still shielded.

Merde, but the girl was getting good at controlling her mental abilities.

Wanta make a bet? Marsh asked, and proved she *could* put the sound of gritted teeth in mind-to-mind communication.

Silence followed.

"Ugh!"

A smothered giggle came through the link, followed by an all-too audible yelp of surprise...from the direction of the ruins.

"Dan! You put me down! Put me down, *NOW!*" Aisha's piercing shriek bounced off the ruined buildings and echoed through the rubble.

"That little rat!" Marsh exclaimed, picking a patch of shadow a hundred meters from the wall and stepping into it.

I'm coming, Mordan.

Aisha wailed again. "You are a bad kitty, and I don't...I don't *like* you anymore!"

Marsh could feel Mordan's amusement. She bolted in the direction of the kat's presence. *How was your hunt?*

There will be food for the winter, was the kat's satisfied reply, *and the cubs' skills are improving.*

The kat was standing in the hollowed-out lower floor

of a ruined building. Rubble formed small towers and a low barricade to the rest of the Desolation, except for the rear, where some of the upper floor remained. There were multiple exits leading to faint paths, and Marsh's heart beat faster. It wasn't the most defensible of positions.

Aisha dangled from Mordan's mouth. The little girl's arms were crossed, and fury filled her face.

When Marsh came to a halt before her, the kat dropped Aisha at her feet.

"Oh no, you don't!" Marsh grabbed her as the little brat tried to bounce away.

"But, I promised..." Aisha began and froze.

"Promised what?" Marsh demanded.

"Not to tell?"

"Uh-huh...but if you don't tell me, it's not going to happen," Marsh insisted.

Aisha frowned, and Marsh sensed a wisp of conversation she couldn't quite grasp.

"Aisha, you know that isn't fair, right?"

The child stuck out her tongue and shrugged Marsh's hand off her collar. When the woman reached for her again, she knocked the hand away, smirking.

"All's fair in love and war," she said, repeating one of Gustav's favorite sayings and stepping away.

Marsh lunged after her and ended up on the ground. Mordan fell beside her.

"Aisha!"

The child's giggle drifted back to them as Aisha scurried through a gap between two piles of rubble and disappeared.

She has learned much. Mordan's disgruntled tones echoed through Marsh's skull.

Roeglin? Marsh sent and was rewarded by his immediate response.

Yes?

I really *need a druid who can manipulate stone.*

Aisha? he asked, and Marsh was grateful for the concern in his voice.

She's fine for now, but she won't be when I get my hands on her.

Laughter sputtered along the link between them. *I'll be right there.*

And the druid?

I'll bring Brigitte.

The thought of what the shadow mistress would say made Marsh groan. *Do you have to?*

"Already done," Roeglin replied, and Marsh twisted her body to look back the way she'd come.

"Shadow-stepped," he explained.

"How'd you know where to look?"

"It wasn't hard to figure out," Roeglin explained, then relented. "I climbed to the top of the gate and looked for Mordan. I guessed if she wasn't out there chasing Aisha down, then she was in just as much trouble as you were."

As he spoke, Brigitte stepped out of a patch of shadow at the edge of the ruins. At first, her appearance made Marsh tense, but then she recognized the woman's sapphire eyes. They were the one thing that made it obvious she wasn't a shadow monster, despite her midnight skin and hair.

"Good morning, Marsh," she greeted her, crossing to

Mordan and laying a fingertip against the stone circling the kat's ankles. "She's getting sneakier."

"She did it without taking her eyes off my face," Marsh told her.

Brigitte finished what she was doing with the kat and approached Marsh.

"Ooh, that really *is* nice work," she observed. "I wonder if…"

Marsh groaned, and Brigitte chuckled.

"All right. Give me a moment, and I'll get you out of there."

Marsh waited, then felt the pressure of stone against her shins ease.

"So, how did she manage to do *that* without either of you noticing?" Roeglin wanted to know.

Marsh shook her head and scrambled to her feet, scanning the surrounding ruins. "I don't know, but I'll figure it out. She was *just* talking to us."

"So, she didn't do anything to your mind to prevent you from feeling it?"

Marsh glanced at Mordan. *Did she?*

The kat lashed her tail. *I do not think so, but the stone did not touch me until I moved.*

"It was the same with me," Marsh confirmed, and Brigitte nodded.

"She circled their feet with stone, but the stone did not touch their feet or ankles until they went after her," she confirmed.

Roeglin snickered. "That little wretch." His face sobered. "Do we know why she was out here?"

Marsh shook her head. "She would not tell me, and I

couldn't get a glimpse of what was going on inside her head. You've really helped her improve her shielding."

"But I haven't," Roeglin protested. "We've been focusing on drawing memories and turning them into pictures..."

Marsh stared at him. "You haven't been teaching her to shield?"

He shook his head.

"How about how to communicate with more than one person so one can't hear what she's saying to the other?"

His eyes widened. "That's an advanced skill!"

"So that wasn't you, either?"

"No," Roeglin replied, but the crunch of several pairs of boots on stone alerted them to the approach of others, and they turned.

Gustav came into the clearing and stopped. Izmay and Henri were not far behind him. He took in the situation with a sweep of his eyes and then scanned the perimeter. "Which way did she go?"

"Who?" Henri asked, then saw the remains of the stone shackles around Marsh's feet. "Oh." His brow furrowed with concern. "Is she okay?"

Marsh rolled her eyes. "Of course, she's okay. She gave us the slip and went that way."

"So, are we going after her?"

Mordan let out a rumbling growl and padded toward the exit Aisha had taken. When she reached it, she stopped and looked back at them over her shoulder. Her tail flicked with impatience, her ears flattened, and then she snuffed the air and stalked in the direction Aisha had taken.

Henri looked uncertainly from the kat to Marsh and

then at Gustav. "So, *are* we going after her? I mean, she's too little to be wandering out here all by herself."

Marsh stared at him.

Izmay snickered. "Oh, *sure* she is, and *you* can tell her that, 'kay, sweetie?" She patted his armored shoulder and trotted after the kat.

Gustav, Zeb, and Brigitte moved out after her. Henri hesitated, staring open-mouthed after them. He turned to Marsh.

"What did I do to deserve that?"

Marsh shrugged. "I dunno. Maybe you should ask her."

He gave an exasperated groan and followed Izmay and the others, leaving Marsh alone with Roeglin.

They exchanged glances.

"You coming?" Marsh asked, and Roeglin reached for her hand.

It wasn't hard to find the rest because Bristlebear and Silvermoth emerged from the bushes at the clearing's edge to show them the way.

That kat thinks of everything, Roeglin muttered, his words coming clearly over the link between them.

Mordan snorted, sending the impression of a disgusted tail twitch through their minds.

They chuckled, releasing each other's hands as they moved from a walk to a trot.

Aisha's trail led from where Marsh had found her and into a thicker cluster of ruined buildings.

I'll murder the little brat, Marsh muttered, slowing to duck through a ground-floor entry that was mostly intact but covered with vines.

I'll help, Roeglin offered, but his eyes were on the

narrow passage ahead of them, and he sniffed the air in much the same way the kat or a wolf would.

Marsh did the same. If there was one thing she'd learned, it was that ruins were like caverns. Each had their own distinct scent, indicating when a ruin was something's home or undermined by water and rot. This one smelled musty and abandoned, but otherwise okay.

Or as okay as any of these ruins were.

Marsh shuddered. The things that had happened in some of them had left echoes. She hurried forward until the tunnel gave way to a larger space. Enough sunlight filtered through holes in a distant ceiling to reveal a large inner chamber.

"Whoa," Roeglin breathed, turning his head to inspect it. "I wonder what this used to be."

"Who cares?" Marsh muttered, heading for the room's center. "She's over there."

Aisha stood at the end of the room, her small face screwed up in concentration as she called rivers of stone from the ground, dragging them over the existing walls and filling the myriad cracks and gaps she found along the way. The only exceptions were the windows—those she left clear.

Mordan and the kits were stalking the perimeter, ears twitching, as they snuffed at the myriad scents they found. The child was pointedly ignoring them, making smoothing motions with her hands as she repaired the walls.

Gustav, Brigitte, and the shadow guards had fanned out around her, covering the cats and the two remaining exits. Henri stood back, crossbow unslung as he eyed the darkened entrances coming off the balcony running several meters above the floor. Vines crept over the walls, but the floor remained clear of vegetation. Rubble was another matter.

"You couldn't have tidied up in here, could you?" Henri demanded, and Aisha flinched.

"Walls first," she told him, her small voice serious. "I like it here."

"Uh-huh. You gonna ask Roeglin what he thinks?" Henri wanted to know.

"Maybe." It was as good as a no, but the guard didn't argue. He looked around as Marsh and Roeglin stepped into the room. "You two took your sweet time."

Roeglin and Marsh ignored him as they picked their way through the fallen pieces of concrete and strewn rock.

"What are you doing out here, Aysh?" Marsh asked.

"Practicing," Aisha told her, and Roeglin snorted.

"Are too!" the child insisted, gesturing toward the wall. "See?"

"Sure, you are," Marsh replied, and put her hands on her hips, carefully surveying the area. "Now, tell me. What are you *really* doing?"

"Practicing!" Aisha repeated in a determined voice. She turned to the stairs. "See?"

Without waiting for an answer, she drew more stone from the ground, this time pulling the rubble into her construction. She kept one eye on what she was doing while warily regarding Marsh with the other.

Dan? Marsh asked, reaching along their link.

Others have been, was the hunter's short reply. *Human, a small pride...* She paused. *And Tok.*

At the mention of the mantid's name, Marsh stilled. *Is he still here?*

No. The kat looked around. *But he is not far.*

"Search the area," Marsh ordered. "We are being watched."

"Wanna give us a clue what we're looking for?" Henri made it sound like she was being deliberately obtuse.

"Wanna see what you can turn up?" Marsh snapped back.

2

MEETING ADJOURNED

The wolves slipped around the crumbled staircase, finding another opening behind it and plunging deeper into the ruin. The kits and Scruffknuckle made a quick circuit of the chamber and its perimeter before vanishing back through the entrance.

The shadow guards made their own check of the chamber and then looked up. Mordan followed their gazes.

"You want to fix those stairs for me, Aysh?" she asked.

The little girl crossed her arms and scowled. "Noooo."

"Well, will you do it anyway?" Marsh pressed.

Aisha gave a huff of breath and stomped her foot. She unfolded her arms. "Fine," she grumbled and began directing more stone from the rubble to move into the staircase.

"It's made of wood, you know," she said as if Marsh should have been aware of how impossible the task was.

"That's never stopped you before," Marsh reminded her and added, "and not *all* of it's made of wood, just the railing. You *can* fix that, can't you?"

Aisha gave a helpless wave of her hands and sat down. "Can't," she replied. "Too tired."

"We definitely have to look upstairs," Henri observed, and Aisha shot him a filthy look.

Roeglin chuckled. "Definitely," he agreed and walked to the deeper shadows at the foot of the stairs.

Aisha sighed and picked up a fragment of rubble, tossing it at the staircase. "Cheater."

Mordan stalked to the base of the stairs and shot the child a questioning look.

Aisha shook her head and stuck out her lower lip. "No."

The kat twitched her tail and leapt gracefully over the broken section to more solid footing.

"*Arschloch,*" the child muttered.

Henri walked over and stood behind her. He looked at Marsh. "You shadow mages go do your thing. Jakob and I will look after her."

"Can look after myself," Aisha argued, and promptly pulled a dome of stone over herself.

Henri stared at it wide-eyed. "Well, look who got up on the wrong side of the bed this morning!"

"Did not," came as a muffled echo from the dome. Marsh figured the child had left enough of a gap to listen through. She was going to be just fine.

Now to see what the little rat is hiding, she thought, studying the balcony above.

Roeglin and Mordan were moving cautiously along it from the end closest the stairs. Marsh looked at Brigitte.

"Other end?"

"Other end," the shadow mistress confirmed, and they headed for a deeper patch of shadow.

"Guess we'll take the center," Izmay declared, nodding at Zeb.

The gauze band she wore to protect her eyes from the sun was in place, but she still squinted against the sunlight coming in through the stone gaps above.

The balcony was in surprisingly good repair, Marsh noticed and racked her brains, trying to work out which of the nearby ruins it might be. There were some buildings that had weathered the passage of time better than others. The patrols used them as landmarks to guide them through the Devastation.

When it didn't come to mind, she focused on where she was searching. The balcony led into a long corridor with multiple doorways on either side. The chamber they'd come through was probably a huge entry hall. For what, she couldn't imagine.

Either way, it gave them more to search, and they didn't have all day. She glanced at Roeglin and he shrugged, moving toward a large block of stone that partially blocked the balcony. When he stopped and cocked his head, and Mordan sank to her belly and began creeping around the other side of the boulder, Marsh called a sword and buckler to her hands.

Beside her, Brigitte did the same. Izmay and Zeb had already moved into one of the corridors and were cautiously approaching the first door. Izmay glanced back and saw them arming. She tapped Zeb and jerked her head in their direction.

Zeb nodded, and the pair of them drew weapons from the dark. He and Izmay moved away from the door, and they backed up so they had a wall behind them while they watched what was happening. Marsh dipped her head in acknowledgment and got ready to defend Roeglin if she needed to.

Mordan chose that moment to pounce, then Roeglin surged forward, and Marsh tensed.

There was a startled squawk, and Mordan tried a midair pivot to turn back on herself. At the same time, a small figure dove away from the back of the boulder. Roeglin skidded to a halt, jerking his blade up and away.

"Tamlin!"

Mordan landed with a thump and rumbled a protest, stalking past.

"Tamlin?" Aisha's piping voice was part question and part outrage.

Marsh released her blade to the shadows and walked over to the boy. "Care to explain?"

He gestured toward his sister. "Someone has to keep an eye on her. You *know* what she's like!"

"Hey!" Aisha protested. "I'm *right* here."

"I know," Tamlin replied, "and you're a pain in the ass."

"*Hey!*"

"If the shoe fits," Roeglin put in, dispelling his sword.

Marsh cocked her head. "So, what's your sister *really* been doing here?"

Before the boy could reply, the soft sound of movement rustled in the corridor opposite. They all pivoted, weapons appearing from thin air as a tall, thin shape moved out of a darkened hollow to where they could see it.

"Tok!"

The mantid twitched its eyes, and an apologetic shudder rippled over its body.

I am sorry.

Tok! Aisha's squeak of alarm was a dead giveaway.

Marsh walked to the edge of the balcony and looked from the child to the mantid.

"Care to share?" she asked, knowing the bug would pull the meaning out of her head anyway.

"Practicing." Aisha still sounded sullen. She folded her arms and gave Marsh a rebellious look.

"Practicing what?" Roeglin wanted to know.

We are practicing mental magic. Tok intervened. *She grasps the concepts quickly, and her mind-walking required supervision.*

Marsh didn't ask how the bug had discovered that.

We did not ask permission to help, just as we did not ask permission to guard your mind while you slept, Tok explained.

"I beg your pardon?" Marsh snapped, cutting him off before he could go any further.

When you sleep, Tok added by way of explanation.

How do you know that?

Your cries echo through the ruins.

Marsh shot Roeglin a look of alarm.

He nodded. *They do.* He frowned. *Or they did.*

He regarded Tok with mild curiosity. *Your sleep has been undisturbed since two days after you returned.*

He raised an eyebrow. *Did you do that?*

The mantid inclined its head. *We have assigned guardians to ensure she is undisturbed.*

Marsh stared at him, open-mouthed. "Why would you do that?"

After all, it wasn't like her cries were keeping the mantids awake.

"Yes," Henri asked from the ground floor. "What makes her so special that she needs her sleep protected?"

Izmay cleared her throat, and he glanced up at her.

"Not that the rest of us don't appreciate it," he hastily added. "I *like* sleeping through the night."

Marsh hung her head, and Roeglin chuckled. Tok's thoughts reflected amusement.

Gustav cleared his throat. He was staring up at Tok from beside Aisha, his flame-wreathed sword in his hand. "Someone want to introduce us?"

Marsh arched an eyebrow. "You don't remember?"

Gustav shook his head.

"These guys helped rescue us from the remnant that attacked just before we arrived."

Gustav's eyebrows rose, and he shuffled back a couple of steps so he could get a better view of the mantid. Tok stepped forward into a ray of sunshine, and the guardsman gasped.

Marsh watched tension run through his frame, and watched as he assimilated the idea that the monster standing in the upper balcony might be a friend. After a minute, he glanced at Roeglin and cleared his throat.

"So, Shadow Master, when were you going to introduce them to the rest of us?"

Roeglin's jaw dropped, and he glanced at Marsh.

She managed a tight smile and a shrug. "Maybe sooner would be better."

Gustav stared at her. When he saw he'd gotten her attention, he glared. "Darned right it would be better. We've all heard about the battle, and we're all pretty frustrated that the people who were there keep avoiding the answers."

He looked at Tok. "No offense. I can see why they might, but we've all heard about the rescue, and there's more than a few of us as would like to say thanks."

No offense taken. Your reaction and the frustration expressed by your nestmates are similar to views expressed among my people. Tok's answer came as a surprise.

The mantid's eyes swept forward to focus on Marsh and Roeglin.

We need to let our peoples meet. I believe the meeting will be less stressful than we at first believed.

Again, Roeglin's gaze slipped toward Marsh. *What do you think?*

Again, Marsh shrugged. *I don't see the harm.*

"Very well," he said aloud for everyone's benefit. He looked at Tok. "Will three days from now suffice? You and I change the time if it is not."

"Your place or mine?" Henri whispered sotto voce and snickered.

Izmay groaned, but Roeglin laughed, and Tok clattered his mandibles to signify amusement.

I believe it would be better if we were to visit you, Tok replied. *You would be better able to control the area and keep your people safe.*

And you? Roeglin asked. *How do we guarantee your safety?*

The risk will be ours, Tok assured him. *If things go wrong, we will flee.*

Marsh shivered. *I do not want things to go wrong.*

Your people have forgiven much worse than a different appearance, Tok reminded them, and Marsh had to agree.

I will speak with you, Roeglin promised.

And I with you, Tok agreed, *although that is not the matter of most concern.*

"It isn't?" Roeglin sounded like Marsh felt.

Unfortunately, no. You see, I coordinate the child's morning lessons with my return from delivering our trade, and today I would have had to speak to you since your trade is not present, Tok explained.

"It wasn't?" Gustav broke in. "But I set it out myself."

Nevertheless, Tok reiterated, *it was not present upon my arrival. I left our goods regardless but thought it best to draw the matter to your attention.*

"We'll look into it," Marsh assured him. She turned to Roeglin. "I'll take Gustav, Brigitte, and the apprentices and report back to you. We've kept you from your duties long enough."

He was going to have to call those from the caravan together, along with the other community leaders who hadn't been present—and he would probably need to show the leaders the kind of guest they were expecting. She wasn't equipped to do that.

As much as she wanted to, her ability to communicate mind to mind was limited, and she had yet to master the ability to weave memory and shadow to recreate events that had already passed. That and Roeglin didn't need her presence.

Nor could he be in two places at one time.

"Agreed." Roeglin nodded toward her and then shadow-stepped to the ground floor.

He knelt in front of Aisha. "You and I and Shadow

Mistresses Petitfeu and Leclerc are going to discuss your training."

"And Tams," the girl told him, folding her arms and pursing her lips.

Roeglin hesitated. "Fine, and Tams."

Marsh heard the boy's sigh of relief.

I will return to the nest, Tok told them. *We have crops to harvest and must work to expand the growing caverns.*

Mordan gave a grunting rumble, and the mantid cocked his head.

Your friend is impatient to investigate, and I am reminded that my people would also like to thank the creatures that assist our hunts and supply the meat you provide in trade.

He looked at Roeglin. *I will return now, but my mind will be open to your contact.*

"No fair!" Aisha wailed. "We're not done!"

The mantid hesitated, then leapt over the balcony's edge to land lightly beside Roeglin and the child. Marsh noticed that Henri's and Gustav's hands dropped to their weapons but stopped and rested there.

I am afraid we must be, Tok told the little girl. *There are other matters that require our attention, and I have introduced you to the skills you need to master. I expect you to practice them before the dawn.*

Aisha cast a sly glance toward Marsh and Brigitte. "But they aren't supposed to know."

I think they know now, and you will have to show them what you have learned so they can know it, too. You will have to show them.

Aisha's face lit up. "Really?"

Marsh, Brigitte, and Roeglin all nodded solemnly.

"After lunch," Roeglin informed her. "I will meet you in the Great Hall, and you will show us then."

"And only us," Brigitte added. "We need to see what you are learning so we can decide if we should ask Master Tok for help with *our* training."

Roeglin sighed. "I will add it to the things we need to speak about," he told the mantid, and Tok's amusement rippled through their minds.

The mantid inclined his head in farewell before taking several steps back and turning toward the entrance.

Until then, Shadow Master.

3

MISSING ITEMS

M arsh, Tamlin, and the shadow guards watched the mantid leave and then descended from the balcony. It was nothing for them to step from the shadows there to the shadows on the ground floor.

"I need to return to the Library," Roeglin admitted.

His face was troubled as though he hated not following through on the investigation.

"I'll report back as soon as we have an idea what's going on."

"Do you think it's remnant?" Henri asked, and Marsh shook her head.

"No, Tok would have said."

"Well, we *hope* he would have said," Henri corrected sarcastically. "Who knows *what* those things deem worthy of reporting?"

Marsh couldn't tell if the man was joking or serious, but Izmay groaned and slapped his arm.

"Don't be difficult, Henri. You know he would."

Henri turned to her with raised eyebrows. "Do I?"

"Ugh. You know you would."

Roeglin looked from them to Gustav and Brigitte. "Go with her."

He shifted his attention to Marsh. "Take the kids, kats, and Scruffknuckle."

Marsh nodded and turned toward the entrance. "Dan!"

The kat had settled on the balcony, but she raised her head and rose to her feet. As Marsh walked out, Aisha and Tamlin in tow, she leapt gracefully down to join them. The kits and Scruffknuckle emerged from the shadows and wove around them before leading the way out of the ruin.

This is a useful space. Roeglin's voice reached her along their link.

Agreed, Marsh replied. *What do you want it for?*

I don't know, but winter is coming, and it would be good to have a place for the mages to practice that isn't under everyone's feet.

He meant a place where the mages couldn't break anything or accidentally target a civilian with lightning or a stone shard, and they both knew it. Still, he had a point. The hall would be an ideal space for them to practice in, and the smaller spaces on the upper floor would be good for other classes.

We'll discuss it when I get back, she told him.

Deal. He paused, but she could feel him thinking. *It would also be a good neutral space for any classes the bugs might want to hold.*

You think that's a good idea? Marsh asked.

We'll know when Aisha shows us what he's taught her. Roeglin told her. *Without a mental mage to help us, we're kinda lost.*

And it's getting dangerous, Marsh finished for him.

"Marsh, we need your head out here." Gustav's voice interrupted their conversation.

Happy hunting, Roeglin told her by way of farewell.

Marsh blew him a mental kiss and blinked back to reality. She'd made her way through the tunnel to the entrance without registering a single step.

Gustav had drawn them to a halt in a sheltered corner just outside. He watched as Marsh blinked her way to reality and focused. "You want to deal with this?" he asked.

"With what?" Marsh questioned and then realized she should have known.

Aisha wasn't happy. She'd stopped in front of them. When she caught Marsh looking at her, she stuck out her tongue.

"You wrecked my day," she declared with all the righteous fury of a six-year-old whose world had gone severely wrong.

Marsh raised her eyebrows. "I what?"

"You heard," the child snarled. "I had *lessons.*"

"You had lessons with *me,*" Brigitte scolded. "Now I know why you've been so tired this week."

"Have not!" Aisha snapped. "Been fine. Been *busy.*"

She said that last word with a meaningful glance at Marsh, and Marsh realized the child was having a go at her for having so much on her plate. She couldn't help shooting a glance at Tamlin, and he cocked an eyebrow in reply.

Smartasses! she thought but wasn't successful in keeping it to herself

Rude! Aisha retorted.

"We'll talk about this when we get back." Brigitte's voice was firm.

Aisha shot her a dark glance, and Brigitte caught her gaze and held it. After a long moment, the little girl huffed a sigh and scuffed her foot.

"*Bien,*" she agreed, and Marsh breathed a sigh of relief.

She was going to have to ask Brigitte for pointers. The shadow mistress seemed to have ways of convincing the children to agree with her that Marsh had no idea how to tap. It made her wish she had a link with the shadow mistress similar to the one she had with Roeglin.

"Shall we?" Gustav asked, his tone suggesting they'd kept him waiting long enough.

There wasn't a single word of thanks to either Marsh *or* Brigitte for talking Aisha down.

Tamlin rolled his eyes behind the guardsman's back, and Marsh stifled a smile. Mordan grumbled at them all and stalked into the nearest stand of bushes, where she disappeared from view. Perdemor and his siblings copied her, and Scruffknuckle bounded in their wake.

Marsh nodded to Gustav. "We shall."

She led the way back out to the road and then to where the trade goods had been laid.

They'd chosen a place equidistant between the Library's walls and the cluster of ruins that marked the entrance to the mantids' "nest." A short track led off the main thoroughfare into what had been the ground floor of a set of shops or joined houses.

The walls between each individual dwelling had long ago given way to decay, and only the stouter outer walls remained. The people from the Library had shaped the rubble into low stone walls and added stout lengths of wooden fencing.

It wouldn't stop raiders or a band of remnant, but it would slow them down long enough for anyone in the compound to seek shelter on one of the ledges created from the reinforced skeleton of the floor above.

The druids from Ariella's Grotto had done a first-class job of creating an area that was open and sheltered at the same time. The arrangement with the mantids meant that they didn't need more than a space where goods could be left for the short time it took for the exchange to be made.

Gustav's people took the Library's trade goods down to it just after the gates opened at dawn and returned at midday to collect what had been left in their place. Today was the first day something had gone wrong.

Marsh muffled a snort. If she thought about it, they'd been lucky to have a whole week before something had gone wrong.

Mordan was circling the enclosure, the kits and the pup at her side. All four of them had their noses to the ground, their ears twitching as they took it in turns to lift their heads and survey the world around them.

Humans, Mordan informed them, raising her head long enough to catch Marsh's eye. *Strangers.*

"Raiders?" Marsh asked.

No. Prey.

Marsh shuddered at the kat's assessment. It was one thing when she classified people as "pride" or "pack," quite another when she called them prey.

I guess you can take the kat out of the Deeps, she thought, *but you can never take the Deeps out of the kat.*

A sense of puzzlement came through her link with Mordan.

I chose to come out of the Deeps, and I have never been a home for them, the kat informed her, and then turned her attention to the matter at hand. *Their trail is clear.*

Looking at the ground in front of where the kat was standing, Marsh could see her point. Faint scuff marks showed where someone, or something, had passed. Following the bent stalks of grass, Marsh spotted the partial print of a shoe.

A shoe? She bent and studied it more closely. *Who in all the Deeps wears shoes out here?*

Even the farmers from Briar's Ridge wore sturdy leather boots.

Gustav came alongside her and stared intently at the ground. "Odd footwear for raiders."

"And remnant don't wear shoes," Tamlin, and hastily added as his sister opened her mouth to argue, "Not usually, anyway."

Aisha closed her mouth and scowled at him. Seeing the child's grouchy face reminded Marsh of something.

"Aisha, you want to scan for other minds?"

Aisha's face brightened. "People's or *everyone?*"

"How about you see what you can find and tell me what's out there?" Marsh suggested.

"Can I peek?"

"Peek at what?" Marsh wanted to know.

"Inside," Aisha replied, and Marsh realized the little girl was asking permission to look into someone else's mind without their permission—something Marsh kept telling her *not* to do.

"Just this once," Marsh agreed, and Aisha clapped her hands excitedly.

Tamlin groaned and rolled his eyes. "You know you've created a monster, right?"

Marsh figured that might be the case, but they needed to know who else was out here and why, and she didn't think the people who'd taken the trade goods would tell them.

"They went this way," Gustav called from the edge of the trading area.

He kept his voice soft, and Marsh felt Mordan's approval of the man.

He is not a bad hunter, for a human, the hoshkat informed her. *If you did not already have a mate, I would consider that one a suitable candidate.*

Marsh's face burned hot, and Gustav raised his eyebrows in question.

"Never you mind," she told him, and Aisha giggled. "And don't you tell him."

"Tell me what?"

"Never you mind," Marsh repeated, and changed the subject. "Which way did they go?"

His lips crinkled with amusement, and he climbed the fence, jumping down on the other side. "This way."

Marsh followed and then watched as Mordan, the kits, and Scruffy leapt onto pieces of rubble on the inside and soared over.

So much for keeping wild animals at bay, she thought and made a note to suggest removing similar blocks of rubble from close to the outside of the fence.

Tamlin and Brigitte watched her climb the fence and then shadow-stepped past her to the other side.

Smartasses.

They chuckled. Aisha's frustrated tone stopped them mid-laugh.

"Like that, huh?" the little girl declared. "Well, *bien!*"

"Uh-oh."

Marsh didn't need Tamlin's murmur to warn her that Aisha was about to do something she might not like. She watched as the child stalked over to the stone wall and rested her hand against it.

"Aisha..." she began, but it was too late.

The stone parted beneath Aisha's fingers, creating a gap large enough for the child to pass through.

"What!" the little girl snapped, joining them.

"You put that back the way it was," Marsh ordered.

"You say 'please,'" the child shot back.

Marsh sighed. "Fine! *Please* put that back the way it was."

"Okay," Aisha chirped happily and skipped back to the wall.

She laid her hand on the wall, and seconds later, there was no sign she'd ever made a pathway through it.

"You're just lucky you didn't break the fence," Tamlin told her. "Evan would have been *really* disappointed."

Aisha's face fell.

"I didn't mean to," she answered, and hurried back to scramble up the wall and check the fence for damage.

"Not broken," she reported back, sounding relieved.

Marsh studied her. "What other minds did you find?" she asked.

Aisha put her hands on her hips. "What lifes did *you* find?" she challenged.

Marsh raised an eyebrow. The kid was all attitude this morning!

Tamlin laughed. "Yeah, *shadow mistress,* what did the shadows reveal when you asked them?"

Marsh fixed him with a glare. "I thought I'd leave asking the shadows up to you," she answered, and his jaw dropped open.

Gustav snorted. "I just want you all to hurry up and tell me what's out there. The longer you delay, the more of a head start they get."

Marsh and the children all rolled their eyes in unison.

"Fine, then," Aisha said and walked up to the warrior. "Make sure I don't fall over."

She sounded so much like Marsh that Gustav stared at her, but Aisha didn't wait for his reply. Instead, she sat down beside him, leaned on his leg, and closed her eyes.

Marsh followed her example, although she did it from where she was standing, and she kept her eyes open. She might not have been able to sense other minds, but she *could* sense other life forces, and she'd done it enough to keep an awareness of her surroundings while she did it.

Well, she was working on it. She swayed and sat on a chunk of concrete. Tamlin snickered, but he chose another piece of rubble to sit on before he searched the air around him for what it might also touch.

"We should have done this at the trade table," he observed. "We might have been able to see what they looked like."

Because the air too held memories sometimes. Marsh

registered the light breeze touching her cheek and doubted they'd have had any luck. The air on the surface was much more *unstable* than the air on the ruins

It would be quicker if we continued the hunt, Mordan grumbled, and Marsh had to agree.

While she had sensed a myriad of small lives around them, she had found nothing as large as the kat's and nothing that resembled a human's life.

"Nothing," she informed them just as Tamlin spoke.

"Nothing here, either."

"Something that way," Aisha announced, pointing west of the Library. "Maybe people, but I can't hear them. They're too far away."

"Which way do the tracks go?" Marsh asked, and Gustav shrugged.

"They took to the rocks," he admitted.

Mordan huffed out a sigh *They went...* she started, but Scruffknuckle bounced past with a happy yap.

He stopped long enough to sniff the ground at Gustav's feet, jumped up on a nearby rock and cast about again, and then leapt down to the stony ground on the other side. With a brief dip of his nose, he bounded into the ruins.

"Pup says that way," Gustav declared, scrambling after him.

Mordan didn't dignify that with a reply, and the others followed.

I wonder how far they went? Marsh thought as Aisha laid her hand on the rock and had it move aside rather than having to climb over.

She said nothing, just let the child catch up and walk alongside her.

"Are we going the right way?" she asked as they crossed an open space leading to a ruin several floors high.

Aisha nodded, her blue eyes solemn. "Up dere," she answered, dropping back to baby speech as she always did when she was worried.

"You know how many?"

Aisha frowned and shook her head.

"Rocks make it hard," she explained

Marsh searched her link with Mordan and discovered the child was right. The link was there, but it wasn't as strong as it usually was.

"Stay with me," she ordered and hurried to relay the news to Gustav.

4

BORROWED ITEMS AND
DISRUPTED PLANS

Gustav crouched in the shadows at the bottom of the stairs. He was waiting for Marsh, even as Mordan was making her silent way up the staircase, her two kits in tow.

"What took you?" he whispered when Marsh and Aisha settled in beside him. Aisha tucked in close to Tamlin and Brigitte.

Marsh ignored the question. "Aisha says up."

He nodded. "Kat does, too."

Marsh glanced after the kat and was in time to see her tail disappear onto the landing above.

"How far up, Aysh?" she asked.

The little girl screwed up her face, closing her eyes to concentrate.

"Not the next floor. Maybe the one—two?—after it."

Dan, did you get that?

The kat sent agreement over their link. It was fainter than it should have been, given how close she was. Marsh nudged Gustav.

"The building is interfering with mental magic," she informed him. "We'll need to rely on our other senses."

"You mean, like a normal person?" he asked, the hint of a smile on his lips.

"Something like that," she told him and shifted away. "Is this the only way up?"

"That's what the kat seemed to think," Gustav replied. "She made a circuit of the ground floor before she decided on the stairs. I got the impression there was only one way up."

Marsh hoped he was right, and slowly made her way up to the next level.

Her link to the kat was clearer there, and she breathed a soft sigh of relief.

Dan?

I am this way, the kat replied, and Marsh got the impression of a corridor to her left and then another staircase. She stopped and focused on becoming one with the shadows.

"Where'd she go?" Gustav's whispered confusion drifted after her.

"Shadow-walking," Tamlin told him, adding wistfully, "I wish she'd show me how."

"I thought you could already shadow-step," Gustav said.

"No, shadow-*walking*," Tamlin repeated. "She becomes like a shadow herself. One of the monastery's scouts taught her how."

"Do you think she'd show me?"

"She could, but it wouldn't mean you could do it."

"I'd like to try, anyway," Gustav told the boy. "*That* could come in handy."

"We can ask her," Tamlin answered as Marsh drifted out of earshot.

Refusing to think about how she was going to teach the pair of them how to shadow-walk, she focused on the corridor ahead. It wasn't long before she heard other voices.

These were hushed and anxious. They were also unfamiliar.

"I don't think we've got anything," came one hoarse whisper as Marsh drifted through the corridor.

It sounded like an older man, perhaps someone around Gustav's age, or Master Envermet's. It was hard to tell. Marsh forced herself to focus on remaining one with the shadow. She needed to get closer.

Her targets remained oblivious and continued talking.

"So, why'd you take it, then?" The woman sounded around the same age as Aisha's mother, but sharper-tongued and a lot less patient.

The man gave an impatient grunt. "Look at us! We're not thieves. We're starving!" His voice softened. "And I was sure we'd figure something out."

The woman glanced up just as Marsh drifted through the door. "Well, figure it out fast, because we're not alone."

Marsh chose a patch of shadows on the other side of the room and stepped into the darkness of the corner, vanishing from view. It was hard to remain blended with the shadows, and Marsh nearly lost her grip on them as she stepped clear.

To her surprise, the people in the center of the room kept their eyes fixed on the doorway, their bodies tense as they listened to the dark. Marsh listened with them, and finally registered what they'd picked up, before—the soft sound of footsteps coming down the hall.

"Get the door," the man murmured, but the woman shook her head.

"It's too late for that," she replied and laid a hand on the shoulder of the young woman crouched beside her.

The girl shrugged it off, frantically digging through her pack.

"Maybe if I can find something to offer them so they won't be mad at us."

The man snorted, nudging the pile of shrooms stacked to one side. "Somehow, I doubt it."

"Well, you didn't *have* to take them all," the woman sniped. "It's not like we're going to be able to carry them far."

He sighed. "I was figuring we'd cook most of them before we left and eat a few more. There aren't *that* many."

Marsh wanted to disagree with him. They'd taken three crates of shrooms. It didn't matter how hungry they were, or what they cooked them into, the woman was right: they were probably *not* going to be able to carry everything they'd taken.

He didn't look like he was in the mood to listen, though. His eyes flashed angrily, and he curled his hands into fists. He didn't argue, however. Instead, he moved so that he stood between the two women and the door.

Others moved out of the corners of the room, and Marsh realized the group was bigger than she'd thought. Three younger men came out of an adjoining room. None of them was armed beyond the short, stout lengths of wood they carried.

One of them looked at the crates.

"I haven't got anything in my pack beside my blankets and my eating equipment," he said, "and I don't think they'll want any of those."

Marsh stayed still and quiet, letting herself slip from the shadows to a more solid form, and waited. In the corridor outside, she could hear Gustav's footsteps coming closer. The older man and three younger ones moved closer to the door.

Marsh bit her lip, resisting the temptation to call out a warning. Gustav was an old soldier. He'd know better than to come through the door without checking first. She pushed aside the thought that neither Aisha or Tamlin was very old and that they were *both* likely to come through the door without checking.

What she didn't expect was Mordan.

The kat came through the door at an angle, knocking one of the younger men off his feet as she passed.

The woman screamed, and one of the men shouted in dismay. The girl scrambled back, taking her pack with her until she fetched up against the wall. Her eyes were wide with fear, and her gaze didn't leave the kat as she pivoted and came to a halt beside Marsh.

The girl stared at the kat, then noticed Marsh.

"Who are you?" she demanded. "And how did you get in here?"

The older man slid a glance at Marsh but kept his attention on the kat.

"When did *you* arrive?" he demanded. His eyes narrowed. "And what do you want?"

Movement at the door signaled Gustav's arrival. "I

think she wants to ask you what you're doing here and why you took our trade goods," he stated, answering the man's question. "I'd kinda like to know that, too."

Marsh noticed that he hadn't drawn any weapons, but Perdemor came to stand in the door beside him.

"What are you?" the man demanded, studying Gustav intently. "Are you some kind of druid or something?"

"Or something," Gustav replied.

He made a show of looking at the others gathered in the room, but the woman didn't give him a chance to ask any more questions.

"Are you raiders?" she asked, her eyes wide in her pale face.

Gustav snorted, his lip curling in scorn. "No. Them, we killed about a month back."

He glanced at Marsh. "Or was it longer? I forget. It's been a while."

"We killed the ones in the Library about a month ago," Marsh agreed, "and I took out the rest of them the week before last."

She looked at the strangers gathered in the room. "Is this all of you?"

The oldest man made a show of looking around and then nodded. "Yup. Looks like it."

"Not true." Aisha's piping voice lanced through the room. "There are two, no *four* more."

The strangers looked at each other, their eyes wide.

"Mind-walker," Gustav supplied before any of them could comment.

"Sounded like a child." The man grunted.

"Am not a child!" Aisha shouted. "Am six, no, *seven*!"

That brought fleeting smiles, some of which remained when Tamlin's voice was heard.

"Six, Aisha. It's not nice to lie."

"Seven." The little girl's mutter was just audible, but the strangers were already turning back to Gustav.

"What do you want with us?" the woman asked. She indicated the packs in front of her. "We were looking for payment."

Gustav cast a questioning glance at Marsh.

She nodded. "It's true, but what I want to know is what they're doing here." She turned to the woman. "I mean, you're clearly not raiders, so what are you?"

"Travelers!" the man broke in quickly. "We're travelers."

"Refugees?" Gustav asked, studying their worn clothes. "Where from?"

"Scruffy, fetch!" Aisha's voice interrupted the conversation, and the pup barked in reply.

Perdemor vanished from beside Gustav, but the soldier ignored him.

"We won't harm them," he said as the men moved toward him.

"We don't know that," one of the younger men snarled.

He swung his club, and Gustav jumped back.

"Have we hurt you?" he demanded, drawing his sword and setting it alight.

The younger man stepped back. "You're a mage?"

Gustav shook his head. "Not by a long shot."

"I am, though," Marsh told them and dropped a shadow dome over the woman.

She squawked in alarm and protest, but Marsh wasn't concerned. She was more worried about the two men turning toward her. While she could drop a dome over each of them, she didn't want to. She needed to restrain them. That became a lot harder when fire appeared in the hands of one of them.

"*You're* mages?" she asked, calling a shield to her arm.

It materialized in time for her to raise it and stop the fireball aimed at her head.

"Why else do you think we left Arcadia? It's not safe for the likes of us."

"Arcadia? Like in the stories? Where in the surface world is it, anyway?"

She blocked another fireball. A shadow dome was looking really good right now, but she'd still have to fight them when the domes came down. What she really wanted to do was tie them up and stop them from making the gestures they needed to get the magic to answer their demands.

The second man came at her with a sword, so she pulled her blade from the shadows and parried his first thrust. It took her a moment to pull more shadow and add a layer of armor to her body, and she deflected three more attacks while she did it.

She needed to do something similar to her opponents but not armor, more like rope. Holding her foes at bay and resisting the urge to return their attacks and teach them a lesson, she called on the shadows.

"Bind them," she commanded, wrapping dark tendrils around their arms and shoulders.

"Blind them," she added, dropping miniature domes over their heads as she wound shadows around their feet.

It was hard to do with her sword in her hand, but with

their arms bound, she was able to release both sword and shield. With their feet bound, they toppled to the floor.

"A little help?" Gustav said, seeing she was free.

He was holding the doorway against the other two men and doing his best not to harm either. It was hard, given he hadn't unslung his buckler and had only his blade to defend himself with.

Marsh nodded, looping shadows around his opponent's feet and drawing them tight with a flick of her wrist. They shouted in alarm and fell, even as Marsh wrapped their arms and torsos.

"Excuse me." Tamlin's voice made Gustav look over his shoulder.

What he saw made him step hastily out of the doorway.

"By all means," he told the boy, and Marsh was surprised when Tamlin and Aisha walked into the room.

Tamlin had his hand wrapped firmly around Aisha's arm, and the little girl's eyes were sheeted white. Marsh watched as Tamlin guided his sister across the room. They were followed by four more figures.

When they'd reached the other side, Aisha turned to the people following and gestured sharply at the floor in the center of the room.

"Sit!" she commanded.

The four strangers sat, their faces turned expectantly toward the child.

"Stay right there," Aisha ordered, and the white left her eyes. She swayed and leaned against her brother. "All good?"

Tamlin wrapped an arm around her and led her over to the edge of the room behind Marsh. He gestured at the people they'd brought in. "You wanna do the same with these guys?"

His voice jerked Marsh into action.

"*Mais oui*," she told him and called the shadows once more.

As she was finishing, Perdemor and his siblings padded into the room. Scruffknuckle followed but stopped beside Gustav, leaning into the soldier's thigh.

"Good boy," Gustav told the dog, patting his shoulder. "Very good boy."

Scruffknuckle panted happily, his eyes dancing with amusement as the kats laid down in front of the prisoners.

"Maybe now they'll talk to us," Gustav suggested, gesturing toward the men.

Aisha's eyes flared white. "Answer the questions," she ordered and slid down the wall to sit on the floor.

Marsh made a note to speak to the child later and ask her how she'd done what she had.

Or maybe I should talk to Tok, she thought, dismissing the shields she'd dropped over the woman and the heads of the two men she'd been fighting. The two men she'd tied up for Gustav watched, fear and anger in their eyes.

"Where are you from?" Gustav asked, and the lead man glowered at him.

"Arcadia, like we said. It wasn't safe for us to stay, so we left."

"What do you mean, not safe for you to stay?"

The man looked around at the others. "We're not nobles, so we're not the right kind to be wielding magic." He shrugged. "I was worried the Hunters had found out, so we left before they caught up with us."

"Didn't Hannah stop that?" Marsh asked, remembering the stories she'd heard from other travelers.

"We're not nobles," the man said as if that explained it. "Hannah changed everything, and we got the blame for a lot of things that weren't our fault. We didn't feel safe there anymore."

"But no one actually hurt you," Marsh said it like it was a conclusion she'd pulled from their words, not a question.

"We didn't give them a chance to," the woman broke in. "They're savages, those people from the Avenue. With them in charge, who knows what would have happened?"

"They couldn't have been any worse than the guy who was in charge before, though?" Marsh asked. "What was his name?"

"Adrian." The man said it like a curse. "We don't know, and we didn't want to risk it."

"So, where are you heading next?"

"The coast." The man swept his hand at the crates. "We usually avoid settlements, but we ran out of food."

"And you thought we had enough to spare?"

"We were going to pay for it," the woman protested. "We were looking for something to leave in exchange when you arrived."

Marsh glanced at Aisha, and the little girl gave her a solemn nod. "It's true," she said, and Tamlin looked down at her with concern.

"You need to rest," he told his sister.

She folded her arms. "Do not."

He ruffled her hair. "Fine, you don't, okay?"

"'Kay," Aisha replied.

The strangers stared at her.

"That has to be the youngest mind mage we've ever seen," the older man told them. "Where did she learn?"

Gustav answered that before Marsh had a chance. "Not your concern, unless you want to stay. You're welcome to since you won't make the coast by winter."

"I thought you said you weren't a druid?" the man challenged.

"I'm not, but the *druids* tell me winter is not far away. One week, maybe two, but no more than that. It'll take you longer to reach the coast."

Marsh wondered how exactly he knew that and marked it as something she'd have to ask him later. She eyed the strangers and then moved a bit closer.

"I'm Marsh," she told them. "What are your names?"

"I don't see why we should give you our names," the man grumbled, straining against the shadows that held him. "It's not like we're free to leave."

"*Bonne*," Marsh growled and snapped her fingers, watching them as the shadows fell away.

To her relief, they didn't move from where they were sitting. She shrugged and glanced at Gustav.

"We can offer you shelter for the winter, or a more permanent home," he repeated. "That's if you want it, but we'll wait over by the stairs to give you a chance to discuss it."

She moved toward the door, only to be stopped by the man's voice.

"How far away is the coast?"

Realizing the question wasn't addressed to her but to Gustav, Marsh kept going. She stopped just long enough to lift Aisha into her arms and then moved into the corridor and down the hall to the staircase. Behind her, Gustav spoke.

"It'll take you the same amount of time to get out of the Devastation as it has for you to cross it so far."

His response was met with cries of dismay.

"And the coast?" the man persisted.

"Another couple of weeks after that," Gustav replied.

"So, we really *won't* make it before winter," the woman stated.

"No," Gustav confirmed, and she sighed, looking up at the man.

"Give us a moment to talk it over," he told them, and Gustav and the kats and Scruffy followed Marsh.

5

A MATTER OF TRUST

I t didn't take the strangers long to decide, but they were still cautious. When the door opened, only the man emerged—and he closed the door behind him.

"I'll need to see your setup," he told them. "Have to make sure it's safe."

Marsh bit back her anger. As insulting as it was that he didn't trust them, it was also perfectly understandable. She exchanged glances with Gustav and nodded.

"It's this way," she advised him, and led the way down the stairs, carrying Aisha.

Tamlin walked on one side of her, and Mordan walked on the other. Brigitte followed her, walking beside the man.

"You never did tell us your name," she said. "Mine is Brigitte."

"And where are you from?" he asked, and then blushed. "I…It's just, I haven't seen anyone like you before."

I just bet you haven't, Marsh thought and made herself keep walking.

Rude, mumbled through her mind in Aisha's sleepy voice.

Shhh, Marsh soothed her, stroking her back with one hand.

"The Four Caverns," Brigitte told him. "They're to the southwest."

"Underground?"

"Underground," she confirmed.

"I'm not sure we came close enough to notice them," he told her. "Not that we would have gone near you if we had. The first time we stopped in a town, someone hid us in the cellar so they wouldn't be forced to turn us over to the raiders, and even then, we were nearly caught."

"How?" Marsh asked.

"The raiders came and took the town. Our host told us to get out, and we ran for it. We don't even know if they escaped. It wasn't like we were looking back."

He quieted, blinking as they left the building and walked out into the sunlight.

"It's like these ruins go on forever," he muttered, looking around them.

"They don't," Gustav told him abruptly, "but they do go on for a good bit longer."

"And they're full of remnant," the man added.

"Yes, although there aren't as many as there were before."

"I noticed there have been fewer in the last week," he admitted. "We just thought we'd hit a good patch."

Gustav grunted and followed Marsh. They didn't speak again until they walked into the dining hall and introduced their new companion to Roeglin.

The shadow master saw them coming and rose from his seat, excusing himself from the table of village leaders. To Marsh, it looked like he'd been holding a meeting with the chief druids, farmers, and guard captains.

"Master Leger, this is…" She hesitated, realizing that their "guest" had yet to give his name.

"Abner," the man supplied quickly. "Abner Mirrow."

"Abner," Marsh finished. "He is the leader of his family."

Now that she thought about it, the men and women traveling with him hadn't *looked* like family.

If Roeglin caught that thought, he didn't show it. Instead, he held out his hand. "Welcome, Abner. I'm Roeglin, one of the community's leaders."

"One of?" Abner's gaze swept the room, pausing briefly on the men and women who had shared Roeglin's table. "Just how many of you are there?"

Aisha stirred against Marsh's shoulder, and she rubbed the child's back again to soothe her.

Bad, Aisha murmured, her small hands forming fists in Marsh's shirt. *Bad, bad, bad…*

Her mental voice trailed into nonsense.

"I understand your people are short of supplies," Roeglin replied instead of answering the question.

Abner dipped his head. "Yes, we were looking for something to leave for the goods we took when your people found us."

"We have other supplies if you need them," Roeglin told him. "I am more concerned with whether you will be able to reach your destination before winter…or find shelter in the meantime."

Abner sighed and indicated Gustav. "Your man tells us

we are more than three months away from the coast, and that winter will arrive sometime in the next two weeks."

"I see." Roeglin pretended to need a few moments' thought, then sighed. "You *could*, if you wanted to, winter here with us—and move on at first thaw."

Abner frowned. "I'd need to be sure it's safe."

Marsh resisted the urge to roll her eyes behind the man's back. What was he thinking? That if he came back to the Library with them, the rest of his family could sneak into the ruins? Somehow she doubted they'd get very far.

After all, she had the kats and the wolves, and her people were in better shape than Abner's family. Surely he'd thought of that?

She felt Roeglin's agreement in her mind and knew he'd drawn most of what had happened in the ruins from her memory. Part of her was grateful they didn't need to speak for him to understand the situation, but another part of her was annoyed at the intrusion.

Mind walkers. They took some getting used to.

Do not, came Aisha's sleepy murmur.

Roeglin's snicker echoed in her head, and she smothered a smile in response.

"Why don't I show you around?" Roeglin offered. "You could speak to whoever you wished and then make your decision."

Noooo, Aisha protested, moving restlessly in Marsh's arms.

"Sshhh." Again, Marsh stroked the child's back to soothe her.

Abner dropped his voice to a whisper. "But we stole from you."

Roeglin's lips twitched into the slightest of smiles. "Out of necessity," he told the man. "The people here have forgiven worse."

"And we can bring the mushrooms back," Abner admitted. "We haven't eaten any of them yet."

"Then no harm, no foul," Roeglin told him.

Tok's people are watching them, he whispered in Marsh's mind. *They'll keep them safe and will watch where they go if they leave.*

Have they? Marsh asked.

No, although they are divided.

Better make this a quick *tour, then*, Marsh told him.

"That will be all right, won't it?" Abner pressed, and they realized they'd been quiet for far too long, although both Marsh and Roeglin had kept their heads down to conceal the fact that they were communicating mind to mind.

Roeglin lifted his head. "Even if you couldn't return the trade goods," he assured the man, "it would *still* be all right. We have good people here."

"So, they'd give us a chance to redeem ourselves?"

"Of course. Please," Roeglin gestured for Abner to precede him out of the hall, "come and meet them."

"Meet them?"

"*Bien ça*, meet them. How else are you going to decide if you are safe here?"

"You're not going to choose them for me?"

Roeglin's eyebrows lifted. "Would you trust them if I did?"

Abner gave him a crooked smile. "No...and thank you."

Marsh went to follow them, but Aisha struggled in her

arms, and she had to stop. She waved Roeglin on, ignoring his look of concern to focus on Aisha.

Setting the child on her feet, Marsh crouched before her, supporting her under the arms. "Aysh? Aisha? Hey, come on, kiddo. You're okay."

The little girl's eyes snapped open, and Marsh found herself staring into two pure white mirrors.

"Not okay," the girl told her and lowered her voice to a fierce whisper. "That is a bad, bad man."

Marsh caught her arm as she lifted it toward the door Roeglin had just closed behind him. Marsh stared at Aisha. "Who? Abner?"

Aisha gave her a solemn nod and then shook her head, her eyes going from white to a dark distressed blue. "No, the one with him."

The one with him? Marsh frowned. *We have to catch up.*

Yes. Aisha wound her hand around Marsh's and tugged her toward the door. *Come.*

Ignoring the odd looks from the others in the hall, Marsh let the little girl pull her in the direction Roeglin had taken. It didn't take them long to catch up.

"And are these *all* the residences?" Abner was asking, his gaze taking in the cottages standing inside the wall.

Roeglin frowned. "Most of them, although we have a few families like your own, who are just passing through, or whose homes haven't been built yet."

Marsh watched as Abner's gaze swung from the gate to the communal mess hall and kitchens, to the dwellings and then around the yard to the large three-storied building that had originally housed the prisoners.

"Do these others share a house or dwell somewhere else?"

The formal phrasing caught her attention. It sounded wrong coming out of the man's mouth, as though he was trying an unfamiliar way of speaking. Roeglin seemed to hear it, too.

"How do you mean?" he asked.

Abner shrugged. "I guess I'm just wondering where my family will sleep," he answered.

Roeglin nodded. "We'd put you in the barracks to start with," he began, only to be interrupted.

"Barracks? You have soldiers here?"

Marsh saw Roeglin's eyes widen and glanced down at Aisha. The little girl hadn't let go of her hand, and she was studying Abner intently. Her small face was pinched with concentration, and her blue eyes were narrowed.

"We have enough to deal with the raiders and keep others at bay."

"Will they stay here?"

To Marsh, the man seemed a little too eager for the information, and she wondered if Roeglin had picked it up. The mage did not reply to her thought, but he was holding Abner's gaze, and Marsh guessed he did not want to reveal his mind-walking abilities.

"This *is* their home," Roeglin told him, "so of course, they will stay."

"And defend it?"

"If they must," Roeglin answered, "although most would prefer to be farmers."

"So, you grow your own food?"

"Of course."

"Then who brings the trade?"

"We have friends who live underground."

Abner's gaze slid to Brigitte.

"The Four Caverns? I thought they were farther away."

"Why do you think we wanted our trade back?" Marsh put in hastily.

Let the man draw his own conclusions...and perhaps get the wrong idea.

Abner nodded as though what she'd said made sense, and he turned back to Roeglin. "Where did you say we would be staying?"

"This way," Roeglin replied and led him toward the repurposed barracks. "The civilians stay on the middle floor."

"And there are soldiers living in all the rest?" Abner's voice was full of awe, and Marsh could understand why.

The building was huge. For the ground and third floors to house nothing but soldiers indicated a large standing force. For a moment, she almost wished Roeglin *would* lie, but that, she realized, could be a two-edged sword.

If Abner *was* part of a force planning to attack, it might not make them go away. It might make them go and find the numbers they'd need to take down a force that large, and then the people they protected would have no chance of escape.

Exactly. Roeglin's head was down and turned slightly away from their guest. *Aisha, show me what you see.*

The child's reply was not reassuring. *Nuffing yet.*

Well, tell me when you do. Roeglin accepted Aisha's word and looked at their guest, his eyes their usual golden-green.

Replying to Abner's question, he said, "No, most of the

lower floor is dedicated to housing cattle and storing building supplies, and we've reserved at least half of the third floor for food storage and crafting."

"And you still have room to offer travelers?" Abner showed a ready grasp of the logistics.

"Yes," Roeglin answered, but did not expand.

For a moment, Abner looked like he might press for more detail, but then his gaze caught on the Library and he stopped.

"What is that?"

"It's a library," Roeglin told him, his eyes wary. "Do you want to see it?"

"Oh, very much, please," Abner's voice became a purr, and Aisha shouted in alarm.

"No! He must not. He is a bad, bad man and sees too much! He has to leave now." She made a grab for Abner's hand, but Marsh was quicker.

She scooped the child off the ground and threw her over her shoulder.

Aisha gave another frustrated squeal and began punching the back of Marsh's armor.

"Down! You. Put. Me. Down! *NOW!*"

As she kicked and squealed, she sent a single image into Marsh's mind—that of an all-too-familiar lump nestled beneath Abner's shirt.

6

AN OFFER OF SANCTUARY

Do you trust me? Marsh asked, carrying Aisha away from the stranger.

Behind her, Roeglin was apologizing profusely for the little girl's behavior. "I'm sorry. She's not usually like this."

Do you trust me? Marsh repeated, but Aisha kept struggling.

As soon as they had rounded a corner out of Abner's sight, she stilled. *Yes.*

So you know what I'm thinking, right?

I hate you, Aisha told her matter-of-factly.

But you'll do it?

Yes.

Good. Here we go. Marsh set Aisha down on her feet and took a firm hold of her hand. She hoped to all the Deeps that the little girl really *would* play along.

"You're very, very tired," she scolded loudly, dragging Aisha back to where Roeglin and Abner stood, "and you're going to say 'sorry' and go right to bed."

"I am not," Aisha declared, dragging at her hand. "I'm not sorry. He is a bad, bad man."

Marsh caught Abner's gaze and rolled her eyes.

"I'm really very sorry, Mr. Mirrow, but she's had a very busy morning and needs a nap. Honestly, I've never *seen* her this tired."

"I'm not tired!" Aisha shrilled.

Marsh used her protest as an excuse to turn away from Abner and reach along her link to Roeglin. Abner was already hurrying to reassure them he understood.

"Believe me, I know children," the man was saying, "so I take no offense. If she needs to sleep, she needs to sleep."

Aisha's voice scaled up a pitch. "I no need to sleep!"

My ears are never going to be the same again, Roeglin muttered, but Abner had already moved on.

"I'm quite happy to have just one escort," he was saying. "I'm sure we can manage without the shadow mistress and the child."

Roeglin made a show of looking at Marsh and then at the Library, and finally, at the sky. "Or we could postpone it until after lunch."

He returned his gaze to Abner. "It's just that if you're thinking of staying, we should let the kitchens know we'll need more for the midday meal, and we need to do that soon. I also need to let the guard captains know we'll have new faces for their men to get familiar with, and the supply master will need to arrange bedding and other equipment. If I tell him, now, your family will have a place to sleep by nightfall."

For a moment, Abner looked torn, and Marsh bent down to lift Aisha from the ground.

"Come on, trouble," she told the child. "It's nap time."

Did it work? Aisha asked, letting herself be carried toward her home.

Yes. The relief in Roeglin's voice was evident. *Good work, Aysh. Now, go tell the healers and Obasi that we need them.*

Abner's voice confirmed it. "I think we *will* stay," he declared and looked at where the sun stood in the sky. "And you're right, it *is* nearly time for the noonday meal."

"Then come with me."

Marsh was approaching the first row of cabins when a familiar figure hurried around a corner and made a beeline toward them.

"Oh, thank you," Calantha declared, loud enough for Abner to hear. "I was wondering where the little scamp had gotten to."

"She's had quite the adventure," Marsh replied, passing Aisha to her mother.

Mother will help me get Obasi, Aisha told her.

You called her, didn't you?

Aisha smiled. *Yup.*

"Well, I'll take over now," Calantha told her. "It will be an early naptime for you, young lady."

"Not tired," Aisha grumbled as Calantha winked at Marsh and returned the way she'd come, taking Aisha with her.

Marsh trotted back to where Roeglin and Abner had paused on the steps to the barracks and supply house. "Her mother was looking for her."

"I can see why," Abner said. "Does the child wander often?"

"Often enough that anyone who sees her knows where she needs to be."

That made Abner chuckle. "Well, that's good to know."

I just bet it is, Marsh thought, trying to work out how much of the man's curiosity was Abner and how much was the puppeteer riding under his shirt.

They found Evan and Alain on the ground floor. The two men were discussing fodder counts and how soon they'd need to start slaughtering for the smokehouse.

"...has to be done before the snows set in," Evan was saying, "and you don't want to do it too close to the barns."

"Oh. I'll get the druids to help. The rock mages should be almost done with the..." Alain's voice trailed off as Roeglin's figure blocked the light from the doorway. His eyes took in the stranger beside the mage. "Can we help you, Shadow Master?"

It didn't take Roeglin long to organize rooms and equipment for Abner's family. The man was shocked by what the community was prepared to give.

"It's too much," he said, repeating himself for the fifth time. "We can never repay..."

"Are you saying your people have all this gear?" Evan challenged, and Abner shook his head.

"No, but..."

"So, are you saying you won't *need* it?" Evan pressed, trying to make his point.

Again, Abner shook his head, his mouth working silently as he tried to find the words he needed.

"Well, we don't believe in anyone going without when we have some to spare," Evan told him firmly, "and we don't expect all of this to last through the winter, either.

You're going to need repairs and replacements, and I expect to see you when you do."

"I hope that's understood," Alain reiterated quietly. "You might be planning to move on in the spring, but you are one of us while you are here and do not need to go without."

"But we can't repay you!" Abner looked close to tears.

"No need," Evan told him.

"Although, if you want to help out, I'm sure we can find something for you to do," Alain quickly added.

Abner relaxed. "Add us to whatever rosters you have," he told them. "We don't expect to be carried."

It was hard for Marsh to keep the frown from her face as she ran through the different tasks and worked out what information they could glean while they were doing them. What if they were all affected?

We'll check first, Roeglin told her. *You* do *remember how, don't you?*

Marsh nodded and saw Abner look toward her.

"Your help will be appreciated," she confirmed, and he relaxed.

They found Gustav and Brigitte waiting outside. Henri and Izmay were with them.

"Heard you might be heading back into the ruins," Henri told them. "Figured you shouldn't do that on your own."

"We're not," Roeglin argued. "The kat…"

He looked around, his expression showing the slow realization that the kat and her kits and the pup were nowhere to be found.

"I don't suppose you know…"

"Probably hunting," Izmay informed him. "It's that time of day."

As if the kats and pup went hunting every day...or went anywhere without Aisha or Tamlin or her nearby.

Abner isn't to know that, Roeglin reminded her, *and I think Mordan is keeping the mantids company.*

The mantids. Marsh remembered that he'd asked to keep an eye on Abner's "family."

The trip back to the ruins was uneventful, which was more than could be said for the time those waiting had had. There was a mantid standing at the top of the stairs. Its eyestalks swiveled back and forth as Marsh and Roeglin approached.

Abner gasped at the sight of it, and Marsh tried to imagine how the man must be feeling at seeing what amounted to a giant insect, some seven-feet tall and as long as a horse. Its segmented body was a burnished red, as were its antennae, and it walked on four feet with two arms held before it.

The triangular shape of its head reminded Marsh more of a mantis than anything else, and its mouth lacked the hard-edged mandibles of most insects but was more membranous and held teeth. From Abner's perspective, the mantid must look like a monster.

Oblivious to the effect it was having, the waiting mantid made a series of rattling sounds accompanied by the rasp of its hind legs against its abdomen.

Roeglin stopped, his eyes flashing white as Gustav grabbed Abner by the arm.

"What in all the worlds is *that?*" the man roared.

"He's a friend," Gustav declared, shaking Abner for emphasis. "A *friend*."

The mantid retreated far enough for them to move past without coming in range of the weapons it carried in a harness crisscrossing its chest. Abner glowered at it as he walked past.

"My family had better be all right," he growled, and the mantid cocked its head, making a curious whistle, followed by a series of clicks.

Abner tensed, but Gustav's grip kept him moving, and they reached the door to his family's quarters. Another mantid stood outside it, but it backed down the corridor to give them room to pass. Abner gave it a frightened look and hurried through the door.

Gustav kept a strong grip on his arm as they went. Marsh followed. Judging by the chorus of voices that greeted their arrival, things had been tense.

"I thought you were never coming back!" the woman wailed.

"Hush, Neela. I'm fine." Abner wrapped his arms around the woman and pulled her close.

Knowing what was under his shirt, Marsh shuddered. She wondered what the bug was doing—and how it had avoided detection thus far.

Did it let its host do what he pleased until it needed something? How easy was it for the bug to override the man carrying it? Did it depend on how long it had been there? What happened when its host was no longer useful to it?

And most importantly, was Abner even aware he was carrying it?

Marsh! Roeglin's mental contact jerked her back to the present, and she watched as Abner told Neela of their offer for shelter for the winter.

"And we don't need to worry what they think about mages," he whispered. "Look at them. So far, every single one of them has used magic in front of us in the open and without fear."

"And the child," she whispered back. "She's not afraid of her own abilities."

"It says a lot," one of the younger men added, pressing close. "We *might* be safe."

"Even with the bugs," another one added, and then frowned. "They *do* know about the bugs, don't they?"

A soft, chittering laugh rattled across the room, and Marsh looked over to where Tok was standing by the window.

What are you doing here? she asked, knowing he would pick it out of her head.

They tried to leave.

They did?

Oh, yes. They were going to abandon the older male and not be here when you returned.

It was news to Marsh. She cocked an eyebrow and stared at the woman.

"You want to tell me what you were doing when the bugs arrived?"

The woman flushed crimson, but she raised her head defiantly as she gave her reply. "We were trying to leave."

"And leave your man behind?"

"It was what we agreed if we were ever found by a larger force. One of us would buy the others time by appearing to cooperate." She glared at Abner. "We were never going to agree to offers of hospitality."

"This one comes with shelter for the winter, food, and blankets and clothing for each of us," Abner told her, and she paused.

"They what?" Neela looked at Roeglin and Marsh.

"Is this true?"

Roeglin bobbed his head. "Yes. If you wish to winter with us, we can offer you quarters."

There was a gasp, and the young woman piped up, "Rooms of our own?"

"An entire room to yourself," Roeglin told her, beginning to smile, "and a cottage, if you wish to stay longer."

"Now, Lissa," Abner warned, but the girl reached out and touched the young man closest.

"Do you hear that, Idron? We could have a place of our own...in a town where we'd be allowed to use our magic."

"Is that true?" Idron asked.

He had dark eyes and thick, dark hair drawn back in a ponytail. He might have been handsome, but his face was pinched with worry.

Roeglin nodded. "Yes. You would, eventually, have a place of your own, and you'd *definitely* be allowed to use your magic to benefit the community."

"It sounds too good to be true," Abner noted. "How do we know we can trust you?"

"Winter is coming," Roeglin told him shortly, "and I think you've seen enough of us to be able to make up your own minds. We can provide you shelter for the winter and see you on your way in spring, or we'd welcome you as part of our community if you wanted to help us build it."

"Either one?" The first young man sounded like he hardly dared believe it.

"Either one," Roeglin confirmed.

"And these?" Abner demanded, gesturing at the three bugs arrayed around the room.

"They are our allies," Roeglin told him. "We believe we have a common foe."

"Yet I did not see any within your walls," Abner noted.

"That is about to change," Roeglin admitted. "Our alliance is new, and we are about to negotiate closer relations."

"What can they offer?"

Allow me, Tok intervened and cast his mental voice wide enough for all to hear.

The Arcadians gasped, crowding uneasily together.

By all means, Roeglin invited, letting the strangers see the change in his eyes as he too projected his voice.

We grow the shrooms you acquired this morning, Tok began, *and we are skilled mind mages, as you can see. We offer our skill at arms, our weapons, and the knowledge of how to use them, and we offer instruction in mental magic.*

He bowed his head, adding humbly, *We hope that is enough.*

"It will be," Roeglin told him. "Will your people be ready to negotiate a final agreement two days from now?"

Yes. It would be our honor.

"You can't be serious!" Abner's mouth was open. "You really think you can trust them?"

"Why not?" Roeglin asked and pointed to the shroom crates. "You did."

Abner stared at the crates in disbelief. "*They* came from the *bugs*?"

The mantids shifted restlessly, and Roeglin intervened.

"They're not bugs. The closest I can come to the name they use for themselves is 'mantid,' and that is how we will be referring to them. Understood?"

"Whether we are winter guests or decide to stay longer?" Abner demanded.

"Regardless of what you choose, you will refer to our allies as mantids," Roeglin confirmed, then added, "There is worse out there."

Abner's eyebrows shot up. "There is?"

Marsh, you need to inspect them for extra passengers, Roeglin reminded her.

I'll do that now. Marsh backed up to the door and focused on the life forces in the room.

The humans and the mantids were easy to dismiss. They glowed a bright, healthy gold...mostly. The mantids' life forces were touched with scarlet, and the Arcadians were more a dull yellow than gold, but they were there.

It was the muddy red and orange life force attached, limpetlike to Abner's spine that drew her attention. Marsh studied it, then walked carefully around the edge of the room, focusing on the strangers in the center.

It was a relief to discover Abner was the only one carrying an unwanted passenger.

Understood, Roeglin told her and turned to the Arcadians with a beaming smile. "We'll go as soon as you're ready. I believe the kitchens are expecting you, and it's nearly noon. They won't like it if we're late."

Idron picked up his pack and reached a hand down to Lissa.

"We'd better hurry then," he announced, keeping a careful eye on Abner. "Being late for lunch is not the kind of first impression I want to make."

His comment made the other youngsters laugh, even as he hauled Lissa to her feet.

Abner managed a chuckle, and picked up his pack, reaching for Neela's and handing it to her. She looped her hand through his arm.

"All right, dear. Let's see if you've finally managed to find us a home."

To Marsh, it sounded like she was desperately not saying "or something worse," but she kept the thought to herself. If the Arcadians stayed, the mantids would be the least of their problems.

There was something lurking in the Deeps below the Library, and come winter, she, Roeglin, and anyone they could spare were going to deal with it.

7

NEW FACES

Keeping that thought firmly to herself, Marsh led the way out of the ruin. Roeglin stopped long enough to thank Tok and his people and then followed—and Gustav kept a close eye on the Arcadians.

The newcomers remained silent as they followed Marsh out of the building. They glanced nervously at the mantids as the bugs exited behind them and then took a different path into the ruins.

"How did you end up making friends with *them?*" Abner asked when the last of the mantids had moved out of sight.

"They helped us when we were being attacked by remnant," Marsh answered shortly.

"And we helped them," Roeglin added.

"I'm not sure I follow," Abner said.

"It's a long story," Marsh told him, not sure she wanted to reveal all of it.

Neela laid a hand on her husband's arm. "Does it matter? They're not going to hurt us."

"But they speak," Abner protested, "and that big one has mental magic. I'm not sure that's safe."

"We've encountered humans who are worse," she reminded him tartly.

Abner heaved a sigh. "I guess you're right."

"If you're still not happy with them when spring comes, we'll leave," Neela assured him, and he nodded.

"Fair enough."

Lissa drew a breath as though she was about to say something, then glanced at Idron. The look that passed between them was unreadable, and she fell silent. They reached the town gates, and Marsh didn't miss the ripple of unease that ran through the group as they entered.

The four women and six men glanced nervously at the walls and the sturdy stone gates, and one of them looked back.

"Are you sure it's safe?" she whispered, clutching the hand of one of the other girls.

Marsh noted the similarity in their looks and assumed they were sisters. Both were fair-haired, with deep-brown eyes and honey-brown skin. Their faces were gaunt from the hardships they'd faced on the road, but they were still pretty.

"It's going to be all right," she said, trying to reassure them.

They cast her dubious looks, and she tried a smile. The doubt remained, and Marsh sighed. She didn't really blame them. Abner had said they'd been avoiding towns since the first one they'd stayed at in the ruins. There probably wasn't anything she could say to help them. They were just going to have to decide for themselves.

"The guard station is on your left," Roeglin declared, gesturing toward the structure. "If you encounter any trouble, that's where to go for help."

He gestured to the right, where the closest cabins could be seen. "Over there is where we're building the settlement. Some of the cabins were there when we arrived, but there's room for more."

"What happens when you run out of room inside the walls?" Lissa asked, and Marsh noticed she leaned into Idron as she said it.

If the two of them weren't partnered, Marsh thought, they soon would be. She wondered how Abner and Neela felt about it.

Judging from the small smile on the woman's face, Neela was happy for the pair. Abner's expression was unreadable, but he also seemed more interested in the way the settlement was laid out than anything his daughter and her boyfriend were up to.

Odd, she thought, not expecting Roeglin's reply.

And we know why. Out loud, he answered Lissa's question.

"That's when we'll ask the rock mages to extend the walls and look to expanding the wall patrols."

"Wall patrols?" Abner was quick to pounce on that, or the bug was, although Marsh wasn't sure why a parasitic insect would want to know.

Don't you remember the remnant? Roeglin asked, and Marsh shivered.

They hadn't encountered any remnant since the small horde that had attacked them on their return to the

Library, and every single one of *those* had had a parasite attached.

They weren't attacking in a big group like that because they'd suddenly discovered cooperation, he observed.

Marsh thought of the larger group that had attacked them when they were escorting the refugees to Ariella's Grotto. They'd been well-coordinated, too.

Right up until you and Tamlin doused them in lightning, Roeglin reminded her.

Speaking of her apprentice... Marsh looked around, realizing she hadn't seen the boy since she'd taken Aisha from him in the ruins. The thought made her glance back through the gates in alarm.

He's with his father, Roeglin informed her. *We have a good administrator there.*

So, not just a mage, then.

No. Who knows what the boy will be?

It was a good question and reminded Marsh that the future wasn't fixed, and that not all their paths were guaranteed.

We're here.

"Fine, keep your secrets," Abner grumbled. "It's not like we won't be able to see it for ourselves."

"Exactly," Roeglin confirmed, giving him a smile. "In the meantime, we'd like to work out your accommodation. Not all of these folk are family, are they?"

At the mage's question, Abner flushed.

"No," he admitted, and his gaze crossed Lissa and Idron, "and some of them are looking to start families of their own once they get somewhere safe."

Whether that last was meant to be information for

Roeglin or a reminder to his daughter wasn't clear, so Roeglin took it at surface value.

"I'll abide by your and her wishes," he informed them and was rewarded by a smile from Neela.

"We want our daughter to be happy," the woman told him, "and if things had been different, she and Idron would have been joined long before now."

Lissa gave a small gasp at her mother's words, and she and Idron blushed.

"We can formalize the relationship if that's what you want," Roeglin told them. "We don't have priests, but we have mages."

"It's something we can discuss later," Abner replied gruffly. "For now, our daughter stays with us, and the boy needs separate quarters."

Roeglin inclined his head and turned to the others. At the end of the discussion, they'd worked out that the two blondes were sisters and needed their own accommodation, and that the five younger men, including Idron, were all officially single.

"You'll be given your own rooms in the barracks," Evan informed them when Roeglin explained the situation, "along with our young folks."

He looked at Lissa. "It's an option for you, too," he added, "if you wish to move out of your parents' home and live independently."

Neela drew a sharp breath, and Abner scowled. Lissa gave Evan a beatific smile.

"Thank you. I'd like that." She caught the look on Abner's face. "Don't you frown like that, Papa. You know I was planning on moving out before everything happened back home."

From the look on Abner's face, it was true, and he wasn't happy about the reminder.

Evan beamed at them. "Good, that's settled then."

He took them through the process of registering for a room and collecting the necessities that had been assigned to them.

"But…" Neela began to protest, just as her husband had.

"We can't," one of the others added.

"I… It's too much…" one of the blondes, Yelen, started.

Evan waved them all to silence.

"This is the standard living package," he told them. "Most of our people came to us with nothing, so we make sure everyone has the basics. If you need something else, come see Alain or me."

That silenced them until Lissa gathered up her equipment and found her voice.

"What do you mean, they came to you with nothing?"

"I mean that many of them were slaves taken by the raiders. When we rescued them, they had nothing, so we gave them a start." He gave it a minute, and Marsh watched the information sink in.

Abner turned to Roeglin. "So, when you say your people have forgiven worse than folk stealing so they don't starve, you mean some of your people used to be raiders?"

It made Marsh hope they could get the bug off him without causing any damage.

Aisha, I need you here.

I'm with Terrence. We are waiting, the little girl informed her.

Stay there, then. We'll be over shortly. Roeglin's voice broke in, calm and authoritative. *Marsh, I need you here.*

Marsh blinked and surfaced. She found herself the center of attention.

"Who were you talking to?" Abner's voice was suspicious.

"Aisha," Marsh told him. "I'm supposed to check in with her at lunch."

"Speaking of which," Evan interrupted. "You all need to stow your gear in your rooms soon if you want to make the mess hall on time."

"Mess hall?" Abner asked. "That's soldiers' talk."

Evan put his hand on his hip and cocked his head. "Yes, I'm one of the raiders they forgave," he told them.

"And we had very good reason to," Alain said, moving past the man. "Evan saved as many lives as he could while trying to keep his family alive. There's not many of us who would have done the same."

"Very few of the raiders volunteered," Roeglin added. "Those who didn't feel sorry for what they'd done didn't live to do anything more."

Abner stared at them. His gaze shifted from Evan to Alain to Roeglin and back to Alain.

"And you were?"

"I was one of those taken," Alain replied, daring him to argue. He looked at Marsh. "She rescued my children, and they came looking—and I'm very grateful."

Idron frowned. "But you're working with..."

He gestured at Evan. Alain nodded.

"I stopped the others from killing him, and then I showed them why."

"You *showed* them?"

"Like this." There was an edge of impatience to Roeglin's voice.

He reached over and touched Alain's forehead, then stepped back to give himself room.

"These are memories," he explained, drawing shadow into the white mist that formed beneath his hands.

The Arcadians watched spellbound as he played the memory of Evan diverting another raider's attention as a family slipped through the gates and vanished into the ruins.

"And they got away?"

Alain's face turned bleak. "No. Their absence was discovered and reported by another guard, and they were brought back."

"But he tried," Idron pointed out.

"And sometimes he was successful," Alain explained. "He kept us as safe as he could without sacrificing his family, and none of us would have asked him to do that."

Abner regarded both men with dark eyes, and Marsh imagined she caught a flash of red in their depths. If Alain, returning his gaze, saw it, he didn't show it.

Instead, he gestured toward the stairs. "Your rooms are on the second floor."

It was as good a dismissal as any, and they left Stores to do as he suggested. Roeglin and Marsh waited on the ground floor until they returned. Some things needed privacy, and Lissa's request for a place of her own was one of them.

When Abner and Neela returned, they were holding hands, as were Lissa and Idron, who descended the stairs behind them. The others followed without comment, their faces somber as they contemplated the choice before them.

Marsh figured winter would be long enough for them to work it out, and the community at the Library would accept their decision regardless.

"The mess hall is over there," Roeglin told them but turned away from it, "and this is the medical center. If you're ever not feeling well, this is where you need to come. I'll introduce you to the staff before we go to lunch."

They followed him, the Arcadians quiet as they looked at the settlement around them. Roeglin stepped up onto the stone porch before the door and turned the handle.

"This way," he instructed and headed inside.

The Arcadians followed, and Marsh was happy to see Terrence standing in front of the counter, and a couple of other healers drifting past the door at the rear of the room. There was no sign of Aisha, and for that, Marsh was glad. What they had to next was—

Now!

She pivoted on her heel and swept her foot through Abner's legs. Roeglin grabbed Neela and pulled her away as Gustav came through a door at the side of the room and pinned Abner to the floor.

Marsh sat on the man's legs, aware of hands grabbing for her shoulders. They were swiftly pulled away as healers came into the room from the back and two side doors.

Chaos erupted around them as soldiers came in from the front door and dragged the non-family members out of the medical center. From the sounds of battle outside, the youngsters weren't making it easy not to harm them.

She ignored the trouble as much as she was able,

working to keep Abner's legs pinned. Neela struggled to reach her husband, but Roeglin held her fast.

"Let go of him!"

"What are you doing?"

"It's a trap!"

"Marsh!"

Marsh pulled the dagger from her belt, and Neela shrieked and fought like a hoshkat to get free of Roeglin's grasp.

"Give her a minute," the mage urged, and Marsh sensed compulsion lacing his words. It didn't affect her, though, and she used the knife to split Abner's shirt and reveal the parasite nestled beneath it.

Neela recoiled in horror. "*What* is that?"

"That," Roeglin told her grimly, "is what we're trying to save him from."

8

DE-BUGGING

"What's going to happen now?" Neela sobbed.

She watched as Abner was lifted and slung over Terrence's shoulder.

"Now we're going to try to free his mind," Roeglin told her.

"How are you going to do that?"

"Like this." Aisha's voice had the woman turning around. Before she could ask the child what she meant, Aisha's eyes turned frosty-white and mist formed beneath the child's fingers.

The scenes that followed had Neela weeping with horror, although she refused to look away.

Roeglin groaned, but he didn't interrupt the child as she showed Izmay and Henri working together to remove the parasite from Gerry's back. In the background, Marsh and Aisha knelt beside the guard's head.

The door to the medical center opened, and the other Arcadians were escorted back in. Some of them sported bruises from their contact with the guards, and some still struggled, but they all stopped dead still at the scene Aisha was drawing from memory.

Gerry lay on the floor of the assassin's cottage, the parasite exposed as Henri and Izmay worked.

"What in the Bitch's name is that?" one of the men demanded.

"It's a brain bug," Gustav told him.

"A what?" the man asked, but one of his companions interrupted before Gustav could answer.

"Wait! Are you telling me Abner had one of those things on him?"

"Yes," Gustav confirmed.

"And that man?"

"He was one of the guards escorting the people we rescued from the raiders to Ariella's Grotto." She paused, remembering. "They didn't want to stay here."

"And where is he now?" Lissa whispered, edging closer to wrap an arm around her mother's waist.

"We took him back to Ariella's Grotto to complete his recovery," Marsh informed her. "The attack happened on the journey, and we couldn't turn back. He'll return when he's better."

"But he *did* survive?" Neela pressed.

"Yes, and we'll do our best to make sure your husband survives, too. I'm sorry we couldn't warn you beforehand."

"And...are the rest of us okay?" Lissa tried looking over her shoulder to inspect her back.

Idron stroked his hand down the length of her spine. "There's nothing there," he assured her.

"I scanned the rest of you," Marsh informed them. "Only Abner carried a puppet bug."

"'Puppet bug?' I thought it was a brain bug."

"Same difference," Marsh replied. "We believe they can control their hosts."

"And after?"

"After what?"

"After you remove them?"

Aisha's memory showed Henri crushing the bug inside the bowl.

"They can't control anything when they're dead," Marsh informed them.

"Well, why didn't you just pull it off him?" Neela demanded. "Why knock him out?"

"Because they send tentacles into their host, and if we don't remove those, the host dies."

"Oh." Neela looked fearfully at the door through which her husband had been taken.

"We're going to do our best to make sure that doesn't happen," Marsh tried to reassure them.

Terrence returned. "We're ready," he said, looking from Marsh and Roeglin to Aisha. He glanced at the waiting family. "Why don't you go with Gustav to the mess? This is going to take a while."

"I'd rather wait," Neela told him stiffly and looked around the room.

"There's a waiting room through there," Terrence told her, gesturing at the door opposite. "Gustav, can you make sure they get something to eat?"

"I'll take care of it," Gustav replied and ushered the Arcadians across the foyer to the waiting room.

Marsh nodded to him and walked over to Terrence. "How bad is it?"

He shrugged. "We won't know until you get started." He paused, giving her a worried look. "Will you be okay?"

"I don't see why not. Why do you ask?"

"Because you've already had a long day," Terrence told her, "and I don't need you falling over in the middle of this."

"It's not like we can delay it," Marsh told him. "The sooner that thing is off his back, the better. We don't even know if it can hear us from in there, or if it will kill him out of spite, or…"

She gave him a helpless look and sighed, pushing past him to take one of the seats that had been placed at Abner's head. Aisha let go of her hand and scrambled into the other, batting away the healer who tried to help her.

"I can *do* this," she declared, settling into place.

Terrence clapped Marsh on the shoulder. "We're ready when you are," he told her.

"Yeah," Henri muttered. "Ready when you are."

Marsh looked up at the sound of his voice, her eyes widening in surprise. He saw the look and laughed, indicating Izmay, who was sitting across from him.

"What? You think they'd get anyone else to do this when we're the only ones who've done it before?"

What he said made sense, and Marsh was relieved.

"Thanks," she told him.

"Yeah. Lucky us," he snapped back and lifted his knife. "Whenever you're ready."

Izmay glared at him across Abner's body, and Marsh smiled. It was good to know that some things didn't change.

Roeglin took the empty chair beside her.

She regarded him in surprise.

"Thought you could do with some help," he explained, then added, "I *have* done this before, remember?"

Marsh nodded. She remembered. There'd been a bug in Briar's Ridge the first time they'd passed through. It seemed so long ago, and so much had happened in between that she'd almost forgotten it.

Mordan nudged open the door and wove her way through the healers, Perdemor and Scruffknuckle by her side.

"Scruffy!" Aisha exclaimed, slipping off the chair to wrap her arms around the dog's neck.

He gave a snuffling groan and settled to the floor. Perdemor flopped down alongside him.

"They're coming?" Marsh asked, and Aisha's eyes flashed green.

"*Oui*," she confirmed. "Dan says they're ready."

Marsh wondered why the kat thought they were necessary, and Mordan replied, *The cubs must learn to hunt, and this kind of prey is rare.*

"And?" Marsh pressed, thinking there had to be more to it than that.

There was.

This one smells...stronger, the kat told her. *We will need the help, and they need the experience.*

"Which is why we have come," Obasi announced from the doorway.

"I don't..." Marsh had been about to say she didn't know if it was safe to have so many inexperienced hunters when Obasi held up his hand.

"The kat asked me to come." He eyed Mordan speculatively. "She said I could have only one hunt mate."

"Hunt mate." It sounded like a term the cat would use, and Mordan wasn't objecting. Marsh caught Terrence's questioning look and nodded.

"That's all of us," she told the healer and hoped she was right.

Mordan sank down under the table, making a soft chirruping noise. Scruffknuckle bounded to his feet and scrabbled under the bed, dragging Aisha with him when she didn't let go of his collar. Perdemor followed in a more dignified fashion and settled at Roeglin's and Marsh's feet. Obasi took Aisha's chair.

"This is Daikari," he said when Terrence brought another for the man with him. "He is another of our healers."

"I didn't know you were a mind mage as well," Terrence said, and Daikari ducked his head.

"It is not my strongest magic."

For a minute, Marsh wondered why he was here, but then Obasi explained.

"After we heard what Aisha did, we thought it might be useful to see if it is something we can teach to other mind mages with healing magic."

"Next time, you will take one of us with you," Terrence told them, and Obasi and Roeglin exchanged glances.

"We will discuss it," Roeglin agreed, "but not now."

He indicated the man on the bed before them. "We need to start before he starts to wake."

"Do we know how long that will be?" Marsh asked, only to be interrupted by a small voice from under the bed.

"I can make him sleep."

"*Bien*. You do that, Aisha, but not for too long, okay? You don't want Terrence to be worried."

"'Kay."

Are we ready? Roeglin asked, and Marsh had the briefest sensation of being led into another mind where the others were gathered.

She nodded, glad to feel Mordan slide along the link between them and brush against her leg.

"Do you understand what it will be like?" Roeglin asked, and Obasi and Daikari nodded.

"I showed Daikari what we faced in Gerry's mind," Obasi explained. "We know what to expect, but do not know how that will translate into reality."

"*Bien ça*. Let's go."

She felt Roeglin and Obasi focus on the sleeping mind before them, but it was Aisha who opened the door.

Be careful, the child warned, slipping through ahead of them.

She didn't go alone, though. The two kats and Scruffknuckle surged after her. Marsh hurried to catch up…

…and stepped into a maelstrom.

Perdemor stood over Aisha's huddled form as Mordan took the fight to the tendrils lashing out at the child from the wall. Scruffknuckle snapped at any that came near, bounding around his child and Perdemor in a blur of fangs and fur.

"Perdy, move!" Marsh shouted, and the kit jumped clear as she threw a bubble around the child.

"No, no, no!" Aisha cried. "I need to…"

"Okay," Marsh agreed, and asked the shadows to

protect the girl but let her move—to armor her as they armored Marsh.

The darkness shrouding the girl shifted, and Aisha stood up. She looked down at the shadows, and her face lit up with a smile. It was a fleeting thing, though, since Mordan was already biting through tentacles as she leapt through the space that was Abner's mind.

Obasi brought Henri and Izmay in close enough that they would know when to start to cut.

Putain a merde! Henri swore. *This is even worse than the last time.*

So, cut carefully, and make it fast, Marsh told him.

Henri rolled his eyes. *As if we'd do anything else.*

Marsh did not dignify that with a reply, and the two warriors faded out to focus on the body of the parasite on Henri's back. She got the impression of Izmay trying to find a space between the creature and the man and of Henri sliding his blade into the gap on the other side.

The tentacles became twisted red vines, their lengths covered in wickedly curving spines. Mordan slid under three and leapt over another, lashing out with her claws as she passed. The vines froze and then doubled back on themselves, their sharp tips all pointed at the hoshkat's side.

Roeglin slammed a shield between them, and Mordan bounded out of the way.

Henri grunted. "This sucker is tougher than the last one."

"Not. Going. To. Do. It. An. Ounce. Of…good!" Izmay declared, grasping a tentacle where it met the creature's carapace.

Marsh looked around them, noting the red patches left behind by the tentacles' emergence and the oozing clear liquid touched by yellow, and she frowned. Aisha followed her gaze and nodded.

"I've got this," she declared. "Basi, Daikari, we do this now."

Marsh wondered who'd put the child in charge, but Obasi and Daikari merely dipped their chins in agreement and began to lift from the floor. Scruffknuckle barked in alarm when Aisha did the same.

"Scruffy! Down!" Aisha commanded, lifting out of range of his teeth.

The pup danced uncertainly below her and then spotted a vine spearing toward her. He gave a growling bark and leapt toward it, crushing it between his teeth and tearing it clear before going after another. Perdemor raced alongside him, slashing and biting as he went.

On the other side of the space that was Abner's mind, Mordan had become a one-kat demolition team. Roeglin fought beside her, protecting the kat's flank just as she protected his. Marsh was suddenly alone, with Aisha rising above her.

The intelligence guiding the tentacles saw it too, and she found herself the center of an attack from several directions at once. Roeglin shouted a warning, and Mordan roared. Marsh pulled shadows from the corners of Abner's mind, shielding herself with some and forming a spinning disk from others. This she directed to cut through the tentacles coming toward her the fastest.

As it spun along the direction she thought for it, she

created a shadow blade and sliced through another of the savage vines.

"Marsh!" Aisha called. "Give me lightning!"

"What?"

"Give me lightning on *all* the vines."

"Don't you dare!" Roeglin shouted.

"Just the vines!" Aisha instructed. "All of them."

Marsh hesitated, and the child sent her a picture through the link between them. "Like dis!"

It was never a good sign when Aisha resorted to baby talk, but Marsh had seen what she wanted and did it. She did not need the child's next command.

"Lightning *now*, Marsh!"

She definitely did not need the compulsion that came with it.

As her hands moved of their own accord, and her mind called the lightning without her bidding. Marsh swore that when this was over, she and Aisha were going to talk.

9

MEDICAL PROCEDURES

"Only the parasite!" Aisha commanded as the lightning began to fall. "Only the parasite!"

There was panic in the child's voice, but there was command, too, and Marsh found herself repeating the little girl's words.

"Only the parasite," she told the lightning, pushing all thought of what had happened the last time she had called lightning in someone's mind.

That time Roeglin had almost died, and she and he had had headaches for days afterward. This time there were more minds at stake. She and Aisha *were* going to have words about mental etiquette when they got out of this.

If they got out of this.

If Aisha heard that threat, she didn't respond. She was already busy implementing the other part of her plan. Marsh slowed the flow of lightning, but the tendrils kept coming. There were decidedly fewer than there had been before, but they didn't let up.

"Call it again, Marsh." This time the voice belonged to

Roeglin, although she could feel Obasi's agreement in the link they all shared.

Focusing on the energy, Marsh called the lightning once more. "The vines, the parasite, the tentacles," she told it. "Destroy them all."

Above her, a tendril lashed out, attempting to wrap around Aisha.

"No!" Marsh cried, and the lightning surged. "*All* the tentacles," she told it. "*All* the parasite!"

"All of it?" Obasi's alarm seemed unwarranted, but the lightning surged again, leaping away from her and lancing down on the tentacles before disappearing through the holes it had made.

"Just the parasite," Marsh told it, willing it to obey as it disappeared from sight.

She frowned, still feeling its presence, but not entirely sure where it had gone.

Henri's startled yelp was all the answer she needed. It was followed by the clatter of a dropped blade and Izmay's savage curse.

"By the Deep's dirty ass! *Marsh!*"

"Well," Henri said a moment later, "I guess we don't need to worry about the *bug* anymore."

"Call it off, Marsh," Izmay instructed. "I'm pretty sure you can tell the lightning to go home now."

"Dismiss the lightning, Marsh." Roeglin's instruction was accompanied by the mildest of compulsions.

It looked like Aisha wasn't the only one who needed a good talking to about mind-to-mind etiquette.

"Dismiss the lightning," he repeated, his voice strained. "Please!"

This time there was no compulsion to his words. Marsh called to the lightning, "Thank you for your service. You have saved us. Return to your home and rest. Return and rest."

The lightning fizzed and then faded, creeping back to the corners of Abner's mind she had called it from. Above her head, Aisha glowed with green and white light, just as Obasi and Daikari did. The three of them spun slowly, radiating streamers of healing magic.

Terrence's voice intruded.

"We can take it from here," the chief healer informed them, "but we need you out before you all collapse."

It was sound advice, and Marsh looked at Aisha. She was relieved to see that the light surrounding the child was already fading. As she watched, Aisha began to descend.

This time, she didn't fall until she'd almost reached Marsh's arms. Marsh stepped forward and caught her, worrying that there was no one to do the same for Obasi and Daikari.

To her relief, the two men descended to the floor of Abner's mind.

"He's waking up," Terrence warned them. "If you're gonna put him out, you'd better do it soon, or you need to be out of there. There's no telling what he'll do if he finds this many people trampling through his head."

"Done." Roeglin's voice sounded weary both through their minds and in the room around them.

Marsh had barely registered it before she found herself dumped back into her own head. The quick reaction of the healer standing nearest her stopped her from falling out of her chair.

"Thanks," she mumbled, looking at where Henri and Izmay had sat.

Had? Marsh looked around the room in alarm.

Terrence chuckled. "Those two aren't very happy with you at the moment," he told her. "You singed their fingers."

She had?

He read the puzzlement on her face. "You don't know?"

Marsh shook her head.

Terrence cocked his head. "Well, I'm guessing *you* were the one who called the lightning. Is that right?"

Marsh nodded, and then she frowned and bent quickly to look under the table and see if Aisha was all right. It was a relief to see the little girl curled up in the middle of Mordan, Perdemor and Scruffknuckle's furry bodies.

The big kat lifted her head and blinked slowly. *The cubs are sleeping,* she informed Marsh. Her tone said the cubs were not to be disturbed.

Marsh pushed herself upright. "Is it okay if they stay there?" she asked, indicating the tangle of bodies under the bed.

Terrence stooped to look and sighed.

"It's fine. We're going to stretcher this guy into one of the recovery wards. His family needs to see him."

Marsh slid off the chair and onto her feet. "I'll help you," she offered, then she swayed, and her knees began to buckle.

She grabbed the edge of the bed, just as the medic who'd steadied her before took her arm and stopped her from falling.

Terrence shook his head. "The only thing any of you are

going to be helping with is returning to your quarters and getting some sleep."

Marsh thought about arguing with him, but there was a glint to his eye that warned her against it. Instead, she shrugged.

"How are Henri and Izmay?" she asked.

"We're *fine*," Henri replied. "No thanks to you. I think."

"Let me guess." Marsh cut him off. "You think I owe you another dinner, right?"

"Give the girl a prize," Henri mocked, but Izmay interrupted.

"This time, I agree with him," she declared stoutly. "You'll be replacing our knives as well."

Marsh's eyes widened. She'd what?

"You heard," Henri told her, reading the puzzlement on her face. "You melted it. You're mending it."

"I what?"

"He's exaggerating," Izmay explained. "You only took the edge off the blades, but you *completely* ruined their temper."

Marsh wanted to say that Henri's temper was already ruined, but she didn't think they'd see the funny side of it.

"Fine," she told them, stifling a yawn. "I'll replace your Deeps-be-damned blades."

"Get out of my medical center," Terrence ordered them, "and go get yourselves something to eat while you're at it. Tell the kitchens I sent you."

Henri grinned, and Izmay smiled, and the two warriors took themselves out of the room before Terrence could change his mind. The healer turned to Marsh.

"And you," he added. "Sit yourself down until we can move the man out of here."

Marsh did as she was asked, not that she thought she had much choice. Her legs were feeling wobbly, and the path to the door was blocked. She settled back on her chair.

"We did it." Roeglin sounded beyond tired.

"Yup." Obasi didn't sound much better.

"That seemed so much worse than the last time," Daikari murmured. "Or was that just me?"

"No," Obasi told him. "*That* was a *lot* worse than the last time."

"I just wish I knew why," Roeglin told them. "That thing *looked* like it was the same size as the last one."

"There were more tentacles," Marsh observed him, "and they had thorns."

"The last one didn't have thorns?" Daikari wanted to know.

Obasi shook his head. "No, it was just all vines. Wasn't it?"

He looked at Marsh.

"Vines is all I remember," she replied, stifling a yawn. "And Aisha and you healing the holes they came out of, and Henri and Izmay removing the bug and crushing it after."

Her stomach lurched at the memory, and Obasi pulled a face.

"Where *is* the bug?" Daikari asked.

Terrence snorted and pointed at Marsh. "I'm going to assume the lightning that burned through the bug was from her, given what I've heard. It's gone."

He reached over to a nearby bench. "And this is what happened to Henri's blade."

Marsh stared at the misshapen edge. *So that was why he and Izmay wanted their blades replaced!*

Roeglin managed a tired laugh. "Just be glad you didn't destroy Abner as well."

"You said only the parasite," Marsh reminded him. "You *made* me only target the parasite!"

He flushed. "I thought Aisha had the right idea."

"You...you..." Marsh sputtered. She slapped his shoulder. "Don't *ever* do that to me again."

"Do what?" Terrence asked, but Obasi and Daikari were frowning.

"You used a compulsion?" Daikari asked. "Against one of your own?"

"She needed to focus," Roeglin muttered, going redder than before.

"Since when has she ever had trouble doing that?"

Roeglin regarded Obasi with wide eyes. "You haven't known her for as long as I have."

Marsh gave an exasperated sigh. "I'm right here, Ro."

"Since when can the girl do a compulsion?" Terrence asked, latching onto the most important question in the entire discussion. "I mean, has she done one before?"

Marsh lifted her head and saw the fear that he'd been manipulated written across his face.

"I think it's something new," she told him and added in a private thought to Roeglin, *We need to talk to Tok.*

He nodded. They watched as the healers loaded Abner onto a stretcher and carried him out of the room. Voices from the foyer signaled the family had seen Abner's arrival.

"Give them space," Gustav rumbled. "I'm sure Marsh and Roeglin will be here soon to tell you how it went."

As a hint they were needed, it was as good as an order, and Marsh groaned. Terrence held up his hand.

"I'll get this," he told them, and stepped into the foyer, closing the door behind him.

In response to his appearance, the voices subsided.

He led with, "Abner should make a full recovery," and followed with, "I'll show you where we'll keep him, but you cannot stay."

"But I should be there when he wakes up," Neela protested.

Marsh heard the sound of footsteps receding as Terrence replied, "First you need to have a meal. This is Tavi. He will watch over your husband until you return."

Neela's reply was muffled by distance, but she heard the heavier tread of boots cross the foyer.

"How is everyone?" Gustav asked, leaning on the doorframe.

"Tired." Roeglin flapped a hand at him.

"Cook says to come up when you're ready, and she'll make you something hot."

He was about to say more, but Terrence interrupted him. "Ah, Gustav. Just the man I wanted to see."

The old soldier groaned and rolled his eyes. As Terrence's quick steps got louder, he turned around.

"Now, Doc—"

"Don't you 'now, Doc,' me, soldier. You were supposed to see me first thing this morning so I could check your recovery. Come through."

"Doc, I really don't..."

"You can either come with me, now, or I'll do the exam here."

"I could just leave."

"You have to sleep sometime, and I can make that happen." Terrence sounded as though butter wouldn't melt in his mouth, and Gustav sighed.

"Doc, you know I'd never—"

"Yes, you would," Terrence told him, "but only if I let you. Now, take off that cuirass."

"A little help?"

"And didn't I hear you were in a fight this morning?"

"Doc…"

Marsh heard a door click shut, and their voices became muffled. She sighed and leaned her head back against the wall.

"Looks like we could be here a while," Obasi observed.

Roeglin slumped in his chair. "The price of being heroes," he replied wearily.

He sounded neither heroic nor proud, just very, very tired.

Terrence didn't keep them waiting long, though. Marsh had barely closed her eyes when the healer returned.

"I thought I told you all to get some sleep?" he grumbled. "Or did you strain something I don't know about?"

Roeglin stood up. "We're going."

He stooped to look under the bed, then reached carefully under to pull Aisha clear of Scruffknuckle and the kats.

Perdemor rumbled a warning, then opened his eyes, mewing in apology when he saw Roeglin.

"It's all right, Perdy," Roeglin reassured him. "We're all worried about her."

"Is she hurt?" Terrence asked anxiously.

"No, but she really pushed her limits," Roeglin told him.

Gustav snorted. "When doesn't she?"

"I'll take her home," Roeglin assured them, but Terrence reached out and took the child from his arms.

"*I'll* take her home," he corrected. "*Gustav* will make sure the rest of you go and get some sleep."

"Gustav will?" the older soldier asked, looking alarmed.

Terrence fixed him with a stern glare. "Gustav will," he confirmed.

10

UNORTHODOX TRAINING

They woke at dusk to the sound of the evening bell calling everyone back inside the gate.

Marsh sat bolt upright, flinging the blankets back and sliding her feet over the edge of the bed.

"It's all right, Marsh. It's just the dusk bell." Roeglin's sleepy voice greeted her from the bed.

She stood up. "Then we're really late for lunch, and I'm hungry."

"Let's hope the Arcadians are at duskmeal. We need to welcome them, and I want to check on Abner."

"And we need to talk to the leaders about the meeting with Tok and his people."

Roeglin sighed. "It's always something."

The saying reminded her of Tamlin, and she giggled. "It surely is. That boy had no idea how right he was."

"Well, he does now," Roeglin declared, getting out of bed, "*and* he never lets us forget it."

Marsh chuckled. "Time to eat."

Roeglin sighed again, but he didn't argue. He just pulled on his armor. Marsh brushed her hair.

"Check me?" she asked when he was ready.

"Always," he told her, running his hands over the straps and buckles.

"Your turn," he said when he was done.

It didn't take long, and Marsh leaned into him for a kiss.

"You know we don't have to go," he murmured, and Marsh playfully slapped his shoulder.

"You know we do," she told him, heading out the door.

The dining hall was busy by the time they arrived. To Marsh, it looked like the whole town was there. She was relieved to see that the Arcadians were there, as well—and that Gustav was with them. If she didn't know any better, Marsh would have said he'd adopted them.

Neela looked worn and tired, and Lissa clung to Idron. The other men and women stuck together and kept a wary eye on their fellow diners. That didn't deter the others from approaching them and welcoming them to the town.

"We're not staying," one of the men roughly declared, but the ex-slave greeting him just smiled.

"You're staying for the winter," he told him, "and that means you are one of us. I'm very glad you're here."

"Why would you care?"

"Because we're a small community, and winter is too long a time to treat you like a stranger. We'll be sad to see you go in spring."

The bluster died on the Arcadian's face, and he held out his hand. "Oliver," he said.

"Fabian," the local man replied, and took a seat beside

him. "Have you decided what you're going to do while you're here?"

"You mean we'll get a choice?" Oliver asked.

"Why wouldn't you?"

Marsh moved on, not interfering. In the end, the Library's people would be its best advocates, and the Arcadians would make their own decisions regardless. She stopped beside Neela's chair.

"How is he?" she asked, and the woman looked up.

She managed a wavery smile. "He's sleeping, but he woke up and seemed okay. He said to thank you."

Marsh patted her shoulder. "I'm glad he's okay."

She went to move away, but Neela reached up and trapped her hand. "Where did it come from?"

"The bug?"

"The thing on Abner, whatever it was." Neela waved her hands helplessly. "Are there any more out there?"

"We don't know where they come from," Marsh admitted, "but we've seen them on remnant, so there are probably more out there."

"That's what I thought," Neela stated. "I don't suppose you know a quick way to the coast?"

Marsh shook her head. "We're hoping to attract traders. Maybe one of them will know a way, but we haven't had any yet."

Neela sighed. "I'm not looking forward to leaving in the spring," she admitted.

Marsh wanted to tell her she didn't have to leave but didn't want the woman to feel pressured. Instead, she slipped her hand out from under Neela's and patted the woman's shoulder again.

"We're happy to have you," she said by way of farewell.

Gustav was talking to Roeglin as the pair of them moved through the line at the servery.

"We introduced them just before you arrived," the guard captain was saying. "None of us were sure when you two would emerge."

He caught sight of Marsh joining them, and his skin burned scarlet. "Uh, that wasn't meant to sound...um..."

Marsh shook her head. "You were right to worry. We were really tired."

"So," Roeglin interrupted, changing the topic, "this meeting. When were the leaders planning to have it?"

"We thought it would be a good idea to hold it over dinner," Terrence cut in. "The kitchen staff set up the smaller hall so we could have a bit of privacy."

The smaller hall was an extension to the main mess hall. The leaders had only started using it recently, as the community had grown and they'd needed a place where they could discuss developments privately.

When they reached it, they found Evan, Xavier, Obasi, and Alain already waiting. To Marsh's relief, their plates were mostly full, showing they hadn't been waiting long.

"This meeting," Evan began. "Why now?"

"Because the townsfolk are already curious," Roeglin told him, "and because the Arcadians we just brought in ran into them when they tried to sneak away."

"They what?"

"When we brought Abner in to look the place over, his companions tried to leave. We understand they had a run-in with raiders and are extremely cautious as a result, but the mantids brought them back and made them wait for our return."

"Where were they going?"

Roeglin froze. "That's a good question. We never got around to asking them that. I'm not even sure *they* had a plan. They were running scared."

"Hmmm. Well, what do you think it'll take for them to stay?"

"Isn't that up to them?"

Terrence sighed. "It is, but we could always do with more people."

"And mages," Marsh informed him. "We need those too, right?"

Terrence's face showed genuine surprise. "They're mages?"

"A couple of the younger ones conjured fireballs when we first met."

"You fought?" Evan asked.

Roeglin nodded. "We did. It took them a little bit to understand we weren't going to hurt them."

Evan cocked an eyebrow. "The kat got involved, didn't she?"

"And Aisha," Marsh admitted. "We really need to speak to Tok about teaching her proper etiquette when it comes to being a mind mage."

"Are you sure we shouldn't get one of the Grotto's folk to talk to her about that? After all, *they're* human."

"True," Roeglin agreed, "but she'll listen to Tok."

Evan frowned and looked at Marsh. "Did you put him up to that?"

Marsh shook her head. "I didn't need to. He knows Aysh as well as I do."

"And the bugs?" Xavier asked. "I mean, we've all heard of the mantids coming to help the latest additions to the community. Not the Arcadians, but the ones you brought back from Briar's Ridge. Are you sure it's a good idea for us to meet them?"

"I think we should have organized it a while ago," Roeglin told him, "when people were still feeling grateful."

"Two days from now," Roeglin told them, "if Tok's people agree to it. That's when I've asked them to come. Do any of you foresee a problem with that?"

"You're not really asking our opinion, then," Alain stated, and Roeglin shook his head.

"I'm sorry, but no. I think this is essential to the progress of our community." Roeglin looked around, as though willing them to understand.

Xavier took a breath, and Marsh prepared to argue on Roeglin's behalf if she needed to. They were interrupted by a series of knocks, then the dining hall door opened, and a woman wearing the colors of the Deeps Monastery stumbled through.

"Shadow Master Leger?" she asked, looking around.

Roeglin stood. "Yes?"

The woman straightened and took several deep breaths.

"Shadow Master Leger," she began, "from Shadow Captain Envermet."

Marsh opened her mouth to express her surprise, but Roeglin held up his hand.

"Continue," he instructed, speaking to the messenger.

"The shadow captain sends his compliments and wishes you to know he will be arriving at dusk in two days' time."

Around the table, eyes widened, but none of them interrupted.

The messenger continued, "He will be accompanied by the future teaching staff of Sunward, the Deep Monastery's surface campus..."

Marsh and Roeglin drew sharp breaths of surprise, but the messenger hadn't finished.

"...as well as a contingent of shadow guard, and druids from the rock mages and Ariella's Grotto. They will be joining the education center to broaden its ability to assist those developing magical talent."

She paused, her face momentarily blank as if she were checking for anything she'd missed. Satisfied there was nothing else, she added, "Message ends."

"Please, come and join us," Gustav invited her. "I will bring you something to eat."

Roeglin nodded, but Gustav was stopped at the door by Daikari. Obasi's assistant was carrying a tray. "I thought you'd need this," the healer-mage explained. He gestured at the messenger. "It would have been a long ride."

Rather than joining the main table, the messenger took the tray and seated herself at a table at the side of the room. Daikari left the room, returning moments later with two hot drinks. "I'm to show you to your quarters when you're ready," he advised her, and she nodded.

"My thanks."

She said nothing more, and Daikari settled into a comfortable silence, sipping his drink while she ate.

Roeglin led the others back to the table. "We really need

to see to the construction of a communications tower," he told them. "It will be safer."

They looked at the messenger. She had crossed the Devastation on her own, and they knew the dangers that lurked between the Library and Ariella's Grotto. One day, a message might not get through.

They had just settled to their meals when Aisha arrived. The little girl held a bread roll in one hand and Scruffy's collar in the other.

"Mama said you were awake," she explained when she caught Roeglin and Marsh watching her.

"To show you what Tok taught me," she went on when Roeglin stared at her. "You were sleeping last time."

That last bit was said in an accusatory tone just as Tamlin came to join her.

"And I came to show you something else," he told them, "but it might be more useful to shadow mages than anyone else."

"Is it useful?" Xavier challenged and blinked as the boy stepped forward, only to vanish from behind his sister and appear next to Roeglin.

Roeglin started back, twisting out of his seat to draw a shadow blade from the air. Tamlin smirked. Marsh stared open-mouthed at the boy, her eyes darting from the unshadowed patch of ground he'd disappeared into to the unshadowed patch of ground he'd appeared out of.

"You didn't... You just shadow-stepped without using any shadows! How did you do that?"

Izmay was also staring at him, the shadow guard having followed the messenger through the door.

"Yeah, I'd like to know that, too."

"It's simple," Tamlin told them and pointed at Marsh. "You told us how, you know."

"I did?"

"Sure, when you told us that shadows were just air that was in the dark."

"I did?"

"Yup," Roeglin agreed. "You said that when we were having trouble pulling our weapons on the surface. It worked, too."

Izmay nodded, and Marsh frowned. It took her several seconds to recall the conversation they'd had on the way to Downslopes.

"Oh."

Seeing she understood, Tamlin continued, "Well, the same is true for shadow-stepping. You don't need a patch of shadow, right? You just need a patch of air. It doesn't matter if the shadows are present or not."

"Let me try that," Izmay muttered, and promptly vanished, only to reappear again in another part of the room. "Oh, man, that is..." She let her words trail off and grinned. "You wait until I show this to Henri.

Marsh's eyes widened. Judging from the look on Izmay's face, Henri was in for quite the surprise. She just hoped he wasn't armed when Izmay pranked him.

"Thank you, Tamlin," Roeglin said, stepping into the ensuing silence. "Izmay, can you organize a training session for the shadow guard?"

"Now?"

"The morning should suffice."

"Yes, Shadow Master."

She turned to go, and Gustav pushed back his chair.

"And me," he declared, looking from the shadow guard to Tamlin. "I want to learn that, too."

Roeglin's face showed a brief moment of doubt, which he quickly smoothed away. Again, he nodded to Izmay, and she frowned, looking at the boy. Tamlin shrugged.

"I can try."

"You don't think I can do it?" Gustav asked, and Marsh's heart plummeted. The most important part of getting the magic to work for you was to believe. The slightest doubt could mean failure.

"We won't know until you try," Tamlin replied.

It was the most diplomatic she'd ever heard him, and her heart surged with pride. Aisha looked from her brother to Gustav and back.

"Not like that," she told the guard captain, and Marsh knew the child had been mind-walking again. Aisha's next two words were the two she most dreaded hearing. "Like this."

Gustav's eyes widened and he stumbled back a step, fetching up against a wall and leaning there.

"Go on," the child encouraged. "*You* try it."

"Me?"

"I can hold your hand," she offered, and Gustav glared at her.

"I can do it."

Marsh drew a sharp breath and Tamlin took a step toward him, but it was too late. Gustav took a deliberate step forward and vanished, reappearing on the other side of the room in front of the child. Before she had time to react, the guard captain had scooped her up and held her out in front of him.

He shook her slightly. "What have you been told about walking through people's minds without their permission?"

Aisha folded her arms and glared at him.

"You needed help."

"And Tamlin?"

"Couldn't say."

"Couldn't say what?"

"He just couldn't!"

Gustav set her down on her feet. "Thank you for showing me how to shadow-step," he told her, "but if I catch you dipping into anyone *else's* head without their permission, I will put you over my knee and take whatever punishment your mother wants to give. It's... It's *rude!*"

Aisha stared up at him with round blue eyes, and then she burst into tears and ran from the room. Gustav groaned and shook his head.

Roeglin sighed. "We'll ask her to show us what Tok taught her tomorrow," he declared.

Tamlin snickered, walking over to Gustav and poking him in the arm.

"You better go after her."

"Why me? *You're* her brother."

Tamlin shook his head. "Nuh-uh. *You* broke her. You get to go find her."

11

A LONG-AWAITED MEETING

Aisha was found, and Roeglin and Marsh tried to make her understand why it was important to ask permission before she walked through someone's mind. It was hard work, and they weren't sure they'd been successful at the end of it.

The settlement was buzzing with excitement by the time the sun rose a second time. Everyone had their morning tasks finished in double-quick time and were waiting by the gates to welcome them.

This is either going to go really well or badly, Roeglin sent to Marsh.

They were standing on top of the gate, dividing their time between looking for the mantids and watching the people of the Library gather.

"They'll be fine," Gustav told him, and Roeglin shot him a sharp look.

Gustav laughed. "Don't look at me like that, boy. I don't have to be a mind-walker to know what you're thinking. It's written right across your face."

"I'm worried about what will happen if Master Envermet arrives before we can warn him," Roeglin admitted. "This meeting could go very wrong in so many ways, it's not funny."

"Here they come," Marsh warned, having caught a glimpse of sunlight flashing red off the mantids' carapaces.

Izmay, Gerry, Henri, Brigitte, and Zeb hurried down the stairs to open the gates, and Marsh, Gustav, and Roeglin followed. By the time Tok arrived in front of the fortress, the entry was clear, and they were there to greet him.

The mantids' arrival elicited gasps of surprise and awe from the crowd beyond the gate, then one of the ex-slaves they'd saved started to applaud. At first, the clapping sent ripples of alarm through the mantids.

Their antennae stiffened, and their eyes swiveled to take in the view beyond the gates. Once they realized the short, sharp sounds were made by the humans slapping their hands together, they relaxed, but only a little.

What does it mean? Tok asked, his thought intruding unbidden in Marsh's mind.

That they appreciate you and thank you for what you did when you protected them from the remnant, Marsh explained.

Oh. Thank you. The mantid bobbed his head and torso, and she managed a slight bow in return. *May I address them?*

Of course, Roeglin told him. He took up position on one side of the mantid, and Marsh chose to walk on the other.

The shadow guard and the children fell in behind them, each one walking beside a mantid as they passed into the town proper. The mantids hadn't come empty-handed. Most of them carried packs laden with shrooms.

People of the Library, Tok announced, *we are very pleased to meet you at last.*

Cheering greeted his words, and he continued, *We have brought supplies for your kitchens.*

The cheering and applause renewed. Several of the kitchen staff came over to take the mantids' burdens. The expressions on their faces were a comedic mixture of gratitude, awe, and fear.

"We do not know how to prepare food for you," the chief chef finally ventured.

May I share the information with you? Tok asked, his tone suddenly formal.

"Okay?" the chef replied, his tone wary.

The mantid didn't elaborate, but Marsh caught sight of the information he'd given the chef and was in awe.

"Er, could you share that with these folk?" the chef asked, and Tok cocked his head.

Very well, provided it will not distress them.

"Oh, it won't distress them," the chef told him, eyeballing the three cooks closest.

They returned his look with wary stares, and a ripple shuddered through Tok's body. Marsh recognized the movement as a sign of unease, or the mantid equivalent of a human shrug.

The exclamations of surprise and shocked looks turned in his direction told her the cooks hadn't known what to expect and were having trouble assimilating it. Roeglin tensed, and Marsh got ready to call shadows to bind them.

They continued to stare, stunned, at the mantid chief, then they shook their heads and grinned.

"We can do that," one declared.

The others nodded, picking up the packs they'd set down at their feet.

"How many are we catering for?" another wanted to know, and Tok looked at him.

The answer passed between them, and the chef shrugged. "Oh. Well, we can do that."

"I told you not to be afraid." Evan's voice reached Marsh, and she looked toward him. The ex-guard had his hand on a mantid's shoulder as he looked up at its face, his expression one of joy. He wrapped his hand around the mantid's bicep. "Come on, let me introduce you to some people."

The mantid cast a glance at Tok, and the lead mantid flicked an antenna. Marsh didn't know what passed between them, but the mantid relaxed and followed Evan into the crowd.

Before long, the other mantids were moving among the people. Some were being greeted by the warriors who'd come to the aid of the caravan, their antennae showing surprise at being recognized and addressed as friends.

"We should have done this from the start," Roeglin observed, and Tok dipped his head in agreement.

We did what we thought was best, the mantid reminded him. *Neither of us was to know our people were so resilient.*

"We should have," Roeglin replied. "They have been through a lot and survived to come out the other side. Why wouldn't they have coped with this?"

Tok flexed his eyestalks and flicked his antennae.

Because we look very different from what your people expect, the mantid explained, his mind voice sounding surprised that Roeglin did not remember.

"I remember," Roeglin replied just as Aisha danced up to them.

She reached up and patted the mantid's carapace. *Hello, Tok,* she greeted him. *I missed you this morning."*

It had been agreed to halt her lessons until after the meeting, and she hadn't been impressed.

I hope you've been practicing, the mantid informed her, and she rolled her eyes.

You would know if I didn't.

The mantid clattered its mandibles and rasped a leg against his abdomen—his species' equivalent of a laugh. *I would indeed.*

Roeglin chuckled, and he and Marsh led Tok to the town square, where they'd set up a space for the humans and mantids to mingle. All around them, the townsfolk and the mantids "talked." Roeglin and Marsh watched them.

"Tok is right," Roeglin said.

"You couldn't have known," Marsh assured him. "The precautions were necessary. They gave us time to get used to the idea our neighbors were very different."

Roeglin lifted his head, his eyes flashing briefly white. Moments later, Evan came over. He gestured at the activity around them.

"And you were afraid." He chuckled. "Take a look at those people!"

"We are," Roeglin answered, smiling, "but it's time to get down to the business of the day."

"You really should have had more faith in us," Xavier told him, joining them. Together they waited as mantids and humans settled in the square. Tok joined them on stage with another, slightly smaller mantid at his side.

Aisha hung off his arm but allowed him to usher her to a seat.

Xavier leaned close. "You know, there was a group of us who were going to corner you and ask you to check on these guys, don't you?"

Roeglin regarded him with surprise. "No."

Xavier grinned. "Well, we were. They saved so many of us that we needed to know they were okay."

He paused and looked out over the square.

"A lot of us owe them our lives. It would be good to see more of them."

The light around them dimmed, and they looked up. To their relief, the clouds were scattered and fluffy, not gathering for a storm. This time of year, that wasn't guaranteed.

"We should build a roof over the top of this," Roeglin observed.

"A meeting hall?" Evan asked, and Roeglin paused.

"Something we could close up to keep the weather out, but leave open when it's nice, like today. Come winter, we'll need a space for everyone to relax in. It might as well be here."

"I'll talk to the druids." He paused. "We really need a carpenter."

"I'll see what I can do when I talk to Master Envermet. Maybe he has one among the new personnel he's bringing."

"Any idea when they're scheduled to arrive?"

"This afternoon. I think around dusk."

I agree that you need a sheltered meeting place. The mantid looked around the square. *And this space would be ideal for the building you have in mind.*

"Can I see that?" Evan asked, and Roeglin realized the mantid was sharing with those who could hear the conversation.

Tok glanced at Roeglin, who sighed. "Sure. Go ahead."

Xavier and Evan's faces lit up.

"I *like* that!" Evan stated, and Xavier nodded.

"It's perfect. I think if we can show this to the druids, they'll be able to work out how to build it."

Tok glanced at Roeglin once more.

"I will show them," Roeglin told him firmly. "Later. Such plans are not for tonight."

We could also do with their help, Tok declared. *This building is a perfect meeting place, and we have found a route that would allow us to move underground between your home and ours.*

Roeglin straightened. "You have?"

We have.

"What did you have in mind?" Obasi had joined them, settling himself beside the table.

"You heard that?" Roeglin asked.

"I believe Tok is broadcasting rather widely," Obasi told him.

The mantid's eyes widened. *Is that bad?*

"No, not yet," Roeglin told him, as Marsh looked at the people close by. All of them were listening a lot more closely than they appeared to be.

Roeglin drew the information from the link between them. "Perhaps you should keep the conversation only to those at the table," he suggested.

Tok's eyes bobbed, and he shifted his antennae as though taking stock of the surrounding situation. One of the druids chatting not far from the table crossed over to them.

He pulled up a seat and looked at Roeglin. "If this roadway passes through the ruins, it might be possible for us to find a place in there to try for some winter crops. The hill is a little too exposed, but if we could find a sheltered space amidst the buildings..."

Roeglin groaned. "Very well." He turned to Tok. "I think we are going to need a second meeting to discuss this project if that is acceptable to you.

It is, Tok assured him, *and I like the ideas this one has for making more growing room.*

One eyestalk swiveled toward Gustav. *And we will need his knowledge of defenses.*

Gustav sat bolt upright. "My *what?*"

Your knowledge of fortifications, the mantid reiterated. *There is much we do not know about that kind of warfare.*

"What about the kinds of warfare you *do* have knowledge of?" Gustav challenged.

Tok's eyestalks twitched in amusement. *We will be able to take care of any matters related to that purpose.*

"There are other measures we can add," the druid assured them. "Between us, we should be able to cover *most* contingencies."

Roeglin opened his mouth to ask what contingencies they *wouldn't* be able to cover but was interrupted by the sudden clang of an alarm bell.

Marsh was out of her seat and reaching for a clear blade as she ran for the gate. She was not alone. The guards were running that way, too, and the druids were already shepherding the civilians toward the Library.

Some of the citizens cast fearful glances at the gray stone building, but the glances they cast toward the gates were just as afraid.

Aisha looked left and right, taking in the fleeing adults. "What about Bear's momma?" she demanded, and Roeglin looked down at her.

"Bear's momma has the safest cottage in all the world," he told her, remembering how the wolves' druid had taken over the assassin's cottage just outside the township's walls. "She has a pit with spikes in it!"

"Oh, yeah." Aisha grinned, and Roeglin took her by the hand and led her toward the gates. She'd be just as safe on the wall with him as she would be with Calantha, her mother. He caught sight of the woman as she hurried away with the druids.

She raised her hand in a slight wave, and he was almost overwhelmed by her trust. It didn't matter that she knew Aisha and Tamlin had faced worse dangers with him in the tunnels. They were still *her* children.

And she is our momma, Aisha told him, *but she knows we need to work, just like you.*

Oh, she did, did she? Roeglin didn't know what to make of that. It made sense, but Aisha was six, and Tamlin just nearing eleven. For them to have steady jobs didn't sit well with him.

What else are they supposed to do? Everyone should work for the good of the nest. Our people begin those tasks as soon as they leave the larval stage.

Roeglin didn't know how to explain human ages to the mantid, and Tok didn't press him.

"What is it?" he demanded.

"We've got a large group of people coming along the road."

"Raiders?"

"They don't look it, but I'm seeing a lot of armor, and they're all mounted."

"Are there any wagons?"

"There are mules." The man handed him the spyglass.

"I don't see anything," Roeglin said after a couple of minutes.

The man took the glass and peered through it. "They've moved into the gully behind those two buildings," he said, pointing at the remains of two tall buildings. "They'll be in view in a couple of minutes."

"Marsh?" Roeglin's voice was hoarse.

"The shadows won't show me," she told him. "They're too far away."

If they were in the gully, then the group was more than a cavern-width distant—much too far for her magic to reach.

"Life forces?"

Marsh shook her head. "Same problem."

He frowned at her, and she nudged him with her elbow. "Minds?"

Aisha bounced beside him.

"I can do it."

He was about to say *he* would do it when her eyes flared white. The grip on his hand tightened, and she let him see what she did. Even so, her shrill shout of joy came as a surprise, and she'd torn free of his grasp and stepped over the edge of the wall before he could stop her.

"Master Ennermet!" she shrieked

12

AN UNFORTUNATE GREETING

"Aisha!" Marsh lunged for her, but the child dropped over the edge...

...and onto the stone she'd conjured from the side of the wall.

"You're fixing that!" Marsh called, but the child ignored her, pulling stone from the wall to form a set of stairs as fast as she took each new step.

Marsh's breath caught in her throat as the child descended at break-neck speed, and she didn't call out again. The last thing she wanted to do was distract the girl at a crucial moment and see her plunge to the base of the wall as a result.

She remembered to breathe again when the child reached the ground.

"Come back here!" she shouted, but Aisha ran away from the base of the wall as fast as her little legs could carry her.

"Deeps dammit!" Tamlin swore, and Marsh glanced

over in time to see him step onto the top of the wall and vanish.

"Deeps be shagged and shaded!" Marsh cursed and chose a patch of sunlit ground in Aisha's path. She stepped to the side but was still disoriented when she found herself on the ground amidst the ruins. The time it took for her mind to catch up with where her feet had taken her was all the time Aisha needed to bolt past her.

"Hurry, Marsh! Master Ennermet is here!"

The little girl's joy was contagious, and Marsh couldn't help smiling as she tried to catch her.

"Aisha, stop!" Tamlin wasn't as amused.

Aisha ignored him, and Marsh ran after her. They reached the top of the rise at the same time Master Envermet did.

Master Envermet's mule was not amused. It gave a startled bray and reared onto its hind legs. Marsh skidded to a halt and called a protective dome over the child as the mule lashed out.

"Aisha!" Tamlin raced past her and Marsh stuck her foot out, tripping him before he ended up under the mule's feet.

She threw a dome over them both and watched through the semi-translucent shield as Master Envermet got his mule back under control. As soon as it quieted, he dismounted and had the shadow guard step down. By the time everything had settled down, Roeglin, Gustav, and the Library's guards had arrived.

Marsh released the shield over her and Tamlin and helped the boy to his feet. When he was upright, again, she looked at the dome covering Aisha.

"I suppose I should let her out," she muttered, and Tamlin nodded.

"She'll be mad at you when she comes out," he warned.

"I'll take care of that," Master Envermet told them. "She needs to apologize to Henry."

"Henry?" Henri asked. "You have a mule called Henry?"

Master Envermet smiled. "He came with that name, and I did not want to change it. Besides, what's wrong with Henry?"

The ex-caravan guard looked at him. "It's *my* name."

"See? It's a perfectly good name," Master Envermet replied.

"It doesn't belong on a mule," Henri grumbled.

The guards around him stifled smiles, and Master Envermet huffed a sigh. "Nevertheless, it *is* his name, and he gets to keep it."

Henri pressed his lips into a thin line but didn't argue. When the shadow captain sounded that determined, the matter was closed.

Master Envermet looked at Marsh again.

"It is good to see you, Master Leclerc, and you, Apprentice Danet. I trust your studies are going well?"

"They are," Tamlin assured him, blushing pink at the recognition.

"Good." Master Envermet dipped his head in acknowledgment, then looked at Marsh and gestured at the dome over Aisha. "If you would."

Marsh sighed but dismissed the shield.

Aisha stood up, dusting her knees as she did so. She glared at Marsh, then focused on the mule.

"That was *rude!*" she scolded it, shaking her finger.

The mule jerked his head up. He flicked his ears forward and then back, sidling to stand behind Master Envermet as he kept a wary eye on the child.

"Hello, Apprentice," Master Envermet said, interrupting her tirade. "Please stop scaring my mule."

"Master Ennermet!" Aisha shouted and leapt forward to wrap her arms around his legs.

The mule snorted, pulling at the reins, and Master Envermet passed them to one of the mages who'd come to stand beside him. As soon as his hands were free, he stooped to lift Aisha from the ground and settled her on his hip.

"Have you been behaving yourself?" he asked, stepping toward Roeglin.

Marsh looked at Tamlin and rolled her eyes. The boy returned her expression, and they both fell in step beside the shadow captain.

"Brigitte, Roeglin," he said, greeting the others as he approached them. "I trust I haven't come at a bad time?"

"We were introducing the settlers to some new allies," Roeglin explained. His eyes flared white, and Master Envermet froze.

"Really? They're our friends?"

Marsh felt a frisson of alarm. The mantids' settlement wasn't far from the approach to the Library. She hoped Master Envermet hadn't mistaken them for enemies and killed them.

He shot her a glance, and his lips curled in a brief smile. "No, but it was close. They watched us pass from the upper floors of the ruins to one side of the paths, but they weren't hostile, so we left them alone."

He shifted his gaze to the woman leading her shadow guards, and his eyes took on a white sheen. Her skin flushed a darker shade, and she glanced nervously at the city gates.

"Perhaps we should introduce our new friends *before* we enter the city," Master Envermet suggested.

"Very well," Roeglin looked toward the fortress gates, and the mantids appeared shortly after.

To Marsh's surprise, they were accompanied by several townsfolk. Murmurs of unease rippled through the newly arrived caravan, but they stilled as Roeglin spoke.

"The Library welcomes you. We also want you to meet our new allies, the mantids. Today we agreed to bind our settlements together and help each other survive in these lands. Together we welcome you."

The townsfolk clapped and cheered the new arrivals as Roeglin went to lead them into the fortress proper. They stopped a few steps later as Bristlebear's pack appeared outside the druid's cottage, the druid with them.

Master Envermet raised his hand briefly to his forehead to acknowledge the wolf and then continued inside.

"There was a human with Bristlebear," he mentioned.

"We found his druid and rescued her," Marsh informed him. "They live in the assassin's cottage. She's happier out there."

"Did the raiders take her?"

"Yes. Some time ago."

"And speaking of animals," Master Envermet continued, "where *are* Mordan and the pup?"

Marsh looked around. *Dan?*

We are hunting, the kat informed her. *You will need extra meat for the evening meal.*

I thought our stores were better stocked than that?

Master Envermet has brought more mouths than were expected.

I brought supplies, Master Envermet intervened, *but no fresh meat. I am sorry.*

Your presence is welcome, the kat told him. *I must go.*

Happy hunting, he wished her as Marsh felt her link go quiet.

They entered the town, and Roeglin summoned the town leaders.

"Alain, Evan, can you make sure they all have a place to stay?"

Alain's eyes grew round as he studied the new arrivals. Evan scowled. Neither of them argued, however, and the new arrivals were quickly integrated into the town's infrastructure and celebrations.

Tok was grateful for the increase in allies and surprised to find another mind mage among them.

Perhaps you would like to take over the child's training, he suggested, only to have Master Envermet rapidly shake his head.

"I am ashamed to admit that she surpasses me in skills. I am grateful she has found a master with the knowledge to teach her." He paused and gave the mantid a careful stare. "With Roeglin's permission, I would like to ask you for training as well."

If Roeglin is happy to allow it, I will train you.

"Only if you train me as well," Roeglin declared. He turned to Master Envermet. "Speaking of which, why *are* you here, and who are these people with you? You look like you've brought your own private army. Did the Monastery send you to start another settlement?"

Master Envermet shook his head. "Oh, no. It's far graver than that. They were concerned for all those who might have magical talent on the surface, and, when I expressed a desire to return to you, the Shadow Master allowed it on one condition—that I established a magical training center of sorts."

His eyes flashed white, and another mage approached. As he got closer, Marsh noticed it was a druid. "This is Sabir," Master Envermet said, by way of introduction. "Selima from Ariella's Grotto sent him to work in conjunction with us to build a druidic arm to the college, and I have brought rock mages from near the Monastery as well."

"Did you have any idea of where you want to build it?" Roeglin asked.

"Do you remember that building we camped at on the way here the first time?" Master Envermet countered. "You know, the one where the wolves found us the day you decided to save the mule?"

Marsh remembered it but was surprised he did.

Master Envermet looked confused. "Why wouldn't I? It was where we saved your life, and it was one of the few ruins that was mostly intact where we needed it."

He looked at Sabir. "The rock mages and druids assure me they can ensure it will continue to stand for centuries to come. That, and it's the only thing with enough structure remaining that's both big enough and close enough to the Library."

"Do we know how far away it is from the mantids?" Marsh asked.

Roeglin frowned and looked at Master Envermet. He shook his head.

"Why do you ask?"

"It would be nice to be able to connect the training center to the Library and the mantids' nest when we connect the nest to the Library, is all," she told them.

Both men looked at Tok, and the mantid inclined its head. *I would like that very much.*

Talks went on long into the night, while the townsfolk got to know the new arrivals as well as their new allies. Aisha fell asleep against Master Envermet's shins and Tamlin dozed in a corner, refusing to leave her.

"Have you met the trader yet?" Master Envermet asked, catching sight of a young woman deep in earnest conversation with Alain and Eric.

"No," Roeglin answered. "What does she trade in?"

"She's looking to establish some kind of stud for horses, mules, and donkeys," Envermet revealed. "I wasn't going to bring her, but I thought it would be nice to have a second avenue of supply."

Roeglin frowned. "I'd prefer it if the horse and donkey breeding was split, but it depends on how much stock she has."

Master Envermet shook his head. "She doesn't have enough stock for that, but we can ask her to build it into her program for later on."

"We'll do that. I don't want another monopoly."

Master Envermet nodded, studying Roeglin's face as though he were seeing it for the first time. Marsh wondered what he saw but he didn't enlighten her, even if his eyes momentarily slid toward her.

"Either way, she'll be looking for shelter for the winter."

Roeglin glanced back at Alain and Evan. They'd retired to a table against the wall, taking the woman with them. Now the three of them were engaged in an animated conversation. Roeglin chuckled.

"I trust them to negotiate a fair deal with her. A hard deal, sure," he added, watching the conversation, "but a fair one."

A pathway is possible. Tok's voice interrupted their observation. *But we have a request.*

They all glanced at the mantid leader. He'd been moving through the crowd and getting to know the people who were to be his people's friends. It hadn't stopped him from overhearing Marsh's earlier suggestion.

"A request?" Roeglin asked.

Master Envermet looked wary. "What sort of request?"

We would like our most powerful mages to join your teachers, the Mantid told him. *Observation suggests that even your strongest mind mages are not equipped to teach the child what she needs to know...or you,* he added, one eye focusing on Roeglin and Master Envermet as the other scanned the room behind him.

"We would be honored," Master Envermet replied, and Roeglin nodded in agreement.

"Honored," he added.

Then we will begin construction in the morning. I have spoken to your chief of druids, and he will organize a roster of people to help us.

"Your people are welcome to stay," Roeglin told him. "The Devastation is not a safe place at night."

It is safe enough for us, the mantid informed him. He turned to go and then paused. *There is one more favor we would ask.*

One of his eyestalks swiveled so he could focus on Marsh. The other remained on Roeglin and Master Envermet.

If you will allow it, I would like to station guardians in the town to protect Marsh. The attacks on her mind are becoming more persistent, and the buildings interfere with our ability to sense them coming.

Marsh opened her mouth to protest, but Roeglin raised a hand to silence her.

"How many?" he asked, and weariness curled along the edge of his voice.

Six, Tok told him. *They will work as a triad, with one on guard at all times and one sleeping.*

"All times?" Marsh croaked. "I thought you only needed to guard my sleep?"

In the past, attacks have occurred on a waking mind, Tok explained.

"Have they occurred on mine?" Marsh wanted to know.

Not as yet, although we are not sure you would be aware of one if it did. That is why we wish to be nearby.

"Why now and not earlier?" Roeglin voiced the question just as it came to Marsh's mind.

The presence is stronger. The attacks are growing stronger, as well.

They were? That came as a surprise to Marsh.

"But I've been sleeping better since I came back," she protested.

That is because we have been shielding you. Trust me, the attacks are growing worse.

"They are?" Roeglin asked. He looked horrified. "I am grateful for your protection, Tok, but I am sorry I have made it necessary."

Tok flicked his antennae. *You have not made it necessary. The attacks have not originated with you.*

"But I am the leader of this community. It's my duty to protect my people, and I have failed her."

Tok made a reproachful series of clicks. *You have not failed her,* the mantid corrected. *Mind protection is a task for those capable of performing it, not for those whose desire is strong but whose capabilities are yet to be developed.*

"I..." Roeglin was at a momentary loss for words, but Master Envermet leaned forward.

"I am here, now," he declared sternly. "Surely..."

Tok laid a long-fingered hand on his shoulder. His mental voice gentle as he interrupted. *Neither of you is able to protect her mind. Nor are the mind mages from the nest known as the Grotto, and the enemy is growing more powerful. We fear the portal is opening.*

"Portal?" Master Envermet demanded, his voice forming a chorus with Marsh's and Roeglin's.

Faces turned toward them from around the room.

This is not the time or place to discuss it, but we fled through an open portal, and it was not one that stayed open always. It will open again, and our old foes will come hunting.

"Your old foes?"

A shudder ran through Tok's form. *This is a discussion*

for another time. Tomorrow, I think, once you have had suffi-cient sleep. In the meantime, I would like to leave my six most proficient guardians.

"Granted," Roeglin answered.

Is mid-afternoon too soon to meet?

As Roeglin agreed that mid-afternoon was an ideal time, Marsh tried to assimilate what she had just learned. There was a portal, and the enemy that pursued her through her dreams was beyond it. When it opened...

She shuddered. Mid-afternoon was not too soon to meet. For Marsh, it wasn't soon enough.

FOREWARNED

R oeglin and Master Envermet spent the morning out at the college site. They were discussing it as they returned to the small dining room after lunch.

"It won't be ready before winter," Roeglin was saying. "I'm sorry, but we need the druids if we're to harvest that last crop before the first snows set in."

"Did they say when that would be?" Master Envermet asked.

"The next four to six days, no later," Roeglin replied. "It's going to be close."

"And the tunnel the mantids want?"

"There might be suitable sites on the route, but they won't be ready, either. That, I'm afraid, is our next priority."

"As well as finding this portal Tok was talking about." Master Envermet sighed. "We have a lot of work ahead of us, especially if we are to secure the Library."

"Yes. It makes me wish I hadn't killed every raider who didn't surrender."

Master Envermet shrugged. "You did what you needed to do, and the world is a safer place because of it. This is not something you could have foreseen."

Roeglin shook his head. "I saw what was below. I should have investigated sooner. It's been a month and a half since we took the place."

"It's been a month and a half of getting your people back on their feet and in a position where they can deal with the weather that's coming. They need to eat if they're to be of any use to you in defending their home."

"They need to feel safe, too."

"Are you telling me you can't lock the ways beneath the Library?"

"No. We could do that, or I could get one of the rock mages to seal it with stone. We could ignore those tunnels until next summer if we needed to."

"But the tunnels lead into the Devastation," Master Envermet reminded him. "If you blocked the way into the church and Library, you wouldn't know when something came through, or what it was or how many. It takes precedence."

"We should have gone in sooner."

"Don't forget you had to wait for Marsh to return, and the children. They're part of your core team."

Roeglin looked around, making sure the room was empty. He even looked under the tables to make sure Aisha hadn't snuck in unseen. When he discovered they were alone, he continued, "I haven't asked Marsh for a permanent partnership," he admitted, "and I-I don't know if I should."

Master Envermet regarded him with surprise. "Whyever not?"

"Because of this. The town takes a lot of my time, and I'm often busy. I... It's not fair to expect her to..."

"To what?" Master Envermet asked, a small smile playing over his lips. "Accept your work the same way you accept hers? To be there as much as you're able? To take time out of her day to see you, the same way you take time out of yours? I'm not sure what she'd be doing differently if you *did* make the partnership official."

Roeglin sat back in his seat and stared at him. "When you put it that way..."

"You have an entire township of work to do," he agreed, "but it shouldn't stop you from finding a partner to run with. Ask Bristlebear how he manages his relationship with Silvermoth when he has an entire pack to oversee."

Roeglin opened his mouth to protest that it was different for animals, but Master Envermet wasn't finished.

"Or the Shadow Master how he manages to coordinate with the Rock Mistress."

Roeglin's jaw dropped, and Master Envermet gave a small smile at his surprise.

"That, I grant you, is new. My point is, you will find a way to manage to find time, and your feelings won't stop just because something seems to be sensible or fair."

He paused. "Besides, don't you think Marsh should have a say in whether she thinks you're too much hard work to run beside?"

Roeglin closed his mouth. Master Envermet had a point. He might not like it and asking Marsh what she thought might scare him twenty times Deeper, but what the shadow captain had raised made sense.

He was about to thank the man when Marsh arrived with Tamlin and Aisha in tow. Master Envermet started smirking, and his blue eyes danced with mischief. Roeglin hoped he wouldn't say anything to Marsh, at least not until he'd had a chance to.

The smirk vanished. *Not likely,* the shadow captain informed him. *That is the sort of thing* no one *should interfere with.*

On hearing it, Roeglin felt some of his tension ease. He watched Marsh tilt her head, listening as Aisha chattered about some game Scruffknuckle and Perdemor had played with Perdy's siblings.

"Dan was not impressed," the little girl was saying. "Her tail did that thing, and her ears were right against her head. She was *mad!*"

It sounded like the kits and pup had *really* upset the adult hosh, and that took some doing. Roeglin wondered what it had been, and if he'd be hearing about it from Obasi or Evan later. Usually when that much mischief occurred, one or another of his foremen knew of it and weren't impressed.

"Did they break anything?" he asked, and the little girl shut her mouth, her eyes going wide.

"Nuh-uh," she told him, and Marsh rolled her eyes.

Roeglin sighed. "I'm going to be hearing about this later, aren't I?"

Aisha took a big breath, and Marsh nudged her.

Roeglin made a show of burying his face in his hands. "I am. I *know* I am."

When he looked up, the little girl was smiling. "Maybe…"

He groaned, but before he could say anything, the door opened again and Tok came through. He brought with him three other mantids. These moved to occupy the empty end of the room.

I have brought the mages you will need for your academy, he informed them.

Master Envermet studied the new arrivals, taking in the color of their carapaces and the blood-red markings and the lighter slashes of yellow. *It is a pleasure to make your acquaintance,* he told them, making sure everyone in the room could hear him.

One of them cocked his head and made a soft churring noise.

That is correct, K'tch, Tok replied. *That one will be your student.*

The mantid's eyes swiveled to focus on Master Envermet alone. When the shadow guard's eyes turned white, Marsh knew the pair were having a student-teacher moment. She cast a glance at Roeglin, but the shadow mage's attention was on Tok.

"Can you explain the danger?" he asked, and Tok inclined his head.

One eye remained on Roeglin and the other turned to K'tch. The other mantid flicked his antennae and settled back on his haunches, and Master Envermet's eyes returned to their usual blue. The other two mantids remained silent.

Your world does not exist alone in the galaxy, Tok explained, *and there are others who deem it ripe for conquest.*

Those others are scattered, but there are some who would own more of them—and who have the ability to open a gate between them. That is what you are facing here.

"An invading force?" Master Envermet asked, and Roeglin looked at Marsh.

The enemy we fled from is an enemy of Death's. It will seek to destroy your world in order to destroy her.

"I don't know who Death is," Roeglin observed, "but if this enemy was going to destroy this world to attack her, why did you come here?"

That is simple. When we fled, we had a limited choice of portals, and we chose this one.

"Knowing it led to a world your enemy would want to destroy?"

We chose it because it is a world that Death will fight to protect, and what she protects is safer than any other place in the universe, no matter who its enemies are. Of all the destinations a portal could lead, this was our best option for survival.

"You couldn't make it back to your own world?"

Tok's eyestalks sagged, and his antennae drooped. Sadness crept through his mental voice. *Our world was not an option.*

Marsh wondered if it would ever become an option, and one of Tok's eyestalks turned toward her.

It was our world we fled. Again, sadness laced the mantid's tones, and Marsh found herself at a loss as to what to say. Tok swiveled both eyestalks toward Roeglin and changed the subject. *You had questions?*

"I did." Roeglin gestured toward Aisha. "Are any of your mages capable of doing what Aisha does?"

In what way? Tok asked.

"Making other people do what she wants, whether they want to or not?"

Tok's eyes widened in amazement, and one eyestalk twisted to regard Aisha. The little girl was sitting up very straight and very, very still, her blue eyes innocently wide.

When did you do that? he asked her, and she lost her look of mock-innocence, narrowing her eyes at Roeglin.

Tamlin snickered, and Aisha turned her gaze on him. The boy laughed out loud.

I do not understand your amusement, the mantid stated.

Tamlin grinned at it. "It's funny to watch her go from trying to act innocent to severely upset because she's about to be found out and can't do anything about it."

Aisha's body gave a short, sharp jerk, and the boy yelped. He bent down.

"Just because I told them why it was funny, it doesn't mean you can kick me," he grumbled, and Tok swiveled his other eye toward the child.

Why are you angry? he asked.

"Because it's not nice to tell," Aisha told him. "Telling on other people is *bad.*"

Tamlin and Roeglin snickered, and Master Envermet smirked. Marsh just shook her head and watched the drama unfold.

So is not answering a question when it is asked, the mantid pointed out.

Aisha scowled at him.

So, did *you make others do as you wished?* Tok asked.

The child nodded.

And did they want to? The mantid's mind voice was gentle.

"Dey were trying to run away," Aisha told him. "Dey had to stay so Roeglin could talk to them. Dey *attacked* us. I made dem stop."

Marsh groaned. It was always a bad sign when Aisha resorted to baby talk. She said nothing, though, letting the mantid handle it. After all, he *was* her teacher in this.

Was there any other way?

"No. Dan was gonna eat them, and Perdy had his claws out. Dere was gonna be blood!"

Blood? Is that bad?

"Dey were not bad people," Aisha argued. "They was just scared!"

I see, and Marsh guessed the mantid really did see, given that he could mind-walk as easily as she breathed.

That thought earned her an eye-twitch, but he didn't take his attention off the child.

So you made them do what? Tok asked.

"I made them come back to where they could talk to Roeglin," the child said and gave the shadow mage a pleading look. "I did."

Roeglin nodded and patted her shoulder comfortingly. "Yes, you did, and you had them all sit down so they wouldn't get hurt."

By "them," Tok observed curiously, *how many do you mean?*

"She returned four young adults bent on escape to where we were waiting," Roeglin told him. "Four!"

And is that bad?

"No, but it is unsettling," Roeglin admitted. "None of us know how to instruct a student with that much power."

Can any of you do the same?

"No," Roeglin admitted, "and therein lies the problem. We can't instruct her on etiquette *or* control if we don't know how to control the ability ourselves—and humans take offense to being made to do things against their will."

My people do not approve of such things, either, Tok assured him, *but, under the circumstances, I believe she acted appropriately.*

"Even in reading their minds without their permission?"

You do as much when approaching a new group of humans, Tok reminded him, his mental voice gentle.

Aisha gasped. "But...but you say that's rude!"

Roeglin groaned and shot the mantid a look, but Tok was unrepentant.

"It's a judgment call," the shadow mage explained, as much for Aisha's benefit as the mantid's.

Tok gave the curious chitter that was laughter for his kind.

It seems a human would be best to teach a human child which factors should be noted, although I think your offspring has a strong grasp of them already.

Aisha bounced in her chair, looking pleased with herself. Tok fixed her with a stern gaze, if that was how the tension in its eyestalks could be interpreted, and the child stilled.

It is not considered polite to scan another's mind without their permission, he admonished, *except when you need to know that an unknown mind is not planning hostile actions. Am I understood?*

"'Kay." Aisha gave the mantid a wide-eyed look.

No, that does not include when you are playing a game with the other children, Tok added after a moment, and Aisha blushed scarlet.

Tamlin chortled with glee. "*Told* you it was rude, Aysh!"

She stuck out her tongue.

Roeglin cleared his throat. "Now that that is clear, I have one more question."

Tok inclined his head. *Ask.*

"Is the child strong enough to protect Marsh from whatever is hunting her in her sleep?"

The mantids rustled in alarm, hind legs scraping protest against abdomens and center legs rasping briefly against their thoraxes. Tok held up a hand and they stilled, but all eyes were on Roeglin.

Marsh waited, holding her breath as the mantid leader contemplated Roeglin's question. After a minute, Tok blinked.

At this time," he stated, his mental voice solemn and firm, *I detect no human with the capabilities required to protect Marsh's mind, but...*

Again, he held up a hand, this time to still the ripple of movement that flowed through the humans.

I am willing to test the humans who wield mental magic to see if there are any strong enough to undertake the training required to become a guardian.

Aisha bounced in her seat and looked excitedly at Tamlin. Her brother frowned, his face pinched with worry.

The mantid continued, *I must warn you, however, that even among my people, the guardians are the elite of all our mages, and that is among a race gifted with mental magic. I expect those qualities to be much harder to find among humans.*

It was not the news Marsh wanted to hear, and she eyed

the mantids worriedly. If they were all that could protect her, what would happen when they were able to return home?

By that stage, the being that threatens you will be gone, Tok told her kindly, *and we would not leave you undefended.*

14

SHADOWS FROM THE PAST

The conversation turned to the training center for mages, with Obasi joining them partway through. He brought a handful of druids interested in teaching and explained that he would not be able to spare them all at once.

Tok bowed his head in understanding, and Master Envermet smiled.

"I brought more with me," he reminded the Grotto warrior, "but we would appreciate it if there were classes for the warriors, too."

He glanced at Marsh. "I need Brigitte if she can be spared, and I'd like you to come to demonstrate how to draw weapons from the shadows. I'm sure there are more with the same ability."

"Two of the Arcadians have an affinity for fire magic," Gustav told them after he'd been summoned, "and Jakob, Zeb, and I can do a little with flame."

His voice turned wistful. "We could always learn more, though. It might help us avoid setting the ruins alight."

He cast a teasing glance at Marsh, and she blushed. Tok drew the memory of when she'd set the cavern alight from her mind. Again, mantid laughter rippled through the room.

After it died away, Roeglin turned the conversation to a more serious topic. "I need to know what it meant to be taken Below," he decided, looking at the guard captain. "Gustav, I'm sorry, but you were here longest. Do you know what it means?"

Gustav paled but shook his head. "I'm sorry, shadow mage, but I don't. I *do* know that the worst of the guards looked forward to it and would taunt those selected with its coming. They weren't done with me the first time people were taken Below after I'd arrived. They still had questions about where I'd come from."

"Which you weren't answering," Roeglin finished for him.

"No," Gustav replied. He managed a small smile. "I was being very uncooperative."

"For that, we're grateful," Roeglin told him, "and we're glad to have you back."

"It *is* a threat you will need to deal with," Gustav told him. "I got the impression that those taken Below weren't just left in a pit, but were *given* to something."

"Maybe Evan or Xavier can tell us more," Marsh suggested.

"Agreed," Roeglin said, and his eyes flashed white. When he had summoned them, he looked around the table.

"I know we could find out just by going and looking to see what's down there," he admitted, "but I'd like to get an idea of what we're looking for before we go back in."

Evan and Xavier came at the trot and gave Roeglin a worried look when they arrived.

"What do you need?" Evan asked.

"Take a seat," the shadow mage told them. "I need to pick your brains."

"You need a particular memory?" Evan asked, "Or do you just want to rummage around in there?"

Roeglin's jaw dropped, and he stared at the man in shock. "I beg your pardon?"

"Do you need me to remember anything in specific, or do you want to go looking for what you need?" Evan repeated.

"I just wanted to ask you a question," Roeglin told him, "but I guess I *could* go rummaging around in your head."

Xavier gave a false shudder. "Ugh. I wouldn't, boss. You don't know *what* you'll step in inside there. Rummaging would be a pretty risky business if you ask me."

Evan elbowed him. "He speaks for himself, but seriously, Roeglin, what do you need to know?"

"What did it mean when someone was taken Below? Were they taken to a specific location? Handed to another batch of raiders? Fed to a monster? What?"

Evan looked at Xavier, and the man shrugged.

"To be honest," he replied, "neither of us knows what you found under the ruins. I mean, we know there were dungeons and they kept prisoners there."

"And tortured them," Xavier added, folding his arms across his chest. His eyes momentarily took on a faraway look. It ended when he shook himself and focused his gaze on Roeglin. "We didn't know."

"The screams didn't bother you?" The comment was

out before Marsh could stop it, and she immediately regretted it.

Evan gave her a wounded look. "There was a lot that bothered us," he answered softly, "and not a lot that we could do to stop it, but we never heard a thing coming out of the Library. The dungeons were a fair way inside, and the doors were thick."

"I understand," Marsh told him, red-faced. She regretted her words. "I'm sorry."

He gave her a grimace. "It's okay. All we know is that the Below is under the Library, and the only entrance to it is inside."

"That and we were asked to bring prisoners to the chief's office and leave them there," Xavier elaborated.

"Especially mages," Evan added. "Anyone who showed an iota of magical talent was to be brought."

His eyes grew wide and his expression haunted. "I hid everyone I could."

Xavier nodded in agreement. "You gave me the courage to do the same. Until I saw you hide that druid, I just tried not to see. After that, I tried to keep them safe as well. It was hard."

Tok hissed and the other mantids drew back, rising on their hind legs and curling their antennae in distress.

Evan snorted. "You know it's rude to look without asking permission, right?"

Tok's antennae quirked.

The matter is important for us to understand. Your kind has done no worse than some of our people, and you did much better than many. I can see why you were forgiven and what constraints we must consider if we are ever able to return to our world.

Marsh didn't know what to think of that, so she shrugged. "Is there anyone left who might know more?"

Evan shook his head. "No. They all fought, and some were trying to kill the prisoners when you reached them. You showed them the only kind of mercy they deserved."

Marsh remembered some of the fighting she'd seen and some of the men she'd killed.

"If I'd known, I'd have tried to take a few alive."

"Wouldn't have done you any good," Roeglin told her. "I'd have killed the ones you left."

She looked at him in surprise, and he gave her a guilty shrug.

"What can I say? I lost my temper."

Xavier's quiet voice broke in. "The guards from the dungeons used to laugh about what happened down there," he murmured. "They'd come off a shift, talking about what they'd done, or what they were planning to do."

He shuddered. "It was always worse to hear when they came out after taking people Below. I asked them once what happened to the prisoners they took Below, and they asked me why, did I want to find out for myself?"

He paused and swallowed hard, then continued. "One told me it was better I didn't find out for myself, and another offered to help me learn firsthand. A third just said they left the prisoners in a place called the Arena and closed the doors. He said they didn't go back until the screaming stopped and the place had stayed quiet for two turns of an hourglass."

"So how did they know when it was time to make a delivery?" Roeglin asked. "Was it on a regular schedule, or was there something else?"

"Something else," Evan told him. "The boss would get a message. We never saw the messages or what they were written on, but he got them, and he'd call a special assembly. He'd ask those of us on the surface to turn in anyone who'd shown magical ability, and then he'd take a stroll through the pens to find anyone else the Others might want."

"Others?" Marsh latched onto the title. "Who were they?"

"No one knows. We just called them that because we figured they weren't us." He shrugged. "We never imagined that they might come from another world entirely."

"How did the boss choose?" Roeglin asked. He gestured at Gustav. "After all, it's not like Gustav is very magical."

"No, but he *did* fight them, and that was more than enough to make him a candidate for the dungeons and a gift for the Others."

Marsh remembered the condition the soldier had been in when she'd arrived. "You would have thought they'd have kept him in better condition," she mused, but Xavier shook his head.

"The injured ones showed the Others our 'strength' or something like that. That's as much as I could get from the guards when I asked them the same question. One of the others said I should ask the boss."

He shuddered. "No way *that* was happening."

"Not that any of us asked him much," Evan added, and Xavier nodded.

"Yeah, he always looked sick until it was done."

"Sick? How do you mean?" Marsh was having difficulty imagining anything that would make Kearick sick unless it was a loss of profit.

"Well, he was always a bit pale after a message came through," Xavier told them.

"And sweaty," Evan added.

"Pale and sweaty and jumpy," Xavier elaborated. "The slightest noise would make him start. It was like he thought something was watching him from the shadows or waiting to leap out at him."

"And talk about a temper!" Evan exclaimed. "I mean, he was mean most days, but until a delivery Below had gone off successfully, he was worse. The slightest infringement could set him off, and it didn't matter who you were. You could be sentenced to a night staked out for the remnant, or a stint in the dungeons, or a public beating by the guards. It all depended on what crossed his mind at the time."

Marsh shivered. That was not a side of Kearick she'd ever seen. Sure, he'd shouted when he was upset, but he'd never meted out physical punishment, and she could not imagine the Kearick she knew *ever* feeding someone to the shadows.

"It took him a couple of days to settle down. We all avoided him until he got over it. It was the only thing we could do."

"Apart from the guards that waited outside, did anyone go in with the prisoners and talk about it?" Roeglin asked.

Evan and Xavier exchanged glances.

"No one went into the Arena that we ever heard about," Xavier told him, "and believe me, I asked."

Evan frowned. "Gustav was down there for one delivery." He glanced at the guard captain. "Ask him."

Gustav shook his head. "I was down there, sure, but they kept the doors closed and locked as if something might get in."

He paled. "It didn't keep the sound out, though. They reminded me of it when they came back. Said that was what was waiting for me next time someone was needed Below."

He fell silent, staring across the table at nothing. The memories scrolling behind his eyes were not something Marsh wanted him to share. They waited until he blinked and came back to the present.

"If you're going down there, I'm coming, too."

"Going where?" Marsh asked, doing her best impression of Aisha trying to look innocent.

It had the desired effect, and Gustav chuckled.

"The Arena, or whatever Evan called it. You're going to go there and then look for the portal." He leaned back in his chair and surveyed them both. "I'm going, too."

Marsh exchanged glances with Roeglin and Master Envermet, and Tok's eyestalks waved as he studied each of them.

"Me, too!" Aisha declared.

Tamlin sighed, and the little girl glared at him. He raised his hands. "I'm not going to stop you."

"You're not?" she asked, her small face comical in surprise.

"Nope, but I *am* coming with you to make sure you don't get into trouble, okay?"

She frowned, considering it. "'Kaaaay."

Master Envermet rolled his eyes and pushed back his chair. "If that's decided, do we have anything else we need to discuss?"

They looked at each other and shrugged.

"I can't think of anything else," Marsh told them, standing.

She glanced at Roeglin, directing their attention toward him. He was the leader of the township, after all.

Roeglin followed her example and stood. "I'll meet you all at the Library as soon as you are ready. It's time we took a proper look at what is down there."

Tok clicked a question. *Where would you like us to wait?*

"You're all coming?"

As well as being among my most powerful minds, these are also my advisors. We need to assess the location.

"And you're already familiar with portals," Roeglin concluded.

He led them outside and pointed at the Library. "Meet us at the main doors. We will not take long to prepare, but..."

But you need your armor and extra weapons, the mantid concluded for him.

"We do."

And the child?

"She has defenses of her own."

And defenders, the mantid noted, flicking an antenna toward Tamlin and then to where Mordan, her kits, and

Scruffknuckle were emerging from around the corner of a building.

The kat flicked her ears toward the mantid and then flicked her tail, her gaze scanning the gathered mages and guards. When she found Aisha, she padded solemnly over to the child and circled around her.

Aisha giggled and then hugged her. The kat gave a long-suffering sigh and looked at Roeglin.

"I think she wants you to hurry," Gustav observed, and the others laughed.

"Then we'd *all* better hurry," Master Envermet suggested, and they made for their quarters at a jog.

Tok watched them go and then leaned down to the kat. *Is she still safe?*

Mordan looked up at the insectoid's face and blinked at him. *Of course, my human is safe.*

And then she yawned, showing the mantid her fangs.

The other mantids chittered nervously, but Tok merely inclined his head in acknowledgment and then straightened. *We will wait.*

It did not take long for the humans to return. Tok looked them over, silently approving of the armor they wore. He eyed their weapons and gave an internal shrug. The shadow mages would not use them, preferring to take their weapons from the air around them—and the one who used fire to coat his sword would soon ruin its temper.

"It's this way," Roeglin told him, unaware of his internal thoughts. Tok was aware of being studied. "The entrance will be a tight squeeze for you."

Dipping into the human's mind, Tok saw what he meant, but he also saw little choice.

He and his people needed to see the site of the portal, and they had no alternative means of reaching it. When they had escaped through it, none of them had intended to go back, and their flight had been too rushed for any to remember what path they had taken.

15

THE DELIVERY POINT

The Library had been cleaned since Marsh's last visit. Even so, she could still see the faint shadows of bloodstains on the floor and some of the walls. She followed Roeglin through the door, and the sight made her pause.

Roeglin continued on a few steps, then turned back.

Are you okay?

Marsh nodded, looking around. To her left, she could see the large desk the children had hidden under. It had been pulled out from the wall, and benches had been added so more people could sit around it. The late afternoon sunshine created a pool of light and warmth on the wall behind it, but not on the table, and the bookcases had been rearranged so that it now sat in a space of its own.

"I like it," Marsh told him. "It's…"

She shrugged. "We need to keep moving."

Without waiting for him to reply, she led the way to where she remembered the stairs started. Roeglin followed, letting her absorb the other changes around her.

For one thing, everything was tidy—the books had been reshelved and overturned furniture righted. What concerned her most, however, was the locked door leading to the small room above the stairwell. The raiders had used it as a secure checkpoint, but it was empty now.

Marsh moved aside so Roeglin could unbolt the door and found herself pushed farther away as Mordan shouldered her way past. She opened her mouth to protest, only to close it again when the cat fixed her with a defiant stare.

"Well, of course, after you, Dan," she answered. "As if *I'd* get in your way."

The kat tossed her head and gave an irritable twitch of her tail but didn't do more. Marsh got the message loud and clear, though, and was tempted to forge ahead of the cat to make a point.

As she thought it, Mordan tensed, and Marsh decided against pushing her. When Perdemor tried to follow his mother, however, she drew the line.

"Don't even *think* about it," she snapped, and the kit hesitated.

When *he* raised his head in defiance, Marsh let the shadows shudder around her, and the kit stepped back. Roeglin opened the door and went to do the same for the next one.

"Nothing's been disturbed," he reported, "and the guards say they've heard nothing the whole time they've been on duty."

"No one's been through since I left?" Marsh asked.

"No, we wanted to wait until everyone was back and we'd had time to discuss what to do."

The bolt gave, and he slid it back. As soon as he started

opening the door, Mordan slipped past him into the darkness beyond. Marsh stumbled as Perdemor and his siblings followed. Behind her, she heard Aisha pat Scruffknuckle.

"Go on," the child ordered. "Go with them. I'll be fine. *I* will look after Marsh."

Marsh smothered a smile and followed Roeglin and the kat down the stairs.

The air felt stuffy and close, and she wrinkled her nose at the lingering scent of long imprisonment and hardship.

"We didn't get to clean down here," Roeglin informed her.

She nodded in reply, letting her eyes adjust to the dark. This time they moved more slowly, inspecting each cell with care and looking for more than the survivors they'd been focused on last time. They found nothing, apart from what they had left behind.

Marsh glanced back at Gustav. "Are you okay?"

His face was pale and his eyes wide, but he nodded. Marsh noticed that his hands rested close to his weapons as his gaze roved the blackness.

She nudged Roeglin. "I'll scout ahead."

He opened his mouth as if to protest, then closed it again, giving her a nod. "Let me know what you find."

Marsh didn't dignify the instruction with a response but stepped past him, becoming one with the shadows as she did.

I am never getting used to that, he told her and let her see herself as he saw her.

The image made her shudder, and she had to fight to stay blended.

She looked like a ghost, a slightly darker shadow in the

midst of shadows. Not quite there, but very real none-theless. Her eyes gleamed, blacker than the rest of her, glittering like wet marble. With one last look at Roeglin, she trotted through the shadows and down the corridor, checking every cell and alcove and peering into every guard station.

Not only was the Under-Library complex empty, but it felt abandoned. The echo of footsteps moving in her wake did little to dispel that notion. Marsh worked her way through the cells until she reached the bare wall opposite the room that had held Kearick.

There she stopped. It was impossible to know what lay beyond the door. To fill the time, Marsh ran her fingers over the area she'd seen Roeglin touch until she found the hollows. She had decided not to try to operate it when he arrived.

"Waiting for us?" he asked, eyebrows raised.

"Thinking about it," she replied, and he smiled.

I can see what's going on inside your head, you know.

That's rude, she told him, smiling back.

Aisha groaned, and they both turned to her.

"You're not supposed to be looking, either," Marsh told her.

Tamlin wormed his way to the front. "Are we going through or not?"

He reached for the space where Marsh's hand rested, but Roeglin stopped him. The mage looked at Marsh. "Ready?"

She nodded and slid her fingers into the slots, feeling the stone shift slightly when she reached the bottom. Just as Roeglin had done, she flexed her fingers. The door opened into the short corridor they remembered, and they followed it to the large, hollow chamber beyond.

The padlocks on the grate remained in place, blocking the nine-foot drop into the pit. Three yards across, it secured the six-foot opening but still gave a clear view of the bottom of the pit and the three empty archways opening into it. None of them could see down the tunnels leading away from the arches, but that they had expected.

Marsh took a deep breath and looked at Roeglin. "Shall we?"

There was a snort from behind them, and Henri said, "Oh, sure. Let's. After all, it's not like you have *company* or anything."

Marsh blushed in spite of herself, but Roeglin sighed.

"What's the worst that could happen?"

Gustav groaned. "You *had* to ask."

Roeglin flashed him a grin and bent to lift the edge of the grate.

"I could do with a little help," he suggested, as Tok and the other mantids moved forward to assist. "How did they deliver anyone down here?"

Evan gulped, his eyes wide. "I think they just opened the grate and pushed them in," he said.

Roeglin stared at him and then looked down into the pit. "The mages can shadow-step there," he declared and frowned, "but the rest of you might need a rope."

Marsh stepped forward and held out her hand. "I can take people through," she told them.

Tok came to peer over her shoulder. *It is not too far for us,* he noted.

He cocked his antennae forward, letting them wave

gently over the opening. After a moment, he added, *And we won't need to return this way. There are other paths to the outside.*

As long as you can fit. Marsh kept the thought to herself, and if Tok heard it, he gave no indication.

Evan came alongside her. "I'll go with you," he said.

"And I'll take Aisha through," Tamlin stated, reaching for his sister's hand.

Tok looked into the hole. *We'll go first*, the mantid offered. *We can defend those arriving and keep a watch on the tunnels.*

"Do you have the energy to take me as well, boy?" Gustav asked Tamlin.

The boy looked him up and down and then nodded.

"And can you show me how, while you're at it?" the old soldier pressed.

Before Marsh or Roeglin could intervene, Tamlin shook his head.

"No, but I can have Aisha show you, and we can practice later." He cast an uncertain glance at Brigitte and Marsh and Roeglin. "That's if it's okay?"

Brigitte also looked at Marsh and Roeglin. "It's up to you," she advised them. "Both children are up to this."

Marsh nodded. "Look now and practice later," she agreed, "in case you tire yourself out."

Gustav frowned as though puzzled as to how that would happen, but he didn't argue. Marsh figured he'd work it out soon enough...if he could actually make the magic work. So far, the man hadn't shown any interest in learning more than the limited fire magic he could manage.

Are you ready? Tok asked.

Marsh stepped back to give the mantids access. "Yes," she replied.

She and Roeglin watched as the large insectoids gripped the edge of the pit and lowered themselves through the hole headfirst before dropping the rest of the way to land lightly on the floor.

This shadow-stepping is of interest to us, Tok commented as he moved away from the opening and stationed himself facing one of the doors.

The other mantids mirrored his action, each choosing a different archway. The fourth mantid filled the remaining gap, although what it had found to focus on was out of sight. Marsh only hoped it wasn't something that would kill them.

She relaxed when the mantids settled to stillness and nothing else moved.

It is safe, Tok assured them. *I sense nothing in the passages beyond.*

Mordan went next. One moment, the big cat was there, and the next, she had padded forward, vanishing into thin air and reappearing in the center of the circle below. The kits and Scruffknuckle moved with her, and Marsh wondered when the four of them had acquired Tamlin's ability to step through clear air.

I showed them, Aisha explained, her voice gliding along the link between them.

Master Envermet rolled his eyes as he stepped out of the darkness and knelt beside the child.

"Care to show me?" he asked, and their eyes flashed white.

"I didn't see any shadows," Gustav murmured, and Tamlin chuckled.

"Shadows are just air that's in the dark," he told the man and offered Gustav his hand.

The captain took it, obeying when Tamlin said, "Walk with me."

Marsh watched them take a step and vanish. Izmay held out her hand to Henry and Xavier, taking them to a point to one side of Tamlin, Gustav, and Aisha. Zeb followed with Jakob, leaving Marsh and Roeglin to go last.

With one last look at the empty corridor and silent cells, they exchanged glances and stepped through the shadows to the center of the arena. It was bigger than it looked from above. The fourth mantid, she discovered, was keeping watch on a door they hadn't seen.

"Do you know where it leads?" Marsh asked, but Evan shook his head. She sighed. "Well, I guess there's only one way to find out."

She strode purposefully forward, stopping just short of it when Henri caught up to her and wrapped a hand around her wrist.

"Let me."

Marsh hesitated, scanning his face.

Henri translated for her. "If there's anything waiting, it's better me than you," he explained.

The door opened onto a set of stairs leading up.

Henri started up the stairs and looked back at her. "Want to hazard a guess where these are going to lead?"

Marsh pulled a sword and buckler from the shadows and followed him. "I know where I *think* it's going to lead. That doesn't mean I'm not going to take precautions."

He nodded and started moving up. Marsh caught the play of a faint smile over his lips as he went.

Smartass, she thought.

Just be careful, Roeglin warned.

Like I'd be anything else.

In the end, care wasn't necessary, although the door hidden close to the library entrance was a surprise.

"I didn't know they *had* another way down," Evan told her when she returned.

Henri snorted.

"I didn't!" Evan protested. "I don't want anything sneaking out of here! If I'd known, I'd have said!"

"We believe you," Roeglin said, laying a reassuring hand on his shoulder, but Marsh didn't miss the brief flash of white that said he'd checked.

She turned to face the doors. "Any preferences?" she asked.

Tok stalked over to inspect the three, but before he'd finished investigating the first, Mordan strolled out of the second.

There is a strange scent in this tunnel, she informed Marsh. *It is strongest this way.*

She flicked her tail, her eyes briefly going to Tok. *I smelled the passage of these, too.*

"Mordan says she picked up a trail down that one," Marsh explained when she found all eyes on her. She nodded to Tok. "She said she could smell that you had passed that way, too."

The mantid's antennae did a surprised flip that was echoed by his companions, and the four of them hurried to the passage the kat had come out of.

16

THE THREAT FROM BELOW

As soon as they stepped through the arch, they discovered a passage that looked like it ran around the circumference of the pit. Roeglin gave a soft whistle and held up his hand.

"Henri, Izmay, take our left. Zeb, Jakob, go right. I need to know."

My people will join you, Tok said, and one of the mantids moved to join each pair of humans. *They can relay what you find.*

Henri's mouth tightened as he looked up at the mantid that joined them.

I am K'tch, it said by way of greeting.

The insectoid that joined Jakob and Zeb gave his name as Etk'k. Both waited for the humans to take the lead.

Roeglin looked at Xavier and Evan. "You don't have to come with us," he told them. "You can take the stairs back to the surface and let them know what we've found so far."

The men exchanged glances and looked back at Roeglin.

"We'd rather stay if it's all the same," Evan told him. He gestured at the closest tunnel. "Time we saw what happened to those we betrayed."

That last word came out as a croak and he cleared his throat after, his skin burning a deep red.

Xavier nodded in agreement, his face the same shade.

Roeglin studied their expressions before nodding. He said nothing in return, though, just turned and walked into the corridor.

K'tch's voice touched their minds. *We have met each other and are returning. Henri says to relay that the tunnel goes beneath the stairs but has no openings into it or the center.*

"Understood," Roeglin replied, his eyes gleaming white as he spoke. "Can you, Henri, and Izmay investigate the first tunnel, and Zeb, Jakob, and Etk'k the second?"

It shall be so.

Marsh felt the mantid's mind leave and forged ahead. As she did, she realized she hadn't seen the children since Mordan had led the way back through the arch. She reached along the link.

Dan, are the cubs with you?

The kat's reply came back immediately. *Of course. They cannot be left unattended.*

Marsh blushed at the kat's reproof and toyed with the idea of scolding the two youngsters. She brushed it aside as Roeglin's fingertips touched the back of her hand.

"Ready?"

She nodded, returning the touch before blending with the shadows. "Time to become a ghost."

"You're lucky the children know who you are," Roeglin informed her.

"And that they're not likely to panic," she reminded him.

They cautiously made their way along the tunnel, shadow blades drawn and shields ready. The tunnel curved slightly left, but they had only traveled for a short distance before they heard the sound of soft footsteps.

Roeglin hesitated, raising his hand to signal a halt.

Go ahead, he instructed Marsh. *I need to know what we're walking into.*

Done. Marsh glided forward, her shadow-blended steps making no sound on the cavern floor.

Behind her, Brigitte dropped back to guard the rear, and Evan and Xavier readied their blades. Marsh moved swiftly, starting to feel the strain of staying blended with the shadow. The tunnel felt subtly wrong, but she couldn't work out why.

Following the sound of the footsteps, she moved steadily toward them. The steps seemed to be getting closer and sounded as though they were coming from in front of her. Marsh was all too aware of Roeglin riding behind her eyes—and Master Envermet keeping him company.

She reached a junction of tunnels.

Wait there. Roeglin's order was short and abrupt. *Stay out of sight.*

As if she'd do anything else.

I know you.

Well, there was that.

Marsh shook his presence away and moved close to a wall. The footsteps were drawing closer, even though they no longer sounded like they came from the tunnel ahead.

The tunnels that joined the chamber gave two potential points of origin.

The only problem was that it sounded like there were steps coming from down both of them. Worse than that was the soft skitter she could hear behind them, as if not everything headed her way was human. She sank into the deep shadows by a wall and waited.

A few feet behind her, Roeglin, Evan, Xavier, Tok, and Brigitte did the same.

The footsteps drew nearer, then suddenly stopped.

"There's a chamber ahead." Henri's hoarse whisper cut the black, and Marsh relaxed. Now, she understood what had happened.

"Tok, can you let the others know we'll meet them at the junction?"

As soon as her words hit clear air, the footsteps stopped.

"Marsh?" Zeb's soft call reached her from the closest tunnel.

"Ahead of you where the three tunnels meet."

"Well, not quite," he said a few moments later.

The sound of his voice made Marsh jump and Zeb chuckled, stepping out of the shadows on the opposite side of the chamber.

"Sorry, Marsh. Etk'k said there was a presence ahead. He didn't say it was you."

"Mantid guards my head every night," Marsh grumbled. "You'd think he'd recognized what my head felt like."

"He says that's not how it works," Zeb relayed. "That it can be hard to tell what head waits for you when there is so much else to focus on."

"Yeah, and K'tch says the same." Henri's voice interrupted them, and the big man stomped around the corner.

He was followed by the mantid warrior. The creature flexed its antennae toward the single tunnel leading away from them.

The cubs and their guardians are not far, K'tch informed them.

Marsh felt her heart unknot.

Aisha? she sent along the link she had with the little girl.

Hurry up, Marsh! We've found something! At the excitement in the child's tone, Marsh dropped out of the shadows, landing with a light crunch on the stony tunnel floor.

Now that she was paying attention, Marsh noticed the floor leading into the room showed signs of wear. As she crossed the junction to the tunnel leading out, she saw it showed even more wear.

"They brought them through this way," she murmured.

Henri snorted. "Now tell us something we *don't* know."

"Or they all came and went this way," Jakob offered.

"You're thinking they didn't take anyone away?" Xavier's voice was full of horror.

"It's a possibility," Henri agreed. He looked around. "But if that was the case, they'd need somewhere to stash the bodies."

Evan gasped, and Roeglin scowled at Henri.

"What?" the big ex-guard demanded. "All I'm saying is that it's a possibility."

Izmay rested a hand on his shoulder. "It's a possibility that we didn't need to hear right now. Let's hope for the best."

Henri sighed. "Yeah, I suppose you're right. Besides, I don't see anything like a burial pit or smell—oof!"

He stepped a little farther from Izmay, rubbing his ribs. She scowled at him for a moment longer, then smiled at Evan. "We won't know until we look."

She followed Marsh into the tunnel.

"Where are the kids?" she asked, coming alongside.

"With Mordan," Marsh told her, not caring that her voice said exactly how she felt about that.

Izmay snickered. "We'd better hurry, then. Maybe get there *before* they find us some trouble to get them out of."

She kept moving while she was talking, and Marsh nodded. Keeping Tamlin and Aisha out of trouble was a full-time task, even *with* the kat taking point.

Rude! Aisha commented, having picked up the conversation along their link.

So's listening to a conversation that doesn't concern you.

Did so!

Yeah, well, Marsh couldn't fault the kid on that one. The conversation kinda *had* been about her.

You know what I mean.

Yup. Aisha's brief acknowledgment became excitement. *We* found *something!*

What?

"Hurry. The kids have found something." Roeglin's urgent whisper reached her, just ahead of the hurried footsteps that followed. Marsh and Izmay kept moving forward, blades ready, but slightly faster than caution would dictate.

Aisha and Tamlin were crouched on either side of a stone doorframe that had been built into the tunnel walls.

Made from precisely cut blocks of a reddish-colored stone, it framed the corridor beyond.

"That doesn't look like it goes anywhere," Jakob mused.

"The tunnel or the door?" Henri demanded. "Because that tunnel has to go *somewhere*."

"You want to step through and prove the point?" Jakob challenged, and Henri's face turned thoughtful.

He eyed the doorway carefully, coming close enough to touch what it was made of.

"That's like no stone *I've* ever seen," he noted. "It feels strange."

"That's not really stone," Marsh observed, tilting her head one way and then another. "It's... It *looks* more like crystal."

She raised her fingers to touch the smoky pink surface, but Tok reached out a clawed hand and pushed her gently away.

It is better not to touch, he advised.

Henri pulled his hand away as though he'd been burned. "You coulda warned me!"

You are not psychic, the mantid told him. *You can do no harm.*

"Well, what can *she* do?" Henri demanded belligerently.

Draw attention was Tok's succinct response.

The others came over to inspect the gate, but the mantids hung back, conversing in a series of chirps, clicks, and scrapes.

Marsh felt her nose wrinkle as though there was some kind of scent in the air. She couldn't define it, though. It seemed to come and go.

After a few moments, Tok cocked his head.

Where did the kat say she detected our scent? he asked.

"From here," Aisha answered, pointing at the door.

She walked down the corridor, moving her hand to indicate the floor. "Along here."

The mantids turned their heads as the child walked past them. Marsh frowned, following Aisha's progress.

"Where are you going?"

"Nowhere," the girl answered, coming to a halt before a section of wall. She turned her attention from Marsh to Tok. "It stops here."

Tok looked at Mordan. The kat had risen to her feet as the child moved away from her place by the door. Now, she padded after her.

The mantids' scent goes from the gate to the child. It stops at the wall. She paused and cocked her head, tail swishing slightly. *The scent of the Others is stronger there than elsewhere, like they stayed in that place longer than anywhere else.*

Marsh frowned. "Aisha, is there anything special about that section of the wall?"

"Special?" the little girl asked, but she didn't wait for Marsh to answer. Instead, she inspected the wall very carefully, placing her hands on the stone. "Oh!"

"Oh?" Roeglin asked.

"Gimme a minute," the child ordered, reaching into the wall. "Dere's a fing."

Baby talk? Marsh frowned and glanced at the wall. As she did, the rock around the edges of the wall shifted under Aisha's hand, and the sound of breaking metal echoed briefly around them.

"Oops."

The mantids had crowded around the hole and were looking down it.

Yes. This was the way we took, Tok confirmed. *But why was it concealed?*

"To stop those taken from trying to escape?" Evan suggested. "I mean, I know *I* would run if I came face to face with *that!*"

Marsh had turned away from the door to see what Aisha was breaking. Now she turned back, registering the soft red gleam starting to light the tunnel.

This is not a good place to be, Tok observed, receiving several disbelieving looks from those around him. *They will be coming.*

"Who will be coming?" Roeglin demanded as the first shrieks split the air.

Master Envermet came alongside him, drawing his weapons from the air.

"Aisha, get out of here. Tamlin!" Marsh shouted, arming herself from the shadows and pulling a thick layer of shadow armor around herself.

Roeglin grabbed the back of her tunic and pulled her slowly back as Master Envermet moved between them and the door. "We need room to fight," he told her.

"Fall back to the junction!" Gustav ordered. "Kat! That means you, too."

Mordan rumbled at him but bounded to Aisha. The little girl didn't argue but scrambled immediately onto the kat's back, burying her hands deep in Mordan's fur.

The kat didn't stop to see if she had a good grip. She bounded down the corridor with her kits and Scruffknuckle by her side. Three of the mantids hurried after them, but Tok and Etk'k slipped into the side tunnel.

Henri and Izmay took one look at them and slid in after them.

"You're not getting all the fun!" Henri told the mantids, and Izmay grinned.

It will not be fun if they see us, the mantid advised, guiding them farther down the tunnel and around a slight bend. *We will emerge after they pass.*

"You know what's coming?" Roeglin asked, not stopping as he and Marsh reversed quickly past the opening.

The image that floated into their minds in response was enough to turn Marsh's stomach. The creature looked like an orange-furred humanoid with spindly limbs. It was almost cute, save that its head was bare and shaped like an elongated egg, its eyes dark almond-shaped discs, and it had no nose that she could see.

Worse still were the small blue tendrils around its sharp-toothed mouth and the tentacles that emerged as a twisting orange and blue mass from its back.

"What in all the Deeps is *that?*" Henri demanded.

Death has called them "Ooken," Tok informed him, *but they are merely the enemy's tools.*

"Well, *poutain a merde!*"

"We *can* kill them, right?" Jakob called back through the tunnel.

Yes, they can die, but they come in numbers.

Marsh shook off Roeglin's hand and bolted toward the cavern at the junction. The noise was getting louder, and she didn't want to be out of position when the creatures making it reached her.

"We need to block the door!"

"I can do it," Aisha called back. Mordan would have carried the child back up the tunnel if Marsh hadn't snatched her from the kat's back as she passed.

Mordan skidded to a halt and doubled back on herself. The light behind them turned scarlet and then dimmed to a sullen crimson glow. Master Envermet arrived at a run, standing with them as he faced the tunnel.

Here they come. Tok's warning didn't tell them anything they didn't already know.

Marsh reached the mouth of the junction and whirled around. The creatures came through the portal in a rush. If Marsh hadn't known any better, she would have sworn they knew they were there, because they raced down the tunnel.

If they noticed the gap in the tunnel wall, they didn't stop to investigate it. It was as though they were sure of the team's location.

"I'd like to know how they knew we were here," Gustav muttered, watching the furry mass screeching toward them.

He raised his blade and frowned slightly, smiling as flames rippled along it from tip to hilt. Jakob chuckled, doing the same. Henri groaned, drawing two blades and finding a space he could work in. The mantids shifted, finding their own places.

Marsh glanced at Roeglin and grinned. He grinned briefly back, then the creatures were upon them. As the first of the monsters followed them, Aisha's shout of defiance was accompanied by a ripple of stone spikes erupting from the floor.

"No fair, Aysh!" Tamlin protested, making it hard for Marsh to resist the urge to look for the pair.

Mordan roared, and the Ooken paused.

They were uglier in real life than they had been in the mental image Tok had shared, and the rancid odor that accompanied them made Marsh wish she couldn't smell. As the floor erupted beneath them, they took to the walls, using their tentacles to full advantage.

Marsh stared as the nearest survivor used its tentacles to navigate the wall and come up and over its head.

"How many of them *are* there?" Jakob asked, his voice faint with disbelief. It was rapidly followed by anger. "Oh no, you don't. You might smell worse than a shade, but you don't scare me. Zeb!"

"I got you!"

There was a brief flare of red light, followed by an Ooken screech, the smell of singed fur and burnt fish, and Jakob's victorious shout.

"Come, get me, you ugly sons of the Deep!"

It was the most vocal Marsh had ever heard him. She was tempted to look back, but she was too busy. Ookens didn't fight fair. They came from all directions, lashing out with their tentacles and slashing with razor-sharp claws.

"Aysh!" Tamlin's shout of alarm was almost Marsh's undoing.

Marsh glanced around in time to see the child disappear into the rock wall, and only Roeglin's quick thinking saved her. A shadow shield slammed down in front of her, catching three Ooken in mid-leap.

Focus! They will be fine! The shadow mage's voice growled through her head, and she saw he was right.

Several Ookens tore at the wall Aisha had stepped into and a smooth dome of shadow had appeared where Tamlin had stood, but the children were untouched.

We are okay, Aisha informed her. *Don't make me come out there.*

Marsh choked back a bark of laughter and parried a murderous slash of claws with her blade. Looking past her attacker, she saw more Ooken emerging from the portal.

Just how many are they sending? she thought.

Tok answered, *They will keep coming until they think they outnumber you ten to one.*

So they're cowards as well as smelly?

Tok chuckled. *We will join you in battle shortly. They will either stop emerging, or they will investigate their broken technology and force us to act.*

Just tell me when you think they're all here.

Tok caught a glimpse of what she was planning. *You do not fight fair,* he observed.

They started it, Marsh snapped back. *I'm just going to finish it.*

Tok chuckled in mantid fashion. *Henri will not be pleased.*

"Henri will Deeps-be-damned just have to get over it," Marsh snarled out loud, earning a curious glance from Roeglin.

"Eyes. On the. Fight!" she rapped out, slashing through another tentacle with her blade.

That one would have wrapped itself around the shadow mage's head.

The Ooken on the ceiling screeched in outrage and dropped. This time, the shadow mage was ready. He sidestepped, dropped the buckler from his forearm, and pulled a second blade from the shadows, slashing the half-dozen tentacles that tried to ensnare him.

As the creature hit the floor beside him, he drove one blade between the ridges on its misshapen skull and swept the second blade hard against its neck. In the short struggle that ensued, he used the first blade to keep the Ooken where he wanted it while he removed its head from its shoulders.

It took several strokes, and he had to kick the monster clear when he was done.

In the meantime, Marsh fought to keep his left flank clear, feeling inordinately relieved when one of the mantids protected his right. This time the insectoid warriors weren't using their slingshots, but the short blades they carried strapped to their torsos.

They did not bother with shields but fought with both hands and their feet. Marsh hadn't realized their feet were clawed as well, or that they'd developed a fighting style that used all six limbs. If she hadn't been so busy trying to defeat incoming attacks and destroy their source, she'd have been fascinated.

Focus! Even Roeglin's mental voice sounded breathless, but Marsh took his advice and kept her attention on her opponents.

There were far more of them than she liked. It was almost as though the death of one spawned another two.

"Where do they keep coming from?" she asked, blocking another attack with her shield but wincing as the tentacle looped past the shadow and wrapped around her forearm.

"Let! Me! Go!" she shouted, punctuating each word

with a sword strike. The last syllable ended on a thrust that buried her blade in the Ooken's throat. She kicked it free, turning so that its body and her tentacle-wrapped shield arm formed a barrier between her and the next attack.

Movement alerted her to the danger coming in from behind, but it ended with a shout from Zeb and several meaty whacks.

Marsh dispelled the shield to the shadows and tried to shake the tentacle loose, but it was wrapped too tight and small barbs were embedded in her arm, keeping its coils in place.

"Sons of the Deep!" she cursed, forced to send her blade back to the shadows.

Rather than distract Zeb or Roeglin, she dropped to her knees and pulled a dome of shadow over her head. "Give me a minute."

"I got you," Zeb reassured her, and she saw him take out another of the furry monsters on the other side of the dome.

Roeglin was fighting on the other side, but he was more than holding his own and Master Envermet was guarding his back.

As she worked the tentacle loose, Marsh observed the battle through the walls of the dome. What she saw wasn't good.

Tok, are they done yet?

Almost. The last of them should cross in three...two...

As the mantid reached *one*, there was a startled roar from one of the kits, followed by three more roars of outrage and a torrent of angry barking.

"Mordan!" Roeglin shouted. "Marsh! You have to stop them. They've taken one of the kits!"

His warning was followed by a treble shriek. "You put dat down! You give dat back! You give dat! Back! *NOW!*"

"*Merde!*" Marsh came out from under the dome without looking to see what was waiting.

"Duck!" Only Jakob's warning and the flash of movement she caught from the corner of her eye saved her.

Marsh ducked, and a clawed hand slashed through the air where her throat had been.

Jakob's "I've got it!" was followed by the sound of heated metal meeting flesh and the dying screams of another monster.

"Marsh, we need the lightning! We need it now!" Roeglin's voice was hoarse.

Hurry. We will try to save the kit. Tok's voice had never been more welcome.

Marsh took a quick look around the battle zone and glanced up the corridor leading to the gate, and then she dropped to her knees. As she did, she reached for the lightning in the shadows.

"I need you," she told it, pushing that need into her request. "I need your strength and your vengeance. I need your swift strike. Those creatures must die."

As she spoke, she pictured the Ookens in her mind. "Kill them all. Sear them from the cavern. Let none leave alive."

Mordan's roar was accompanied by others and followed by Ooken screams.

"Help me *NOW!*"

As the lightning answered her call, she became aware of a second presence in her mind.

Aisha!

The little girl reached along her link and then picked up another—Tamlin's.

He will help you.

Marsh wished she'd thought to call on the boy. They'd been practicing contacting each other, but Marsh's ability was still growing, and Tamlin struggled with even the most basic of connections. With Aisha holding the link open, their minds touched.

As one, they reached for the energy lurking in the cavern's shadows, finding it also in the mushrooms and the rocks. She paused. There was a surprising amount of lightning lurking in the rocks.

"Come," she commanded it and felt Tamlin reach out with her. What was less comforting was the feel of Aisha's nimble mental fingers reaching out to touch the lightning in the stone.

"Ooh, *pretty!*"

Tamlin summed it up. "*Merde.*"

There was no time to debate the consequences. They had a kit to save.

"Come!" Marsh told the lightning. "We need you. Take only these."

Again, she showed the lightning the targets she needed it to take. "Just these."

"Only the Ookens," Tamlin echoed.

"Kill them all," sounded no less sinister in Aisha's childish tones. "Just the Ookens."

"Hurry it u—" was as far as Roeglin got before Marsh released the lightning.

"Just the Ookens," she told it, forcing her mind to stay focused on the tentacled invaders. "Kill only them."

"Only them," Aisha echoed stoutly.

"Just the Ookens," Tamlin agreed.

Roeglin's voice filtered through her concentration. "Uh, Marsh?"

She didn't answer him, but he felt her brief attention.

"You can stop now."

His words were followed by Jakob's fervent tones. "You can. You really, really can."

17

FOREARMED

They had saved the kit, but only just. Aisha ran to where he lay. Of the Ooken carrying him, there was nothing left, and the kit had been dropped just in front of the portal. The child wrapped her small arms around his head and neck and tried to drag him farther away.

"Not safe," she mumbled. "It's not safe here. Not safe."

She was still mumbling those words when Henri came and knelt beside her. The warrior didn't say a word but gently lifted the kit from the floor.

"Where to?" he asked the child, and she looked around uncertainly.

"Um."

There is no debris in the side tunnel, Tok advised them, and Henri carried the kit to where he, Izmay, and the mantids had hidden earlier.

He was accompanied by an anxious Mordan and the remaining kits and the cub. As he passed, Marsh cast an anxious glance at the kit in his arms.

His eyes were open, and his breathing came with a

rasping unevenness that indicated a long, hard run, or fight, or shock. Strips of fur were missing from his body, and the exposed skin was laced with circular cuts and bruises where the numerous tiny mouths lining the tentacles had bitten through.

"Will he be all right?" she asked, turning to the mantids.

They cocked their heads, chattering between themselves, and then they looked back at her. Marsh waited for their response, startled when they all tensed and Tok darted toward her, pulling his blades free.

She ducked, dodging to one side as he lashed out in a two-strike combo that saw him reach past her and slash through the tentacles that had extended out of the portal. There was an unearthly shriek from the other side as the mantid struck.

The red light flared a brilliant shade of crimson and then went out, and Marsh found herself staring down the corridor that lay beyond, her breath coming faster than needed.

"Can... Can this thing open two ways?" she asked, looking at the frame where the portal had once stood.

In theory, yes, Tok told them.

"Then we need to see where that tunnel leads," Marsh stated. "We need to know *every* direction they can attack from."

She glanced at the tunnel that had been hidden. "Why couldn't we see it?"

They have technology that creates an illusion over what is really there.

"Technology?"

You would know it as ancient magic, the mantid explained. *They have a lot of technology.*

Tok tilted its head, staring pensively at the portal's empty frame. *They will bring more of it the next time they come.*

"So, there *will* be a next time?" Roeglin asked, his tone suggesting he knew it was inevitable but hadn't wanted it confirmed.

I am sorry, but there will, the mantid confirmed.

"And it will be worse than this time?"

I am afraid it will, Tok replied.

"Then we need to block as many of their access points as we can."

"We could just destroy the gate," Marsh suggested and pointed at the rock. "Do they need the frame to make it work?"

Tok stilled, every line of his body showing he was giving the question serious consideration. *They should not,* he answered, *but perhaps they need it as a focus for the coordinates. It is as if they wish to remain unknown, so they are trying to conceal its presence. The ground provides natural shielding.*

"Shielding?"

From both sight and to conceal the energy released by its activation.

"Energy?" Marsh asked. "Like lightning?"

Tok glanced at one of the other mantids. A brief exchange followed, then Tok looked back.

Yes, exactly like your lightning.

"Can the portal be destroyed by lightning?"

Again, that pause, and another brief exchange.

We think so, but it would take a direct strike in a more concentrated form than we have yet seen you summon.

The other mantid chittered, ending its words with a rasp of its legs against its thorax.

K'tch says you would need to direct the power of a storm into the portal in order to destroy it.

"Or I could just bury the exit point beneath a ton of rock," Marsh murmured, eyeing the cavern and the passage on either side.

She glanced at Roeglin. "That would solve your access point problem too, wouldn't it?"

The shadow mage gave her a nervous look and dipped his chin in agreement. "Let us hope it won't come to that."

Before they could discuss the situation any further, Aisha re-emerged from the tunnel, Tamlin by her side. The injured kit walked behind her, staying beside Henri and giving the warrior the occasional questioning glance.

Marsh groaned. "Oh, no. Tell me he didn't."

Roeglin snickered. "That would be the most ironic, wouldn't it?"

Henri, for his part, seemed oblivious to the fact he now had a kat following his every step.

"We heading up now, boss?"

Roeglin shook his head and gestured at the corridor beyond the portal's frame. "We need to see where that goes."

"Do we?" Aisha asked, and Roeglin gave the child a wary glance.

"Yes, we need to know where the monsters might come out if they go that way instead of this way."

"But we can't walk through the portal," Marsh added. "We need a way around it."

"I can do it," Aisha told her, coming over and laying her palm on the wall beside the doorway's red stone.

Before Marsh had time to respond, the cavern's natural rock had moved aside, forming a perfectly arched stretch of tunnel around the framework.

"Dere."

Catching the more juvenile speech, Marsh cocked her head. "You feeling okay, Aysh?"

Aisha opened her eyes very wide and nodded. "Yeeees."

Tamlin snorted, but the little girl kept her eyes on Marsh.

Marsh returned the look. "Uh-huh."

The effect of those two syllables was instantaneous. Aisha scowled and stamped her foot.

"I *am* fine. Fine like you and Roeglin and Brij and Tams."

"Hey! What about me?" Henri interrupted before Marsh could respond.

"You're always fine," Aisha told him. "Izmay says so."

That brought sputtered laughter from the rest of the team, and Marsh felt Tok searching for the reason. She let the mantid find it, and the insectoids started laughing, too.

Izmay slapped Henri on the arm. "You *had* to ask!"

She was blushing, but she was smiling, too.

Roeglin alone stayed silent. He was staring pensively at the empty portal.

Marsh noticed and sobered. "What's wrong, Ro?"

He scowled. "Now they know," he replied. "They know

we're here and that we'll fight. They know our capabilities, too."

That is correct, Tok confirmed.

"And next time, they'll come in numbers," Roeglin added.

The mantid dipped its head in acknowledgment. *Of course.*

"And you did not warn us."

Until now, I did not know how close the portal was. The mantid sounded apologetic. *And I did not know if they had followed.*

Etk'k whistled and clicked at him, and Tok shuddered in apology.

Etk'k is correct. It is something we should have known. He gave a soft whistle of regret. *We were hoping to arrive somewhere far from human habitation.*

"Given that they have been taking our people and our creatures," Marsh retorted, "how likely was that?"

Tok repeated his apology, his antennae flattening to one side before drooping. The other mantids moved closer to him, making noises Marsh thought were meant to be comforting. K'tch touched her antennae lightly to Tok's and he whistled acknowledgment.

"Your coming doesn't matter," Marsh told them. "These...Ookens were already here. They were already coming because we had stopped their supply lines."

She gestured at the tunnel beyond the portal. "We need to know if they could have come through and observed us. The wolves and Mordan can tell us if there's a fresh trail."

The kat's disgusted affirmation made her smile.

I can tell to the heartbeat how long ago they came...if they came. She wrinkled her nose. *They have a* very *distinctive scent.*

"And can you tell if they took anyone in the meantime?" Marsh asked.

Of course. Their scent isn't strong enough to defeat me. The kat sounded offended that she'd asked.

Marsh gestured toward the tunnel. "After you."

Mordan stalked forward, but Perdemor and his siblings pushed past to accompany her before Marsh could move a single step.

Roeglin laid an arm across her shoulders. "I guess that shows you, then."

She shrugged clear and stalked after the kat and her kits. The others followed without a word, the mantids splitting into two groups.

Tok and K'tch moved with them, but Etk'k and another mantid remained behind. Master Envermet stayed with them. "Henri, Izmay, if you would," he murmured, and the two warriors stepped away from the tunnel. "We need to watch the portal."

"I don't see why Aisha can't just blanket the Deeps-be-damned thing in stone and be done with it," Henri grumbled.

Master Envermet eyed the warrior with surprise. "It's an idea," he allowed. "I'll ask her to do just that when she gets back."

"But you don't think it'll work?" Henri asked, and Master Envermet shook his head.

"I think they will have a means of blasting their way through."

Henri curled his lip. "That doesn't mean we have to make it easy for them."

"No, it doesn't," Master Envermet agreed, laying a hand on the warrior's shoulder and eyeing the portal.

They watched as Marsh and Roeglin disappeared around a bend in the tunnel. It seemed to take forever before they returned, and when they did, it was at a run. Their appearance was followed by a sudden rumble and the telltale cloud of dust from a cave-in.

Mordan skidded back around the corner after them, Aisha clinging to her back and giggling hysterically while Tamlin ran alongside.

"If Dad wouldn't tan my hide," the boy was saying between breaths, "I'd put you over my knee."

For some reason, that made the child laugh more.

She chuckled. "Your face!"

Mordan came to a stop beside Marsh, the look on the kat's face making the meaning of her chirping growl plain. Marsh wrapped her arm around the child's back and lifted her off.

"What did you *do?*" she asked.

"She dropped the tunnel on the other side of the portal," Tamlin explained. "Said it would stop the 'bad monsters' from getting out."

"And?"

"We were standing in it at the time."

"Not my fault!" Aisha protested. "It should have stopped!"

"Stopped?"

"*Oui,*" Tamlin commented, poking her, "It *should* have stopped, but it didn't."

Aisha pouted. "Don't be mean."

Marsh held the little girl up in front of her and Roeglin.
"Don't you *ever* do that again," she told her.

"Ever!" she added as Aisha stared back.

Aisha looked at Roeglin.

"At least, not without a *lot* more warning," the shadow master added.

Brigitte laid the flat of her hand against his shoulder and gave him a none-too-gentle shove. Marsh elbowed him in the ribs, then set Aisha firmly on the floor.

"Look what you did to poor Mordan. You owe her a bath!"

That earned her a wounded look from the kat.

Marsh shook her finger at the hosh. "I mean it, Dan. You are *not* coming into *anyone's* room until you're clean."

She surveyed the other animals.

"None of you are."

She had a point. The four kats and Scruffknuckle were coated from nose-tip to tail in rock dust, and Aisha wasn't in much better condition.

"You need a good scrub, too," Marsh told her. "Your mother would kill me if I returned you to her in *that* state."

"Would not." The little girl pouted.

"Would so, too," her brother confirmed, and Master Envermet had to agree.

With that settled, they made their way into the tunnel around the portal frame. Master Envermet waited until they'd reached him before he put forward Henri's suggestion.

"I was wondering if we shouldn't try to block the portal with stone," he said, earning a sharp look from Roeglin.

The shadow mage looked from the captain to Aisha and then at Marsh. "What do you think?"

"I think they'd break through," Marsh replied, echoing Master Envermet's assessment. She added, "But it's worth it if it slows them down."

Henri snickered, and the mantids cocked their heads.

"What?" Marsh demanded.

"You sound exactly like him," Henri told her, indicating the shadow captain.

Master Envermet rolled his eyes. "So, are we going to try it?"

As he asked the question, they heard the sound of rock grinding as it moved. Master Envermet's eyes widened, and Marsh and Roeglin turned in time to watch a curtain of stone descending over the door and its frame.

"Need a heartbeat," Aisha told them, ducking back into the tunnel she'd created around the frame.

Marsh and Mordan followed, pausing at the tunnel's exit to watch as the little girl blocked the other side of the portal.

"There!" Aisha said with satisfaction as all evidence of the portal vanished behind a wall of light gray stone. "All done."

"Block this tunnel, too," Marsh told her. "Just to be sure."

Aisha put a hand on her hip and cocked her head. "Uh-huh, and what did your last slave die of?"

From the tunnel beyond came the sound of Henri's startled laughter. It stopped abruptly with an *oof* as if he'd just had an elbow driven into his ribs.

Marsh groaned. Of all the people the child could have chosen to emulate…

"Insolence," she told the child. "Now, seal the Deeps-be damned tunnel before I kick your tail."

Aisha giggled and focused on the ceiling overhead. The tilt of her head showed she was watching as Marsh and Mordan left the tunnel, but only when Marsh had rejoined Roeglin did she mutter quietly to herself.

Roeglin sputtered with laughter, and Master Envermet snorted.

Do I want to know? Marsh asked them in the privacy of her head.

Well, she asked, "Which army," Roeglin began and broke into laughter.

She did? Marsh couldn't keep herself from smiling.

We're not supposed to be listening, remember? Roeglin reminded them, still chuckling.

Aisha's voice interrupted Marsh before she could think of anything to say.

"All done," the child declared and walked over to Mordan. "Time for your bath."

There was glee in her tones as she buried her fingers in the fur of the kat's scruff, and Mordan shot Marsh a reproachful look.

Like this is my *fault!* Marsh protested, but she couldn't argue with the kat's logic.

It is your *cub*

18

KEEPING IT CLEAN

The mantids took their leave at the uncovered tunnel.

We believe this leads out to the Devastation, and we will find our path back to our nest, Tok informed them.

He waved his antennae as though testing the air. *And night is falling. Your people will be worried. We will meet in the morning.*

He paused, inclining his body toward Roeglin.

With your permission, of course.

Of course, Roeglin allowed. *Your presence and your counsel will be welcome.*

With a happy flick of his antennae, Tok led his people into the tunnel.

Henri gave Roeglin an anxious look. "Should we go with them? Iz and I would be fine to make our way back."

Roeglin frowned, considering it. "Perhaps not this time," he decided, "although I might ask them to show me the exit so we know which way the Ookens might come from."

'You don't think they'll come at us from out of the Library?" the soldier asked.

"I think they'll come at us from every direction they can," Roeglin told them. "We need to know what those directions are."

Henri grunted his agreement, and they returned through the tunnels to the Library stairs.

"I'm glad we don't have to try to climb back up there," Gustav noted, indicating the grate as they passed beneath it.

"No, but we need to go back and secure it," Roeglin told him. "I'm not saying they can't get past it if they have a mind to, but—"

"I know," the old soldier interrupted him.

"Why make it easy?" they chorused, their voices joined by everyone else.

"I'll go back and do it, boss," Henri offered.

"We'll go with him," Zeb agreed, laying a hand on Jakob's shoulder.

"Thanks, man. Thanks a shroom-shagging lot," the ex-caravan guard muttered, but he didn't look like he minded.

"You are very welcome," Zeb told him, breaking away to follow Henri and Izmay as they turned to descend again. Brigitte followed without a word.

Marsh and the rest made their way through the guards' foyer and into the Library. Marsh hesitated. "I'll stay and make sure they lock it," she offered, but Roeglin shook his head.

"Brigitte's with them," he explained. "I'll ask her to make sure."

Marsh nodded, breathing a sigh of relief. It only took a

momentary flare of white for him to contact the shadow mistress and receive her confirmation.

"It's done."

Marsh smiled her thanks and looked at Aisha and the kats. The smile faded, and she sighed. "You know I have to deal with this, right?"

Roeglin put his arm around her waist and pulled her close. "*We* have to deal with this," he told her.

Master Envermet snorted. "I'll let the kitchens know you're going to be a little late," he informed them and pointed at where Scruffknuckle and Perdemor had almost reached the Library door.

The way the kit and pup were moving told Marsh they had no intention of waiting around for a bath.

"Scruff!" she called. "Perdemor! Come back here."

Mordan chuffed in amusement as the pair of youngsters returned, disappointment in their every line.

Gustav and Jakob arrived as she and Roeglin were heating the water.

"What?" Marsh had asked when Mordan had cocked her head in question. "You don't think I'd try to wash you in *cold* water, do you?"

From the look on the kat's face and the twitch of Mordan's tail, she'd been thinking exactly that. Scruffknuckle huffed out a deep sigh and flopped down on his stomach, resigned to being bathed.

"Let Jakob and me take care of that," Gustav told them, summoning a small ball of flame.

"By all means," Marsh told him, stepping away to give the two soldiers room to work.

Brigitte arrived with two druids and some soapweed.

"This should make it easier," she explained, setting down a bundle of clothing beside the cleaning supplies. She smiled, stripped out of her robe, and snapped her fingers at the nearest cub.

"Come on, kitty. Time for your bath."

The kit lifted his head and flattened his ears to the side, only to have Mordan pick him up by the scruff of his neck and carry him over to the shadow mage. The big kat dropped him at Brigitte's feet and then walked over to Aisha.

She didn't give the little girl time for protest, but gripped the collar of her tunic and pulled her under the next water outlet.

"Hey!" Aisha protested.

"Hey!" she shouted again, when Gustav and Jakob turned the water on, drenching them.

"Wanna get naked?" Roeglin asked, waggling his eyebrows at Marsh.

The mischief on his face made her laugh, and she stripped out of her armor and clothing. "Come on, Scruff. Let's get you clean."

The pup glared at her, while Roeglin stripped out of his clothes. He gave a yip of surprise when the shadow mage lifted him off the ground and staggered under the next outlet.

"Deeps, pup, but you're getting *big*," Roeglin told him, turning under the water until they were both soaked.

"I told you they'd forget." Master Envermet's voice reached them from the edge of the communal showers.

Marsh looked over to see the shadow captain, Henri,

and Izmay place several piles of clothing on the shelves in the dry changing area opposite.

"Yes, you did," Henri grumbled, reaching into his belt pouch and pulling out several coins. He dropped them into the shadow captain's outstretched hand. "You really did."

Izmay laughed and slapped his shoulder. "I brought *us* clothes, too," she told him.

"As if losing a bet with the captain wasn't enough."

"I'll be getting naked…"

Henri rolled his eyes. "You'll be getting clean and dressed, too."

"Picky, picky, picky," Izmay teased and looked at the remaining cubs. "Come on, you two. I *know* you can understand me."

The injured cub got to his feet and padded slowly over to Henri, and Izmay sighed. "Fine."

She turned to the other one. "You coming or not?"

The kit returned her sigh but walked into the next empty stall, where she waited patiently until Izmay had soaped her all over and then rinsed her fur clean. As soon as she figured she was done, the kit dabbed Izmay on the nose with her tongue and stalked back out.

Izmay was about to follow when one of the druids who'd come with Brigitte stepped forward with a towel. "Come here, cub."

The cub looked the woman up and down, sighed again, and allowed her to rub it dry. Seeing it was well taken care of, Izmay turned to the more important task of washing the tunnel dust and Ooken remains out of her hair.

Marsh's lightning might be effective, but it wasn't the tidiest means of killing she'd ever seen.

She smiled as Henri joined her. "You know we're not alone, don't you?" she murmured as his lips brushed her hair.

He laughed softly and held her close. "I just wanted to wash your back."

Izmay rested her head against his chest and hugged him back before pushing him away and turning him around. "A likely story," she told him, running soapweed between his shoulder blades.

Around them, kats, pup, and people got clean and dry, then Jakob interrupted them.

"Water's not going to stay hot forever," he warned, and Izmay looked up to see him and Gustav step away from the cistern.

"We're nearly done," she called back, hastily rinsing the last of the soapweed from her skin.

"We are?" Henri grumbled, and she slapped his chest with the flat of her hand.

"Yes, sweetheart, we are."

He gave a disappointed sigh and followed her over to where Roeglin and Marsh were almost dressed.

"Took you long enough," Marsh quipped.

"Do I need to remind you how many meals you owe me?" Henri retorted, and Marsh chuckled.

Roeglin laughed too and Henri got dressed, watching as the pair of them straightened each other's clothing.

"Dinner's on," Master Envermet announced, returning from wherever he'd disappeared to once he'd delivered their clothes.

He didn't stay long this time either. Henri and Izmay arrived at the mess hall as the rest of them were sitting down. The room was redolent with the smell of well-seasoned meat and vegetables, underpinned by the odor of drying kat and dog, but no one seemed to care.

Roeglin was filling in the township's leaders on the threat Below.

Alain and Obasi looked worried.

"And you say they'll come back?" Alain noted. "Do we have any idea of how long we have?"

"Or how many there'll be?" Obasi added.

Roeglin shook his head. "All the mantids could tell us was that these were the creatures they'd fled from and that they'd be back in numbers."

"But you said Aisha had sealed the portal," Alain protested. "Won't that hold them?"

Roeglin shook his head. "We don't think so. We think it will only buy us a little time."

He raised his hand as Alain opened his mouth to say more.

"Marsh has a plan for shutting down the portal permanently." He gave Alain a direct look. "I'm sorry, but she'll need Tamlin's and Aisha's help."

The man groaned. "Now, why doesn't *that* come as a surprise?"

Roeglin shrugged and gestured around the dining hall. "We *are* looking to train more mages, but right now, they're the strongest we've got."

"I know." Alain sighed, sadness momentarily clouding his face. "I don't have to like it, but Calantha says we should be grateful our children can help. And I am, but..." He gestured helplessly.

Roeglin gave the man's shoulder an awkward pat. "I'm sorry. We'll do what we can to make it safer for all of us."

"It won't do us any good to leave?" Obasi asked. "We can't evacuate?"

Roeglin shook his head. "I'll check with Tok when he arrives in the morning, but I got the impression these creatures are here to hunt. If they *are* the things the raiders were delivering their prisoners to, they won't stop until they've got their supply lines up and running."

He looked around the table. "And we all know what *that* means."

Murmurs of acknowledgment ran around the table. They knew. The raiders had been the scourge of the surface and then tried extending their operations of enslavement underground. If the Ookens were the force behind the raiders, running away wouldn't save them.

Obasi and Alain looked at the other leaders. "What do you need us to do?"

"We're still going to need supplies for the winter, regardless of what is coming," Roeglin replied, "and we're still going to need a sheltered pathway linking our settlements, so we don't lose contact when the snow arrives."

He looked at Obasi. "Do you have any idea of when that will be?"

"The closest we can guess is any day now." The druid warrior smiled sheepishly. "We're speeding the growth of the last crop now." He looked at Master Envermet and Alain. "I can spare some people to help with the pathway, and maybe prepare some areas along it for winter crops."

"And if we don't find any?"

"I'll speak to Tok and see if his people can help us turn the dungeons below the library into shroom vaults."

"Shroom vaults?"

"Indoor spaces for growing shrooms," Obasi explained, "but they're not suitable as they stand at the moment."

We would be glad to assist. Tok's mental voice had them reaching for weapons and pushing back their chairs before they registered who it was.

Roeglin looked at the door. "What brings you back so soon?"

We returned safely to our nest and realized we'd left your mate unguarded. After this afternoon's skirmish, she will be hunted with greater diligence.

It wasn't what Marsh wanted to hear.

"So, you'll be staying?" she asked, blushing as she cast a quick glance at Roeglin.

Henri barked with sudden laughter. "Better you than me."

19

FRIENDS IN NEED

The mantids did not need to share a room to protect Marsh's mind.

It would be better if you slept where you usually lie, Tok informed her. *We can rest nearby. Two of us will remain alert at all times, and two will sleep. If you are hunted, we will be awakened to assist in your defense.*

"Thank you," Marsh told them.

She was about to close the door between them when Mordan stalked past. The kat looked up at Tok and made a soft sound of query. The mantid started and stared at the kat.

After a moment of exchanging looks, the mantid responded, *Of course, you can stay. We would be honored by your assistance.*

Mordan brushed against his legs as she stalked by him into the neighboring room. Marsh breathed a sigh of relief and shut the door, turning to where Roeglin had already settled in her bed.

"You don't have to stay if you don't want to," she informed him, and he gave her a wicked smile.

"Since when has that ever been the case?" he challenged, and she blushed.

He wrapped his arms around her as she slipped into bed. "Besides, I can guard your mind better from here than a room away."

"That's what you always say," Marsh murmured, folding her arms over his as she closed her eyes.

"I have my reasons," he told her, settling to sleep beside her.

They left the lamp to flicker out on its own as if its yellow flame would be enough to keep the darkness at bay.

It wasn't.

Marsh fled, the darkness rising behind her. This time it was worse, like a storm ready to sweep her away. She still couldn't tell what hunted her, but she knew it was there, and getting closer all the time.

She caught sight of a cottage up a small rise to her left. Light gleamed on the porch and shone golden and inviting from behind its curtains. She turned toward it as the only shelter she'd yet seen.

The darkness behind her grew, its presence closer, sapping her will to run. It tried to drain her of hope, to convince her there was nothing she could do except sink to her knees and await its arrival. That the pain it offered was all she could hope to live for.

Tendrils of cloud twisted around her head and tried to entwine her arms.

Marsh brushed them away, seized the more stubborn ones with her fingers, and tore them from her scalp, yelping with pain as hair came away too, but she didn't stop.

Fight it, Marsh. Roeglin's voice came out of the dark, almost her undoing.

Her stride faltered, and he shouted in alarm.

For the Deep's sake, don't stop! Make for the cottage.

The cottage, huh? Marsh eyed the tiny building and half-turned toward it, only to find her way blocked by a snarling hoshkat.

Dan?

The kat growled, swatting at her as she drew closer. Marsh tried to swerve around her, only to have another form block her path. She dodged and continued to run.

Do not stop. The wind whispered in a chorus of voices, and she swore she heard Roeglin there, too. She'd have stopped to ponder why he was contradicting himself, but there was no time. She raced on, trying to outrun the storm.

Ahead of her were mountains, towering hills cloaked in trees and ruins. Her lungs burned, but she knew there would be shelter there. Those ruins had survived the savagery of many storms. Surely, they'd survive this one.

And once inside... She pushed herself harder, feeling the wind rising around her, more solid than air had a right to be. She fought that too, drawing a blade from the storm's darkness.

She woke, gasping, held tight, with Roeglin whispering in her ear.

"Wake up. Please wake up!"

"I'm here!" Marsh looked around wildly, registering the lantern, now burning brightly, Roeglin's grip of iron,

Mordan's anxious presence by the bed, and the mantid standing in the doorway.

"What happened?"

"Do you know what type of stone blocks our minds?" Master Envermet asked, stepping through the door. He glanced at Marsh as Roeglin let her go. "Welcome back, by the way."

"There's a what?" Marsh asked, scrambling to catch what he'd said.

"A stone that interferes with mind magic," Master Envermet reminded her. "If we could discover which one it was, we could build you a room made from it, and maybe stand a chance of giving you a good night's sleep."

Marsh fought to steady her breathing. She'd only been running in her dream, for the Deep's sake! Why did it feel like she'd been running for real?

"You're only coming up with this, now?" she demanded between gasps.

"I'm sorry. It was only when I tried to ask Sulema for aid that I realized the answer might be closer than we thought."

"Did you get through?" Roeglin asked, his voice rough with worry.

He didn't touch her, though, and Marsh was grateful. She wrapped her arms around herself, trying to get a grip on what had happened.

"I don't care what rock you surround me with," she announced. "I want them gone, even if it means I go hunting."

She straightened. "As a matter of fact, that's exactly

what I want. I want to hunt down the thing that is hunting me."

She pushed herself to her feet and advanced on Tok. The mantid backed up nervously, raising his hands before him.

Like that would protect you if I wanted to harm you, Marsh thought. *You're just lucky I know you are my friends.*

Tok relaxed a little. *Then what can we help you with?*

Tell me where to find him.

Tok shrugged helplessly, flicking his antennae nervously. *You know where he is. He is beyond the portal.*

How can I open that? Marsh pressed.

You cannot. You must wait for the portal to open, and then you must get past what comes out.

Marsh raised her forefinger, intending to tap the mantid's chest, but Roeglin intervened. He stepped between them.

"Is there any way we can draw him out?" he asked.

The mantid curled his antennae and turned them this way and that as though seeking some sort of scent. A fine shiver ran through him.

We would need to find something he wanted above all else, some kind of bait that would entice him to open the door sooner rather than later, something that would bring him here in person, and not just his minions.

"And?" Roeglin demanded.

I will need time to think of such a thing.

Marsh laughed. "You don't need to think of anything. He is coming because he needs to be first."

Roeglin gave her a look of concern. "The first to do what?"

"The raiders, the resources," she explained. "He's been gathering what he needs in order to establish a base here. That is what he wants to be first for. He wishes to be the first to establish a base. There is someone he wants to please."

Tok regarded her with attentive antennae. From the quiver that ran through them, Marsh figured he was communicating with his fellow mantids. The closest she could get to their response was...worried?

They were worried by what she was thinking?

Yes, Tok replied. *The first move is to always establish a base on the target world. If what you say is true, the invasion we feared is coming, and he wishes to claim the right to rule. There will be others thinking of doing the same.*

"How do we fight them?" Master Envermet demanded. "How do we beat them?"

We cannot defeat them, Tok replied, *but Death can. She will come. We only have to hold them back until she notices and arrives.*

Roeglin slid out of bed and stood beside Marsh.

"How do you know this anyway?" he asked. "Last I remember, you were running and screaming."

"And pulling a sword from the black," Master Envermet reminded him. "Don't forget that. If you hadn't had such a good hold on her, you'd have been a dead man."

"Worth it," Roeglin responded, his face hard. "Worth every second of it."

He laid his hands on Marsh's shoulders and looked into her face. "How did you know?"

"The storm," Marsh began, her voice trembling at the memory. "It kept catching hold of me, and every time it did, some of what he intended leaked through. He wants to be the first to arrive. He wants to claim the Devastation as his territory."

"What else did you find out from the storm?" Master Envermet demanded, his voice harsh.

"That he's chosen the Library as his base, and he will be the one to lead the invasion forces." Her voice grew softer, but there was a core of iron beneath it. "He doesn't think we are enough of a threat for him to need to arrive later."

That is both good and bad, K'tch observed. *We might stand a chance if he gives us even a little more time to prepare.*

"He thinks we're weak?" Master Envermet asked.

To Marsh, he sounded almost outraged. She nodded. "He does, which is why he believes it will be safe for him to arrive with the first troops."

"That indicates more than a little arrogance," the shadow captain replied. "A lesson might be in order."

"As long as it's his last," Marsh told him. "We don't want him putting anything he might learn to use."

Master Envermet's mouth twisted sourly. "Agreed. This lesson will be his last, and there will be no graduation."

Tok shifted uneasily, and Marsh looked at the mantid. "What is it, Tok?"

I need to return to the nest. My people must prepare for war. He looked at Obasi. *If you send the people you have in mind, my cultivators will be ready to assist them in any way they require.*

The mantid paused. *We too would appreciate your particular skills to speed the crops if you have the energy to spare.*

Obasi closed the distance between them, taking the mantid's hands in his. "You only had to ask. We cannot spare many, but I can find you six, at least two of whom are quite gifted with handling shrooms."

Tok shifted his hands so one rested on the outside of Obasi's grip and held his hands in return. *Your people's aid would be welcome.*

Something in the mantid's tone made Marsh wonder how much difficulty Tok's people faced with the coming winter.

We will need warmer quarters and have been unable to spare the people to prepare them, the mantid surprised her by answering. *With the help of the Grotto's druids, we will be ready for the cold season.*

He shuddered, and this time it was not an apology. *I wish we had pried earlier, for then we would have understood the hardship ahead of us. This "cold" in your thoughts is much more severe than anything we have experienced.*

"We will be glad to aid you," Obasi reassured him. "If you will come with me before you leave, I will ask my people to accompany you on your return."

His offer was met by restless shuffles among the other mantids and a myriad of soft clicks and whistles as they discussed the offer. Obasi waited patiently, his eyes glowing white as he followed the conversation in his head.

Marsh wondered what he heard, but decided if the mantids had wanted her to hear it, they would have included her in the conversation. Tok cocked his head as though catching her thoughts.

I am sorry, we did not think it of interest.

"You can tell us later," Roeglin reassured him, "or Obasi can. He has permission to send you the people he can spare."

You trust him to do that? Tok asked.

Roeglin dipped his chin in assent. "Of course. If I did not, he would not be responsible for the area I have asked him to take charge of."

Tok flipped his antennae in amusement. *Of course, he would not.*

There was relief in his mental tones that made Marsh smile.

Then we will take our leave.

"Go in peace, my friend," Roeglin told him. "Do you require an escort to see you safely home?"

"Thank you, but no. The wolves keep watch for us."

"Speaking of a watch," Roeglin added, "we will set one on the portal. I don't think mental magic is disrupted between here and the Below, is it?"

Master Envermet shook his head.

"Then, Master Envermet, can I ask you to head that effort?" Roeglin asked. "It will take men away from the new college, but I will provide extra help once this threat has been dealt with."

Master Envermet gave him a slight smile. "I would be honored to help with the defense of what is to be my home," he said and looked at Obasi. "I can organize a watch, but I will need to borrow warriors who can fight with their minds as well as other abilities."

"Come with me," Obasi told him. "I will introduce you to my impi leaders, and they will find you the people you need."

"I'll let Alain and Evan know you will be needing guards from them," Roeglin added. "I take it not *all* your watchmen will need mental magic?"

"No," Master Envermet said. "I will meet with Alain once the first watch is set."

"Have Zeb and Jakob go with you," Roeglin told him. "It will help to have men who've seen the Ookens in the flesh."

"That it will," Master Envermet agreed.

TOO LITTLE FOR LIGHTNING

Marsh watched them go, glad of Roeglin's presence by her side. When they were the only two in the room, she sank onto the edge of the bed and rested her elbows on her knees. Cupping her chin in her hands, she stared at the empty doorway.

"Are you okay?" Roeglin asked, and she gave him a reluctant nod.

"I think so. I'm just tired, is all. Do you think it'll come if I sleep now?"

Roeglin regarded her with a curious gaze. "Do you?"

Marsh thought about that and shook her head. "I think it has other things to do at this time of day."

"Are you sure?" Roeglin asked, then smothered a yawn of his own.

Marsh nodded. "But then, you and *I* have other things to do at this time of the day, too."

She pushed herself upright, dragging a clean pair of socks out of her drawer and pulling her boots out from under the bed.

Roeglin watched as she put them on, then sat down beside her. "You don't have to be the strong one all the time," he reminded her, and she managed a shaky smile.

"Tell me that when this is over," she told him. "That'll be when I let myself sleep instead of getting our people ready for war."

He pulled back from her and arched an eyebrow. "So you think it's war, do you?"

Marsh nodded. "I really think it is. That storm or whatever was in it? It was ready for war. It wanted everything we had, and then it wanted everything else."

She stood up. "I'd better go talk to Aisha and Tamlin. We've got to work out how to pull the power out of a winter storm and get it that far Below."

Roeglin's hand brushed hers and she stopped.

"Have you thought about asking the druids?" he asked, giving her a crinkly smile.

His laughter touched her mind, and the sense of mischief that he was suggesting the obvious and knew she probably hadn't thought of it. He was right, and it made Marsh smile.

"You think I should?"

"I really do. I mean, you're not going to be able to guarantee having a storm blowing around when you need one." He shrugged. "Maybe one of them knows how to predict when there'll be one. We don't *need* to wait for the gate to open, do we? I mean, we *can* blow it up *before* the monsters come back, can't we?"

"What are you trying to say, Roeglin?" Marsh asked.

"I'm trying to say that if we can guarantee destroying the gate even if we can't guarantee destroying the threat beyond it, then we should consider doing that rather than leaving it too late. Remember, storms aren't guaranteed."

Hearing the worry in his voice, Marsh cupped his cheeks in the palms of her hands.

"I'll remember," she told him. "No vengeance for my nightmares if we can get rid of the source of them by destroying the door first, I promise."

"You do?"

"I really, really do," Marsh told him, trusting that he could see the truth of her words in her mind.

He confirmed it by pulling her into his arms for another hug. "That's what I love about you," he murmured. "You trust me to look when you need me to."

Marsh gave an abrupt laugh and stepped back, slapping the flat of her palm against his chest. "Ha! Deep's ass, I do. I know you'll be looking whether I like it or not. I just wanted to be sure you were looking *that* time."

Roeglin gave a sheepish chuckle. "Fine, I admit it. I just can't keep my head out of yours."

"Just as long as you keep it in the game as well," Marsh told him and headed for the door. "You know where to find me."

"I do," he acknowledged, "and you, me."

They parted, still smiling, to face whatever the day might bring, and Roeglin couldn't help feeling a little hopeful. Maybe a partnership would work after all.

Marsh found the children at breakfast, then went in search of their parents, the crisp morning air making her shiver as she arrived. Their delight at seeing her turned somber when she explained what the settlement faced.

"You want to put our children back on the front line *again?*" Calantha sounded almost annoyed.

Marsh felt her face heat. "I'm sorry," she began, but the woman waved her down.

"Don't you *dare* apologize, Marsh. To be honest, if getting ready to face that challenge will keep them from giving my *other* children any more ideas, I'd be grateful."

Marsh frowned. "What do you mean, *more* ideas?"

"I mean, Sasha stepped out of a wall and scared seven kinds of the Dark out of me," Calantha exclaimed, waving a spoon at Aisha when the child giggled. "It's not funny, young lady."

Tamlin snorted. "You have to admit, *Maman*, it kinda is."

Marsh watched as Calantha resisted the urge to smile, but the small smile tugging at the corner of her mouth won, and the woman gave a short laugh.

"All right, you two, I'll admit it *was* a bit funny, but that doesn't mean I want her learning how to fight like the pair of you do."

"Learning how to fight was what saved our lives, *Maman*," Tams told her seriously. He laid a hand over his mother's and caught her eyes with his own, reminding Marsh of just how much time the boy had spent around Roeglin. "I don't want her to die."

"Tamlin!" Marsh was shocked, but she could see that his words had hit a chord. "I'm sorry, Calantha, I…"

"You don't need to be sorry," the woman said for the second time that day, "but just because he has a point, it doesn't mean I'm ready to hear it. She's only four."

Tams was relentless. "That's how old Aisha was when she had to learn."

"Was not," the little girl declared stoutly. "Was three? No, maybe two?"

She frowned. "I hid in the rocks when you hid in the shadows."

Tams regarded his sister in wide-eyed surprise. "You did?"

Aisha gave a solemn nod. "I did."

"You little cheater!" he exclaimed, and Aisha giggled again.

Calantha sighed and rolled her eyes. "Well, at least now I know why the pair of you were so good at hide and seek!"

Marsh leaned forward, gaining her attention. "You can send her to the school Master Envermet is setting up. She doesn't have to learn how to fight, but it *would* be better if she learned how to control the abilities she has."

"And hiding in the rocks can keep her safe," Aisha informed her gently. "That was the first thing I learned."

Marsh noticed how carefully the child was enunciating her words and suppressed a smile. This was Aisha's latest tactic—speaking like an adult so the adults would take her seriously. The little devil was learning fast!

Calantha turned to Tamlin. "Is that true?"

The boy nodded. "Marsh wouldn't let us travel up front with her. She said it was too dangerous, so she made us travel with Master Envermet, where there wasn't *supposed* to be any fighting."

"But there was, wasn't there?" Calantha asked, and Tamlin smiled.

"The shadow monsters don't listen to what they should and shouldn't do, even though it *is* what they usually do. Aisha would hide in the rocks, and I would hide in the shadows. We used to secretly copy the soldiers when they practiced fighting, but we weren't supposed to."

Calantha stared at the boy. "Are you telling me you learned to fight when you weren't supposed to?"

Tamlin nodded. His face was serious, but Marsh caught the slight quirk of his lips that said he was trying not to smile. Aisha was looking serious too, but her eyes were bright with mischief.

"Sasha does, too," she stated, and Calantha's eyes widened in horror.

"Since when?"

Aisha's reply was forestalled by the small form that erupted from the wall beside Aisha. "You said you wouldn't tell! You promised!"

Aisha made a brief gesture with her hand and Sasha jerked to a halt, rock entwined around one foot and ankle. "Aysh! You...you Deeps-damn-ded shag room!"

Marsh's eyes widened, and she couldn't stop the laughter that bubbled out of her.

"Fighting *and* cursing," Alain noted, trying not to laugh or look impressed. "She's made fast progress."

Marsh shook her head, her face hot with embarrassment. "I really don't know what to say."

Calantha exchanged glances with Alain and rolled her eyes. She looped an arm around her youngest daughter and squeezed her gently. "No cursing, young lady."

"Aisha does," she muttered, directing a sullen look at her sister.

Aisha's mouth dropped open, and she looked askance at her sister. "I do—"

Tamlin cut her off. "Do too."

"Not as much as you," Aisha argued, and Alain intervened.

"Right. New rule: there will be no cursing in this house, and preferably none where your mother or I can hear it."

"So, we *can* curse, then?" Tamlin asked hopefully.

"I'd rather you didn't," Alain replied. "Think of how often you hear Roeglin or Master Envermet curse."

Marsh did. She blushed even more, and the children started giggling. Alain gave a heavy sigh.

"Fine! Think of *when* you hear them cursing. They understand there's a time and place."

"Sometimes it just slips out," Tamlin observed.

"Like that time Marsh went looking for the raiders without them," Aisha added. "Master Envermet cursed a *lot* that day!"

"Roeglin, too," Tamlin agreed.

"And Izmay," Aisha added, her eyes wide at the memory. "She knows a *lot* of curses."

"And Brigitte," Tamlin chortled. "I didn't know *she* knew so many, either!"

Alain groaned and shook a finger at Marsh. "This... This..."

He gestured helplessly at Sasha, who was listening to the conversation with wide-eyed interest. Calantha shook her head.

"Just try not to curse," she directed and turned back to Marsh.

The children settled.

Once they were quiet and paying attention, Calantha continued. "So, what was it you wanted them to do?"

"I need their help when I call the lightning," Marsh

told her. "There's a door to another world we need to close. The mantids say a powerful surge of lightning should be enough to close it and stop it from being opened again."

"In just that place, or everywhere?" Alain said, asking the question she'd hoped they wouldn't think of.

She sighed. "Just that door," she admitted. "Tok says it won't stop them from opening another door elsewhere."

"Which you'll have to find and then close the same way?" Calantha wanted to know.

"Yes," Marsh told her.

"And you and the children, *my* children, are the only ones who can call the lightning." It was a statement and not a question, and Marsh nodded.

"For now, yes. Blowing up this door should give us time to find others who can learn the same thing. Given how many mages are at the Library, we won't be the only ones for long."

Alain frowned. "I know Tamlin got the hang of calling lightning a little while ago," he began and pointed at Aisha, "but when did my daughter find the knack?"

"That's easy, Papa," Aisha chirped. "I found the lightning in the rocks."

He stared at her, his mouth open in shock. "There's lightning in…in the rocks?"

"Uh-huh." Aisha nodded her head, grinning happily. "Now I can call it, too. Wanta see?"

"Me! Me me!" Sasha cried, bouncing excitedly in her mother's lap. "Show me!"

Aisha opened her mouth to explain, and Calantha held up her hand.

"Don't you dare!" she admonished, her face pale. "She's four! There will be no lightning."

"No fair!" Sasha wailed. "Aysh and Tams can."

"Aysh is si...*seven*!" Calantha snapped, and the two older children gaped at her outright lie. She flushed and continued before any of them could speak. "There will be *no* lightning until you're seven. No arguing."

Marsh considered pointing out that if Sasha was able to call the lightning, they were going to need her no matter how old she was, but she took one look at Calantha's face and decided that was an argument for another day.

She tried not to think that that day would be the one where Sasha had found the lightning for herself. The thought sent a shiver of apprehension through her, and she decided to have a word with Aisha, Tamlin, Obasi, and Brigitte. If Sasha was anything like her sister, she'd need to be watched.

Thinking of Brigitte reminded Marsh of the shadow mage's new-found ability with rocks and stone. She made a note to see if Brigitte could also find the lightning in the stones. If she could, it would be an enormous help in what they wanted to do.

Calantha turned to Aisha. "You are *forbidden* to show your sister how to call the lightning in the rocks. *Forbidden*! Do you hear me?"

Aisha stared at her mother and slowly nodded.

Marsh got the impression that Aisha had never seen her mother so angry or adamant about anything. Her gaze shifted to Tamlin's expression; he looked like he'd never seen Calantha like this, either.

It was going to take something fairly spectacular to

shift the woman on her decision. She kept her expression carefully blank and hoped Sasha *didn't* follow in her sister's footsteps and do whatever it was that would cause a reversal in the decision.

Instead of pursuing that thought, she cleared her throat. "So, I *do* have your permission to train Aisha and Tamlin to control their ability to call the lightning?"

Calantha regarded her with a sour stare. "Of course. *They've* already discovered how to call it. They *need* to be trained."

Marsh nodded, her eyes catching the look on Sasha's face as the little girl listened to her mother's words. She saw when the girl's expression shifted from resentment to determination and failed to stifle a groan.

"What?" Calantha demanded. "I thought you would be happy."

"I am," Marsh reassured her. "Happy and grateful. Thank you."

Alain, however, had followed the direction of her look and seen the expression on Sasha's face. His mouth dropped open, but he hastily closed it, darting a quick glance at Marsh.

She got the impression he had something he wanted to say, but another glance at his wife silenced him. No doubt he'd be seeking her out later. It was not a meeting she was looking forward to.

I'll speak to him. Roeglin's voice was a welcome relief. His next words were not. *You've made a promise, but I have not.*

Well, shag the shrooms and shank the Deeps, she thought and was rewarded with a gasp from Aisha.

Rude! the little girl told her, remembering to keep the exchange strictly between them.

Marsh arched her eyebrows. *Don't make me come over there.*

Don't make me tell Mama what you and Roeglin are doing, the child shot back.

Marsh narrowed her eyes at the girl. *You wouldn't.*

Aisha gave her a beatific smile, and Tamlin groaned.

"What?" his mother asked, and the boy shook his head.

"I just realized I was going to be late for class," he told her, pushing back his chair.

"Me, too," Aisha added, doing the same.

Sasha tried to wriggle out of Calantha's grasp. "Me! An' me!"

Calantha pulled her close and frowned at Tamlin. "I thought Marsh was going to do your lessons today?"

"Well, *you* know that, and *we* know that, but *Brigitte* hasn't been told yet, and she'll make us do push-ups *and* run ten times around the square for being late."

"I'll get Roeglin to—" Marsh began, but Tamlin waved her offer aside.

"It will be better if you come and get us," he told her. "That will give you time to talk to her about other things."

The whole sentence sounded normal to Marsh, despite the significance of her talking to Brigitte about "other things." Marsh had to admire the way the boy kept his face straight. That had to be taking some effort.

Instead of remarking on it, Marsh nodded. "Good point. Go talk to Brigitte. Tell her I'll be over shortly to discuss your training."

She stopped them as they raced toward the door.

"Haven't you forgotten something?" she asked, indicating their parents.

"Bye, *Maman*, Papa!" Aisha cried and would have dashed out the door if Tamlin hadn't grabbed her by her arm.

"Say goodbye properly!" he ordered, and Aisha shot him a look that promised retribution later.

Marsh squelched an internal sigh. It looked like the day was going to be inexorably long.

She watched as Aisha marched over to her mother and gave her a hug and a kiss on the cheek.

"Bye-bye, *Maman*," she said, and then kissed her sister. "Bye, Sasha. Be good for *Maman*."

Her little sister's response was as sullen as any of hers when she'd been thwarted. "Bye."

Tamlin followed suit, and the pair of them left after bidding Alain goodbye.

Marsh shook her head. "I don't know what to say," she admitted, and Calantha and Alain laughed.

"It's just children," Calantha explained and then frowned. "You should know that."

"Yes, but I've never seen them like that."

"Well, get used to it. Those are their normal selves." Calantha paused. "Well, when they're not being precocious demi-mages."

The term made Marsh smile "Precocious demi-mages," she repeated. "That's one way to put it."

Calantha smiled, and Alain pushed back his chair. He glanced out the door.

"Is there anything else we need to discuss?" he asked, and Marsh shook her head.

Alain pushed back his chair. "In that case, I'd better be gone before Evan sends a rescue party."

Calantha raised an eyebrow. "What *have* you been telling that man?" she asked, and Alain chuckled.

"Not from *you*, dear, but the children…"

"No one ever checks to see if *I* need rescuing," she grumbled, and he smiled.

"That's because everyone knows how well they behave for you."

Calantha snorted and slapped his shoulder, but she accepted his kiss and watched him go with a fondness that made Marsh's heart ache. These were the things she was trying to protect: family, love, and her people's ability to live safely to enjoy them.

She pushed back her chair. "I'll try to keep them as safe as I can," she said.

"I know you will," Calantha replied.

Marsh had almost reached the door when Roeglin's mental voice reached her.

The mantids need our help.

21

MISSING MANTIDS

It was hard not to run until she'd closed the door behind her, but Marsh managed it. As soon as she heard it click shut, she broke into a swift jog. The day was no warmer than when she'd first arrived.

When she got to the mess hall, she was not surprised to find Brigitte, Aisha, and Tamlin already there. Master Envermet and the shadow guards were also in attendance, as were Obasi and two of his impi leaders. They all looked up as Marsh trotted through the door.

She slowed to a quick walk, negotiating the tables and chairs in the empty mess hall to stop beside Roeglin. "Sorry I took so long."

He eyed her quizzically. "Did they give you permission?" he asked as Alain, Evan, and Xavier came through the door.

Marsh nodded, and Tamlin and Aisha relaxed.

"Told you," Aisha stated, glaring at Brigitte.

The shadow mistress just smiled. "I had to hear it from

Marsh," she explained, patting the little girl's shoulder comfortingly.

Aisha shrugged her hand away, scowling irritably.

Tamlin just smiled.

"Yes," Alain declared, "but if they blow anything up, I'm holding *you* responsible."

It was difficult to tell which of them he meant, given the way his finger was waving, but Marsh ignored it. She looked from Roeglin to Tok, K'tch, and Etk'k.

The three mantids were so tense they were almost vibrating.

As soon as Alain and the others had found seats, Roeglin turned to the insectoids. "Tell them," he instructed. "We will all help as we can."

Some of the nest are missing, Tok began.

"When?" "How long?" and "What can we do to help?" came back at him in quick succession.

The mantid froze, his antennae flexed in surprise. After a moment to absorb their responses, he continued.

I do not know when the first vanished, but the ones who alerted us did not return to the nest last night, and they were still missing this morning. We have searched where they were meant to be, and we cannot find them.

"Have you asked the druid if her wolves can aid you?" Roeglin wanted to know.

Tok cocked his head. *I have not met this human,* he replied. *The wolves sometimes help us, but we have not had time to ask them.*

"What about Mordan?" Marsh asked, realizing she hadn't seen the kat or her cubs all morning.

I have not seen the kat today, Tok replied, and Marsh

frowned.

"Aysh?" she asked, but the little girl shook her head.

"Perdy and Scruffy left before breakfast," she replied. "I think they went hunting."

Marsh frowned.

Hunting? Roeglin murmured in her mind. *For what?*

That's what I'd like to know, Marsh answered.

"How long ago did they leave the nest?" Master Envermet asked, his voice rolling over them.

Our gatherers leave as the first light touches the sky.

So, *very* early, then, Marsh thought. She shivered. The Devastation was forbidding at that time of day, the darkness permeating every canyon and fallen building, a rival to any cavern's despite the sky above.

And it hid more. In a cavern, the walls limited how many directions the dangers could approach from. In the Devastation, the danger came from *all* directions, not just one or two marked by tunnel entrances. Tok continued, interrupting her thoughts.

They return either as the last light leaves or when they have filled our needs.

The way he said it suggested they did not get back early.

Soft footsteps and the patter of claws on the wooden floor drew their attention to the door.

"Adrienne!" Roeglin exclaimed. "I was about to send for you."

The druid gestured to Aisha. "The child sent through Bristlebear."

At the mention of his name, the pack leader lifted his head beneath her hand. The movement made her smile, and she scratched his head. Looking at the mantid, she asked, "What do you need?"

I have lost nestmates, Tok explained again. *I need to know where to find them.*

"Where did you lose them?" the druid demanded, but Tok's reply was interrupted by a rumbling snarl, followed by the skitter of claws and swift steps as the druid and her pack cleared the door.

As soon as the way was open, Mordan stalked into the room.

The others came, the cat informed Marsh. *Their scent says they left while the sky was still dark and your people slept.*

Marsh knew the kat couldn't possibly mean all her people. There had been a night watch. Why hadn't the night watch seen them?

They came and observed, but took care not to be seen. They observed the paths the pride made.

They what? Roeglin had been privy to that thought.

"They spied on us," Marsh interpreted. "The slimy Deeps-spawned turd-lovers came and spied on us, and then they took the mantids."

They took the mantids before the sun had set.

"Sons of the Deep! How did we not know it was opening?" Marsh turned to Tok. "Can't you sense it?"

We cannot. In that, we are as blind as you.

"With that in mind," Master Envermet interrupted, "have you lost any other nestmates since you arrived?"

We have lost no nestmates from around the nest. Tok's voice was thoughtful.

"But some *have* gone missing." Master Envermet stated, pushing the mantid for an answer.

That is true. We thought them merely overdue.

"How, when you expect them by nightfall?"

These were sent to scout the land for other more suitable nesting and foraging grounds. Their tasks were designed for them to be absent from the nest for multiple day and night cycles.

"Then how do you know they are missing?"

Their voices have been absent from our minds for longer than we had realized until you asked.

"They were supposed to check in mentally?"

Tok inclined his head in assent. *And they have not. We have assigned searchers for them.*

"And they're searching now?"

That is correct.

Master Envermet turned to Adrienne. "Can you help?"

The druid's eyes flared green, and she looked at Bristle-bear. For a moment, the wolf's amber eyes matched hers, then the color faded from both. Several of the wolves who had accompanied Adrienne into the building padded back out.

"It is done," Adrienne informed them. She looked at Tok. "Please tell your people that the wolves are friendly and seek only their welfare."

Again, Tok inclined his head. *It shall be done.*

Mordan rumbled a query at the mantid, and he dipped his antennae in her direction.

Thank you, pride mother, but there are sufficient seeking my people, and you are needed here more.

This time Marsh caught the definite flick of antennae in her direction. She also caught Mordan's look. Deciding not to say anything, she waited for the pair to finish their exchange.

"In the meantime, we will go inspect the portal," Roeglin declared, drawing the attention of all those in the room. "If there has been an incursion overnight, I need to know where it's come from. I need to know it wasn't just a group of Ookens stranded here when we closed it."

We will accompany you, Tok told him. *This matter is of interest to us also.*

"Agreed," Roeglin told him. He turned to Obasi. "I need to know when the next big storm is coming."

When Obasi drew breath to reply, Roeglin silenced him with an upraised hand. "It doesn't have to be perfect, just close, and I need to know how we are going to direct the lightning to the portal."

"It needs to be open to the sky," Obasi told him.

"What does?"

"The target—unless you plan on opening a portal to the portal you wish to target, and I don't know what effect that would have on the lightning."

"Then I need a way of exposing the top of the portal so Marsh and the children can direct the lightning into it."

Obasi froze, then gave Master Envermet an inquiring look. "I have some druids who might be able to help, but it might take the specialized skills of a rock mage."

One of the mages standing with Master Envermet finally spoke. "I believe we might be able to assist."

He looked at Roeglin. "I would need to see the portal and the stone under which it stands."

He frowned. "It is not located directly beneath the Library, is it?"

"I'm not sure," Roeglin told him. "All I know is that we

traveled some way beneath the building. I could not tell you if we remained under it when we found the portal."

"Then I will accompany you…if I may?" This last question was directed at both Roeglin and Master Envermet.

"We would appreciate that," Roeglin answered, and Master Envermet gave an affirmative nod.

"Sylvie will come with me," Brin informed them. "Between us, we should be able to tell you how difficult it will be to reach the surface from the portal's location."

"Will it be difficult?"

"Of course," Brin informed him. "It is only the degree that will vary."

"But you *will* be able to do it?"

"We will know when we see where it lies," Brin replied. "We can give no guarantees."

"We will do our best," the stocky woman standing beside him stated. "Beyond that, we can promise nothing."

"That is all we ask," Roeglin told them. "I understand you came here to teach and to build. I am sorry we must ask this as well."

Sylvie glanced at Brin and smiled. A large stone hammer appeared in her palm and then vanished once more. "Stone-shaping is but one of our callings," she replied.

"We will help instruct your fighters," Brin assured him. "We came seeking a home on the surface. We're not about to let it be taken from us."

"You have our thanks," Roeglin assured them and turned to Marsh. "I need you to train. It will take the three of you to control the lightning of a storm."

Personally, Marsh thought it would take more, but she

wasn't about to say it. Roeglin caught the thought anyway.

Ask Brigitte, then focus on your training. I will have Master Envermet see who else might hold the potential.

Understood, Marsh answered, and hesitated before adding, *Sasha...*

I know, he told her. *Let me think about it.*

Marsh nodded and looked at the children. "We'd better get started."

She looked at Tamlin, Aisha, and Brigitte, and they returned her gaze with brief nods, stepping back from the center of the circle so they could move toward the door.

Roeglin's voice stopped them as they reached it. "Where do you intend to practice?"

If she was truthful, Marsh hadn't thought about it. She wasn't about to tell Roeglin that, though.

"There's a ruin a little way from the walls," she told him, waving vaguely in the direction of the gates. She was glad when he didn't interrupt to point out that there were hundreds of ruins just outside the walls. "We shouldn't hurt anything there."

Etk'k stepped forward. *I will accompany you,* he told them. *That way, if you need to call for help, you will be able to.*

"Thank you," Marsh told him, and left before Roeglin could call her bluff.

Aisha snickered. "Uncle Roeglin will be *so* mad at you," she whispered, leaving Marsh wondering when Roeglin had become an uncle.

The child had an answer for that as well. "If I call him 'Papa,' he will be sad, and my other papa will be confused. 'Uncle' is good."

Her answer made Marsh smile. It would make Roeglin

smile too when she told him. It brought a lump to her throat, though, so she changed the subject.

"Tell me what you know about the lightning in the rocks," she instructed, and Brigitte echoed her.

"Yes. *Please*, tell us about the lightning in the stone."

"It hides there," Aisha informed them. "It's part of the stone and not part of it. It can hide in the stone and in the air and in the water."

She glanced at the sky. "There is a little bit of lightning in everything. You just have to ask it to come out."

"Out of *everything*, Aysh?" Marsh asked, feeling a frisson of alarm.

"Mostly out of the air and the rocks," the little girl replied. "If you called the lightning out of a person, that would be bad."

Marsh's heart sank. The child had druidic magic, too. If there was lightning in a living thing and you called it out of that thing, what would happen to it?

"It would die," Aysh answered. "I told you it would be bad."

"What would die?" Brigitte asked, worried but not sure why.

"The thing you called the lightning out of," the child informed her. "If it was alive. Rocks and air are good, and water, but not people and animals."

"Oh, I see," Brigitte replied in a tone that told Marsh the shadow mistress really *did* see—and that she wasn't happy with the view.

Tamlin glanced at the sky. Clouds scudded overhead, still too far apart for rain despite what the wind promised.

"We really need a storm."

22

PRACTICE MAKES...FOR MAYHEM

"Again!" Brigitte demanded. "Show me again, Aysh."

I'm not sure that's wise, Etk'k protested, but Aisha stamped her foot.

"No, again," the little girl declared. "Brij, it's like sparkles in the rock, and it's shy. You've got to ask it *nicely*!"

"I *was* asking nicely," Brigitte snapped, "and I didn't sense any sparkles."

Her usually blue eyes were black with the effort of holding her connection to the stone she'd just raised from the ground.

"Wait!" Tamlin held up a hand, and Brigitte and Aisha turned toward him.

"What?" Aisha demanded while Brigitte snapped, "What is it this time, Tamlin?"

The boy shrugged. "I was just going to suggest you try to find the lightning in the clear air," he told her. "After all, you talked to shadows for a long time before you discovered you could talk to rocks. Finding the lightning in the shadows might be easier."

They stared at him as though he'd struck both of *them* with a bolt of lightning. Aisha looked at Brigitte, put one hand on her hip, and cocked her head.

"It's worth a try."

Brigitte sighed. "At this point, I'm willing to try anything!"

"Etk'k, are you ready?" Marsh asked.

The mantid flicked its antennae in affirmation, and Marsh felt its subtle presence in her mind. She also felt when the connection between her, Brigitte, and Tamlin joined the connection she had with Aisha.

Are we ready? she asked, and did not need to hear their spoken confirmation.

Brigitte's mind was a presence sharp with interest as Marsh sought the sky for hidden lightning. It was there, scattered around them, and she reached for it, calling it as she went.

"Come," she told it. "I need you."

Aisha's soft "Oh" of discovery wasn't as comforting as she might have hoped. Nor was the moment the child slipped from her mind.

"I've got her," Tamlin reassured her, then he was gone as well.

"I guess it's just you and me," Brigitte murmured.

"Just make sure you call the lightning *outside* my head," Marsh instructed. "Neither of us is going to be much use to anybody if you do it any other way."

"Gotcha. Okay, I *think* I can do this."

"You sure?" Marsh asked, and Brigitte gave a short bark of laughter.

"No, but this is as good as it's going to get."

"Okay, then," Marsh acknowledged and released the lightning back to the open sky. "Show me."

They'd set up a small stone target on the other side of the roof, but Brigitte was ignoring it. First, she had to master the art of calling the lightning. Only after that could she direct it.

"Come to me," the mage ordered, and Marsh felt the lightning slither beneath her touch.

She let it go, then realized what Brigitte had done. "No!"

The mage started, and Marsh grabbed the lightning from her control, directing it to the statue.

"Tell it to go back, Brij!" Tamlin shouted. "Tell it thank you and that you don't need it."

"Return!" Brigitte ordered as Etk'k whistled in alarm.

"Return!" Marsh reiterated, reinforcing Brigitte's order.

"Thank you for helping us," Tamlin added as they willed the lightning to return to the air.

Their skin tingled and their hair stood on end, and when they opened their eyes, they saw it flickering in the air between them, but it *did* go, subsiding into invisibility as they watched.

"*That* was close, Brij," Tamlin told his teacher.

"*What* was close? And why are you calling me 'Brij' when we are still in the classroom?" the shadow mage demanded.

"I am sorry, Shadow Mistress, but you nearly called lightning on yourself," Tamlin informed her. "If Marsh hadn't grabbed it when she did, you wouldn't be very happy right now."

Aisha was as brutally honest as only a six-year-old could be. "You'd be dead."

Brigitte looked from one to the other of them. "I'd be *what?*"

Marsh rolled her eyes and glared at Tamlin. "Tams, why don't you take your sister over there and get her to practice making buzz bunnies?"

"Buzz bunnies?" the boy asked, a mystified look on his face.

"Rabbits made out of lightning," Marsh told him. She didn't bother telling him that she didn't even know if lightning could be used that way.

Tamlin cast her a dubious look but he went, taking Aisha with him.

"Aysh, you know how you can make all sorts of shapes with stone…" Marsh heard him say as he led her away.

Brigitte gave Marsh a tired look. "Thank you," she said. "I didn't realize what I'd done until you shouted, and then I panicked and didn't know how to *un*do it."

She sighed. "I guess I'm just not cut out to control it."

"It's not as easy for some people as it is for others. You just need more time."

Brigitte's blue eyes filled with worry. "What if there *is* no more time?"

Marsh made a show of looking around the rooftop. "I don't see any Ookens here, do you?"

Before she could answer, Etk'k gave a whistle of alarm, its shrill tones cutting through her head like a knife.

"What is it?" she asked, and then didn't need to know.

Marsh! was all she heard from Roeglin amidst the impression of a flood of orange fur and pain.

"Roeglin!"

Aisha's shriek of dismay and outrage came as a surprise. "You give him back!"

The little girl whirled and raced for the rubble leading up to the open second floor they'd been standing on. "Give him back! Give him back! Give them *all* back!"

"Aisha!" Marsh ran after the child. "Wait!"

While she agreed wholeheartedly with the girl, she also knew they couldn't go rushing headlong into what could very well be a trap.

Aisha ducked under her hand. "Marsh! We *have* to go. We can't let them take them!"

As Marsh lunged for her again, she caught sight of movement rippling the bushes nearby. Now, she ran to catch up to the child, instead of just catching her.

"Aisha! We have incoming!"

She trusted the little girl would understand what that meant. Aisha *had* spent a lot of time with the soldiers, after all.

Stone floated up from the ground and began orbiting the child.

"Where?" Aisha demanded. "Show me!"

"Wait!" Tamlin's cry came just in time. "They're friends! The wolves are our friends!"

"Friends!" Aisha cried, and the rocks hit the ground around her in a patter of falling stone.

Bristlebear broke cover and raced toward her, his nose alternating between sniffing the ground and sniffing the air. The wolf's eyes flared green as he passed.

This way. The words were a blur in Marsh's mind, but their intent was clear.

He didn't stop but raced past, leading them down the remains of an ancient road and veering into the rubble of a ruin a block from where she and the others had been practicing calling the lightning. At first, Marsh wondered what he meant, but the sudden familiar screeching identified his prey soon enough.

He and the wolves bounded up the remnants of stairs to the second floor. They were soon overtaken by Mordan and her kits, who raced into the fray with semi-identical roars.

"Hey!" Aisha yelled in frustration. "Those are *mine*!"

She sprinted after the wolves and then surprised Marsh by leaping into the air even as she pulled a pillar of stone from the ground, then drew the flowing stone into a bridge for her flying feet.

"Aysh!"

"Sorry!" As if her apology was ever going to be enough.

The child must have been paying more attention to her thoughts than she'd realized because the stone suddenly extended behind her to form a path. Marsh didn't question the hows or the whys, even if she was suddenly worried by the extent of the child's rapidly developing ability.

It's not nice to be afraid of me, Marsh, Aisha told her, reminding her that the girl could do more than manipulate stone.

I'm not afraid of you, you little shit. I'm afraid for you. There's a difference.

Aisha's delighted giggle was a relief to hear. The crunch of rock being ripped from the walls was not.

Her "Bristlebear! Get! Back! I've got this!" was even more worrying, and Marsh made herself run faster.

It reminded her of her dream, but this time, the nightmare was in front of her and not behind her.

Not funny, Marsh, Aisha told her, punctuating her sentence with the sound of rock being driven into rock with something meaty and metallic in between.

Marsh winced. She might have felt sorry for the Ookens, but she caught sight of three of them leaping over the side of the building, with Bristlebear and the pack in full pursuit.

One of the orange-furred monsters didn't make it. Mordan slashed upward and took it out of the air midleap. Her blow brought it down to the rooftop, and Perdemor pounced and ripped off its head.

Marsh felt her stomach roll as blood and other materials sprayed the rubble around him.

"They're getting away!" Aisha's shrill call brought Marsh abruptly back to the present and she stepped into the nearest patch of shadow, preparing to close the distance between them. As she did, she watched a large, multi-legged form race out from the base of the building, its forelimbs a blur of metal in the afternoon light.

The blades gave the Ookens pause, but it wasn't until Brigitte sent a large shard of stone through its skull that it fell, leaving the mantid free to find its next target. In the meantime, a large gray blur had brought down the leading creature.

The monster screamed and thrashed, but Bristlebear wasn't alone. Silvermoth and Mousekiller were with him, and more of the pack arrived soon after, but even with Etk'k's help, they were struggling.

"Help me," Tamlin murmured, and the air came alive.

"Only the Ookens," he added, directing the lightning into the roiling mass of tentacles, fur, and fang.

Wolves yelped and Etk'k stumbled back, but the lightning did as Tamlin asked, receding at the boy's request. For a few long moments, silence reigned as humans, wolves, and mantid scanned their surroundings for more.

"Was that all of them?" Marsh asked, searching the shadows and crevices for more.

Yes. We have taken down the enemies of the pride, Mordan confirmed. She sniffed the air, sending a querulous growl through the ruins.

To Marsh's surprise, the kat was answered by several light yips and a soft, crooning howl, and Bristlebear and Silvermoth trotted over to nose around at her feet.

Their trail leads that way, but it will be gone by dawn. There is rain coming.

It leads to the portal, Etk'k's voice interrupted after the wolves had moved a few steps, their direction clear. *I can show you the way.*

"Brigitte, Aisha, Tamlin, are you ready?" Marsh asked, noting that the wolf was right. The clouds had slowed, and the wind felt damp against her skin. She wondered how long they had.

"I don't have my armor," Brigitte replied to her question, then added, "but we really don't have time to go back."

"Marsh can show you how to make shadow armor," Tamlin told her before Marsh had a chance to respond, "and Aisha can show you how to use a shield of rock."

"And we always have weapons," Brigitte agreed, pulling a spear of stone from the rock making up the nearest wall and hanging a shield of shadow from her forearm. She glanced at Marsh. "How do you do armor?"

"It's like the shield, only you pull it around your body and ask it to protect you," Marsh explained.

Brigitte's brow furrowed, then darkness shrouded her form. There was a moment where her face completely vanished, then the shadow cleared from there.

"Got it!" she exclaimed triumphantly. "Now, what happened to Roeglin?"

He was taken, Etk'k informed them. A lump blocked Marsh's throat and stole her voice. *As were my people. We* must *get them back.*

It was the first time Marsh had seen him afraid.

"Show me the way," she ordered, glad to see Aisha scrambling onto Mordan's back and two kits and a pup closing around them.

The child wouldn't stay behind, but she was well-protected. Tamlin ran beside them, as close as he could get with the kit and Scruffknuckle in the way. The boy didn't seem to mind, though. Despite the occasional glance to make sure his sister was okay, he kept his eye on the mantid as it led the way over the half-buried street and into the semi-collapsed structure of another building.

Normally, Marsh would try to work out what a ruin had been. Today, she didn't bother. The clouds gathering above seemed only fitting. Roeglin had been taken, and she had to get him back. It made her wonder what had happened.

They were waiting, Etk'k told her. *Tok thought they knew we would come, they struck so fast, and with electro-nets.*

"What nets?"

Nets that hold lightning inside their strands and release it when they strike their target.

"Oh." It made a horrible kind of sense. Lightning paralyzed. Even if a net didn't trap its target, the lightning inside its strands would prevent the person it hit from controlling their limbs.

When they arrived at the portal, the shattered chunks of stone told their own story. The Ookens had blown the barrier from the inside, sending the stone flying almost to the junction.

Pulse gun, Etk'k murmured, and Marsh wished the mantid would make sense. Not even the image the mantid sent by way of apology explained how such a weapon had destroyed the stone.

The stone...

"We need the mages," she gasped, remembering Brin and Sylvie. "Without them, we won't be able to calculate where to direct the lightning."

She gulped, pushing back the sense of despair that threatened to overwhelm her. "I don't even know if there's anyone else who can do what they do if we lose them. We need them to help us close the portal."

Agreed, Etk'k responded, *and we* must *retrieve my leader. Without him, there is no future for my people. We* must *get him back.*

Ahead of her, the portal still shone, sending a dull red glow down the tunnel. Mordan, the wolves, and the children didn't hesitate. They ran into it without stopping, making Marsh's heart leap to her throat.

Etk'k outdistanced her, racing through the portal in a blur of limbs and shadow.

Without him, there is no future, echoed through Marsh's head as she followed. It didn't matter what lay on the other side. She had to get her people back.

Roeglin not least among them.

23

INFILTRATION

I have them, Etk'k announced.

Have who? Marsh used a short staff to block and trap another tentacle, wrapping it around the short bar before asking the shadow to transform into a two-edged blade.

The Ooken shrieked as the tentacle was slashed apart, but it didn't seem to matter. The orange-furred monster had more.

Their minds, Etk'k replied. *Now they cannot tell the others we have arrived.*

How... Marsh began but decided it didn't matter. She disentangled her blade and thrust it into the Ooken's chest. *We need to warn the Four Caverns about these.*

Agreed.

Ruins rose around them, the Devastation of another world. Summer's heat hung thickly in the air, but the difference didn't end there. Instead of the stone being brown or gray or white, everything here was touched by a dull red veneer, and the plants were dead, what few there were.

"What is this place?" Brigitte murmured.

The shadow mistress was briefly wrapped in a tentacle, but her armor shifted, growing sharp-edged spikes that severed the limb even as she drove a dart into her attacker's chest. Marsh killed a second one, then a third.

She searched for Aisha along their link and found the child coated in stone and impervious to attack as she caused spikes of stone to erupt from the closest wall. The kats and Scruffknuckle worked to keep the area behind her clear while she dealt with the Ookens up front.

"Those things don't fight fair!" Tamlin observed from inside a maelstrom of shadow.

He'd adapted his sister's tactic to create a whirling storm of dark fragments.

"Just count yourself lucky that our magic works over here," Marsh snapped back. "We'd be shagged and shroomed without it."

Roeglin? she called, trying to contact him along their link.

I am sorry. The block is non-specific, Etk'k apologized. *The only reason we can speak is that you are linked through me, and we are close.*

So, we need to kill these guys before I can try to talk to Roeglin?

That is correct.

Well, why didn't you say so?

Etk'k had no answer for that, but Marsh didn't need one.

Around her, the wolves fought, her children fought,

everyone fought because Tamlin was right. The Ookens didn't fight fair, and they weren't stupid. They'd attacked as soon as the children and kats had come through.

Only Tamlin's quick thinking had saved them. The boy had thrown a shadow shield over them as the attack came and kept it moving with them as they ran. Etk'k had arrived in time to throw a different kind of shield; she'd have to ask the mantid what he'd done later.

For now, she was grateful he had. She focused her energy on taking down the next tentacled monster, glancing around the battlefield as she did so. There weren't as many of them now.

The kats were working with Tamlin and Aisha, and they'd reduced the initial mass of orange and blue to a scant half-dozen. It was still a lot, but at least the kids and kats outnumbered their foes now.

On the other side of her, Etk'k was using both hands and his feet to take his foes out, sometimes singly and sometimes in pairs. The wolves had divided into two groups, with Bristlebear and a half-dozen packmates protecting the mantid, while Silvermoth worked with the rest to keep Brigitte free and clear.

There was a yelp and Tamlin snarled, "I've had enough of this!"

Merde! Marsh felt her skin tingle with accumulated power.

"Keep it small!" she snapped, smashing her buckler into the Ooken face coming at her.

"Small?"

"I want you to have enough energy to call something bigger when we get to wherever they took Roeglin."

"*Bien.*"

Marsh slashed another tentacle at the same time as she reached into the shadows to touch the energy the boy was gathering.

"That should be enough, boy," she murmured quietly, so as not to distract him and through gritted teeth as she blocked another attack with her shield and ended the Ooken with a savage cut into its chest.

Jerking the blade free, she lost contact with the energy, surprised as tiny shards of power rained down around her, striking her opponents with deadly accuracy and stopping once the last one had fallen.

In the silence of the aftermath, she stared at Tamlin in open-mouthed surprise. "Where did you…"

She closed her mouth and gathered her thoughts. "You've gotten better," she finished.

He grinned at her, moving to tap carefully on the carapace of stone surrounding his sister. "Aysh? You can come out. It's safe."

I have dropped the shield, Etk'k told her. *You should be able to speak to them now.*

He paused. *Tok says to hurry. The facility is remote but has sent for transports.*

As he spoke, the stone armor melted away from Aisha, returning to the ground beneath her feet. She pointed at a worn trail through the rubble. "They're that way. Master Ennermet says to hurry."

Marsh frowned at the child. "And does he say how many Ookens there are, or where they've been taken?"

As if she'd summoned him, Master Envermet was in her head. *He says to picture this location in your head and portal your asses here before any more of them arrive.*

His acerbic tone was accompanied by the image of an open pit in the center of a walled-in courtyard.

He also says to save some energy so you can open a portal for our new friends and us back to the gate, he added. *You remember what the area around that looks like, can't you?*

Marsh had started to run after Aisha, but she jolted to an abrupt halt. "Tamlin! Brigitte! Aisha! We're going to open a portal to them."

"Bear! Dan!" Aisha's childish treble summoned the animals back, and Mordan and the pack leaders relayed the order to return.

Marsh turned to Etk'k and the two shadow mages. "We need to remember this space well enough to open a gate to it. Master Envermet says there are people we have to bring back."

Speaking of Master Envermet reminded her she hadn't heard from Roeglin.

I'm here, he said as if thinking of him had called him to her mind.

Are you okay?

I'll be fine. That was Roeglin at his most evasive.

His words sent a jolt of panic through her. *Ro?*

Just get here.

The connection closed, but before she could react, a gentle touch brought her back to the present.

"We're ready when you are," Brigitte told her. "Etk'k has shared the destination, and we've all tried to remember exactly what the gate looks like from here."

The shadow mistress' words reminded her that she needed to do the same, no matter how much of a hurry she was in to get to Roeglin. Brigitte and Tamlin came to stand beside her as she studied the gate, trying to commit it to memory.

She was guessing there wouldn't be a lot of time to create the portal, and she didn't know what state the mages with Roeglin were going to be in. Deeps! She didn't even know how many of them were injured or dying or...

A small hand patted her side, and she looked down to see Aish reaching past Brigitte to give her comfort. The little girl was sitting astride Mordan's blood-spattered back, her other hand wound firmly in the kat's fur.

"I can fix," the little girl assured her, catching her worry about the injured, "but we must go now."

Marsh gave the child a shaky smile. "Okay, then."

She looked at Tamlin and Brigitte. "Are you ready?"

"Ready."

Taking a deep breath, Marsh tried to picture the location Master Envermet had shown her. Beside her, she knew Tamlin and Brigitte were doing the same. Picturing the pit and the courtyard was difficult at first, despite the distinctive pink shade of the crystal that formed it. The task became abruptly easier with Aisha's help.

I've been practicing, the little girl explained, tweaking the picture in her head. *Master Tok showed me.*

He did?

Yes.

How many more did the Shadow Master say were coming? Etk'k's interruption almost jolted the picture from her mind.

He didn't, Marsh replied.

Go ahead, Etk'k told her, coming to an abrupt decision. *I will bring help from the nest.*

He didn't wait for her to reply but ran back through the portal, Bristlebear and a half-dozen wolves on his heels.

Bear will protect him, Aisha assured her, *and he will come back very soon.*

Marsh hoped so. She also hoped the portal would remain open long enough for them to get back home, but she tried to keep that thought to herself. It was bad enough that Roeglin and Master Envermet walked her head whenever they felt like it, but for Aisha to be doing it, too?

"So, are we going to do this?" Tamlin demanded, and Marsh nodded.

Opening her eyes, she began drawing a doorway ahead of her. Beside her, Tamlin and Brigitte did the same. As they worked, Marsh could feel Aisha helping them keep their destination clear in their minds.

The prisoners were walled in by the same substance as the portal, the crystal a deep rose shot through with milk. The glistening ground beneath them was the same color and smooth. Marsh wondered what Aisha's magic would make of it.

Slowly, three doors formed before them. As soon as they were solid, they floated into each other, merging into one larger opening. Aisha didn't wait for them, or perhaps it was Mordan. Either way, kat and child had surged toward the opening and bounded through before Marsh had a chance to order them to stop.

Tamlin followed. Marsh didn't bother trying to call him back, but raced after him and hoped they'd opened the portal in the right place. She hoped, too, that the Ookens weren't already there and waiting.

"We have to hurry," Master Envermet greeted her as soon as she and Brigitte stepped through.

His greeting jolted Marsh's concentration enough that she let go of the portal.

"*Merde!*" Brigitte exclaimed, and the portal snapped shut.

Marsh gave her a concerned look.

"It's okay. I let it go before it got too much," the mage assured her, looking around. She'd scanned half the courtyard when she gasped and froze.

Marsh followed her gaze and soon saw what she was looking for. Aisha.

The little girl was kneeling on the dead red earth, her hands on the crumpled figure of a shadow mage. "There's no life," the little girl sobbed. "No life!"

At first, Marsh didn't know what she meant, and she recognized Roeglin and didn't care. She bolted across the intervening distance and skidded to her knees beside Aisha.

"What can I do?"

"I need life to fix him," Aisha cried, and slapped at the crystal beneath her. "This ground has no life!"

Relief washed through Marsh as she heard the words and registered that Roeglin was still breathing, then she realized what Aisha had said.

"What do you mean?"

"I mean, there is no life. The land can't help me fix him. This rock can't help, either!" the child wailed.

She stopped as Scruffknuckle nudged her with his nose,

and then worked his head under one of her hands, whining anxiously.

"Is 'kay, Scruff?" Aisha asked, her small face pinched with worry. "He's hurt a lot."

Mordan growled and came to stand beside the pup. Aisha looked at her, then she looked at the wolves who walked over to stand in front of her. Silvermoth gave an imperative yip.

"What's wrong with him?" Marsh asked, and Aisha lifted the hand Roeglin had wrapped across his middle. "Oh."

Her head spun, and her heart went into freefall. Master Envermet laid a heavy hand on her shoulder. "He saved my life."

As if that would be any comfort. Marsh managed a nod, resisting as Master Envermet drew her to her feet. "Give the girl some room."

It wasn't a request, and his grip tightened until Marsh stood, relieved and terrified as the wolves crowded into the space she'd vacated.

"Not too much, Aisha," Master Envermet admonished, his voice audible both in Marsh's ears and her mind. "Just get him on his feet. There are others who need you too."

"'Kay."

"Help me with the others," Master Envermet instructed. "Just don't do too much. Brigitte, we need you."

The shadow mistress had been hovering nearby, her eyes scanning the walls and the people around them.

"We need to heal the shadow mages first," she said, noting how many others shared the space with them.

She looked around again. "Where are they?"

"Where are who?" Master Envermet wanted to know.

"The Ookens," Brigitte replied, lowering her voice as though mentioning their name would summon them.

"Look up," Master Envermet told her. "Tell me what you see."

Marsh obeyed and registered the expanse of crystal above her head. "Is that a-a ceiling?"

"*Oui.*"

"So, we're inside?"

"*Oui.*"

He kept moving as he talked, leading them over to where Henri and Izmay were crouched beside another familiar figure.

"Tok!" Marsh exclaimed, recognizing his form. "Are you okay?"

The mantid gave a soft chitter of amusement. *I have been better.*

"I'll have Aisha come," Master Envermet reassured him.

That would be for the best, I think," the mantid wheezed. His antennae wove above his head. They reminded Marsh of a horse's ears twitching. *They will be returning soon.*

He turned to Marsh. *Are you able to get us back to the portal?*

"I can," Marsh told him. "I just need some help holding a gate big enough to fit us all through."

We should not leave any behind.

"Done!" Aisha's happy shout was followed by a groan from Roeglin. "No complaining!"

"I wouldn't dare," the shadow mage replied. "Now, go help Tok."

Marsh wheeled toward the sound of his voice, and Master Envermet let go of her arm.

"Get them ready," he ordered as Marsh ran past him. He paused and then added, "Izmay, we'll need you, Brigitte and Zeb. Henri, ask Aisha to show you how to borrow energy without taking too much. Brin, are you still with us?"

The rock mage's response was lost as Marsh found Roeglin's arms. The hug was brief, and she choked back tears as she registered the remains of his armor and the fetid damp of the cloth beneath. "What did you do?"

"I'll have Master Envermet show you sometime. Apparently, it was spectacular, and I am twenty times the fool."

Marsh cast a surprised glance at the shadow captain. "He said that?"

"He was really upset that I'd saved his life. Something about being more important to the Library than he will ever be or some stupidity like that."

Marsh wanted to argue that Master Envermet was right, but all she managed was a choked laugh. It was enough to have him on his feet, although the absence of any enemies had her worried.

"Look up," Roeglin advised. "There's a reason they haven't come yet."

Marsh glanced up as he asked, noting the solid pall of gray overhead for a second time. "Master Envermet showed me, but why aren't they here? Where are the guards?"

"It looks like they don't think we can escape."

"And you don't think they're watching us?"

"I don't see how they could."

They watch us. Tok's mental voice sounded stronger. *You do not have time for me to explain how.*

"How long will it take for them to come once we open the portal?"

Not long, and they will come in numbers.

"Then we'd better hurry," Marsh finished, leading Roeglin back to the fallen mantid and slapping him on the shoulder. "Stay there. I'll use you as a marker for the rest."

"Where do you want to open things?" Roeglin asked, stopping her short.

Marsh looked around, taking note of where the largest concentrations of prisoners were. There were an awful lot of mantids, and some other hard-carapaced creatures she didn't recognize.

"Do they all want to come?" she asked, and Roeglin snorted.

Tok's response was amused and perplexed. *Of course. You do not think they* want *to stay here, do you?*

Marsh blushed. In hindsight, it *had* been a stupid question.

"Well, are they safe?" she asked. "Will they..." She searched for a way to ask what she wanted without being insulting.

They will be grateful to be released and will not attack you, Tok told her, *although they might not accept your hospitality when they reach the other side.*

"What? But why?" Marsh asked, remembering the world outside.

This was their world, too. Sadness edged the mantid's voice, and Mash remembered Aisha crying because the ground had no life for her to draw from.

"It can't *all* be dead!"

Tok's silence was almost an answer in itself. When he did answer, his mental touch was heavy with grief. *There are some of us who hope it is otherwise, and many who would like to stay, but I am responsible for my people, and I cannot keep them alive on hope alone.*

Marsh didn't know what to say to that, but she was saved from having to say anything by Master Envermet.

"Shadow Mage Leclerc, we are ready."

24

EXFILTRATION

M arsh looked around the courtyard. She'd found her people, and they were now helping the other prisoners they'd been put with. Apprehension prickled through her. There were *so* many…

They are almost here, Tok warned, interrupting her thoughts. *I can feel their minds.*

Marsh nodded and looked at the mages to the left and right of her. They were only a few.

"If everyone hurries, we can get them to the portal back to the Library. Make them understand they need to go through. They cannot wait."

Etk'k has not returned. Tok informed her. *I am worried.*

"What if the portal is closed?"

I can operate it from this side, Tok told her. *That information was not locked as securely in the Ookens' minds as it should have been.*

"Marsh?" Master Envermet prodded, and Marsh swallowed with a throat gone suddenly dry.

She glanced at Tamlin and Roeglin, who were stationed on either side of her.

We are ready, Roeglin confirmed.

"Aisha?"

The little girl was mounted on Mordan's back and sat facing them. She nodded. "They are ready."

Marsh raised her hands and sketched the portal in front of her. Her actions acted as a signal for the rest, and they too began drawing on the shadow to open a way out of their prison. One by one, six more portals appeared in line with hers. Behind them, the Ookens' captives moved uneasily.

"Tok, tell them no one is to be left. We offer sanctuary to *all* who come in peace. We *will* make room for them." As she spoke, Marsh completed her door, focusing on the area in front of the portal. The shadows writhed and coiled around its edges.

"Please," Marsh murmured, "stay with me a little longer. Keep the path clear between here and home. Please!"

Her mind tingled with Tok's order, but she wasn't listening. Tamlin's and Roeglin's doors were merging with hers, and the shadows twisted at their control.

Is it...just...me, or are these going to be hard to hold? Roeglin gritted out.

"Steady," Aisha admonished, and they smiled.

She scowled at them. "No laughing matter," she snapped, sounding so much like Master Envermet that Marsh almost laughed out loud.

She was prevented by the presence of someone moving past her.

Henri's heavy hand fell on her shoulder. "You make sure you bring my Izmay home," the soldier told her.

"I'll do my best."

"You bring her back, and I'll strike *two* dinners off what you owe me."

"Five!" Marsh retorted, but he didn't stop to argue, and she didn't insist. The shadows were squirming under her control. "Oh...no...you...don't."

She willed the portal to stay open, fighting for focus as more prisoners passed her. Some she recognized from the Library, and others from Tok's nest, but there were more, and almost none of them were human.

Of the ones who were, none of the faces were familiar.

This is going to be one Deeps-spawned mess to sort, she thought and felt Roeglin's agreement. She also felt his complete confidence that they'd succeed.

As the passing prisoners grew fewer, Aisha scanned the area behind them.

"Almost done," she told Marsh. "Almost."

A terribly familiar screech broke the air, and Aisha's eyes grew wide. "They're here!"

It took all of Marsh's self-control not to turn around.

"Master Envermet, tell them to hurry."

Ahead of Marsh, the ranks of the departing prisoners parted, and Etk'k raced through the portal. The mantid skidded to a halt facing her, his antennae dancing between relief and alarm. He raised his head and issued a shrill whistle that echoed around the courtyard.

It set Marsh's ears ringing, but it had the desired effect. The last of the prisoners hurried past her.

"Is the portal open?" Marsh demanded.

It was closed until Tok came, Etk'k told her. *It was hard to get him to cross over before the last were free, but Henri convinced him his presence was needed for bloodshed to be avoided on the other side.*

"Henri?"

He was most persuasive. The one called Jakob went with him. They will bring the druids and also mind mages from the Grotto, and they will find those who can organize shelter for those we bring with us.

His eyes took in both sides of the arena.

Although I do not know how they will manage it.

"They *will* manage it," Roeglin growled, his faith in Alain's and Evan's abilities coming through in his words.

The mantid settled beside Aisha and waited as the prisoners passed to safety. It was not a long wait.

That is the last of them, Etk'k informed them as Aisha shouted, "Done!"

"Zeb!" Marsh ordered, "Go through and hold it from the other side."

"*Oui!*" echoed back to her, cutting through the boom of multiple doors, the slap of suckers on stone, and more screeching.

Marsh felt the portal shiver as Zeb passed through it, and his control momentarily faded before strengthening again.

More shadow mages are coming, Etk'k informed her. *They will help.*

"They can't!" Marsh gasped. "They mustn't come through."

They are already here, on the other side, Etk'k stated. *They refused to stay in their own world while you were in peril. They will return, but only with you.*

"*Putain a moi!*" Marsh swore, and Roeglin chuckled.

"You'd better not disappoint them, then," he said. "You don't want them getting into even more trouble trying to come after you."

"They wouldn't!"

Master Envermet chuckled. "They very much would, and you know it. Who's to cross next? We don't have much time."

"Izmay and you," Marsh responded, as Etk'k drew his swords.

Hurry, the mantid told her, moving past her toward the screeches. *I will not be able to hold them for long.*

"You won't be able to hold them at all," Marsh snapped. "You get your armored backside right back there and wait for us on the other side."

I will compromise, the mantid told her. *I will guard your back and return when you do.*

"Of all the stubborn, hard-shelled, Deep-spawned *roaches* in the world!"

"Done!" Roeglin told the mantid. The portal dipped and bucked as Master Envermet and Izmay shifted their control to the other side. "Marsh! Who's next?"

"You and Brigitte."

Twin denials reached her, and she heard Etk'k's whistle of warning. At the same time, Aisha slid off Mordan's back. Marsh stared as the child pulled the stone from the court-yard's floor and covered herself in a layer of flexible plates.

A shield lifted out of the floor to float in front of her, and a spear appeared in her hand.

"I will hold them," she declared, heading for Etk'k at a run.

"Change of plans!" Marsh shouted, thinking fast. "Roeglin, if I let go of the shadows, can you hold the gate?"

"Can I what?" Roeglin asked, then gasped as Tamlin released *his* hold on the gate.

Marsh had been expecting it and seized the shadows before they left the portal and broke their only path out of the courtyard.

"Stay!" she commanded, sweat beading her upper lip as she grasped the suddenly freed darkness and bent it to her will. "Brigitte?"

"I'll help him."

"Roeglin?"

"Almost there."

Marsh felt the shadows resist Roeglin's call until she willed them into his care.

"Trust him," she whispered, willing them to obey Roeglin as they had obeyed her. "Do as he commands."

"Keep the portal open until we get them back, and then keep it open. We'll all cross together!"

"Got it!"

"Hurry, Marsh!"

"Aisha! Etk'k! Protect Roeglin and Brigitte! Tamlin, with me."

What are you doing? Roeglin demanded.

"Leveling this place! Tamlin, we need the lightning!"

She reached the place where the mantid stood, braced and ready to receive the Ooken attack force. Across the courtyard, the orange-furred horde was now scrambling across the walls, ceiling, and floor toward them.

"Why do they *do* that?" she whispered, hearing the snap and crackle of their tentacles slamming into and releasing from the crystal surfaces as they moved.

"Does it matter?" Tamlin asked as Mordan darted back to him. "Aisha! Get going! We're going to call the lightning!"

The little brat started running, but not in the direction or for the reason Marsh had hoped.

"We are?" Aisha's face was alight with excitement as she approached. "I'll help!"

"Not—"

"Fine!" Tamlin cut across Marsh's denial. "You help, but we need to back up until we reach Uncle Roeglin and Brigitte, okay?"

"Okay!"

Having successfully convinced the little girl to come back with them, Marsh and Tamlin reversed slowly back, the mantid moving with them.

"You see what we're going to do?" Marsh asked, hoping the mantid had been his usual selective self about intruding on her mind.

I see it, but you will have to be quick.

Just make sure Roeglin and Brigitte make it back.

And the child?

Mordan will take Aisha.

As if to confirm that, the kat circled around the little girl, pushing her with her head until the child relented and turned to her shoulder.

"Fine, Dan! Down!"

It was a new command for Marsh, but the kat knew exactly what the little girl wanted. She bowed, lowering her forequarters to make it easier for Aisha to mount. As soon as she was aboard, Mordan straightened and came to stand beside Marsh.

"Now?" Tamlin asked, and the air close to the courtyard's ceiling crackled.

"Now!" Marsh agreed, reaching for the lightning in the shadows along the walls.

"Now!" Aisha shrieked, and the wall sheeted white with power, setting alight every Ooken touching it and then arcing to the other Ooken touching them, and arcing again.

"Sons of the Deep," Tamlin whispered, his voice soft with awe.

"Tamlin!" Marsh yelled, reminding him there were still more Ooken to deal with.

He started as though he'd been slapped and the light along the ceiling flared, falling in sparkling droplets. Marsh swept a hand in a wide arc. Neither of the children had called the lightning that lurked in the air between the ceiling and the floor.

Marsh focused on that, barely hearing the sudden soft "Oh" that came from Brigitte. She felt what the shadow mage did, though. As Marsh drew the lightning from the air surrounding them and Aisha pulled it from the wall and Tamlin took it from the ceiling, Brigitte gave it direction.

The front rank of Ookens reached them, and the lightning fell or coalesced into giant balls that spun and then sharded into horizontal bolts that devastated the Ooken ranks.

Etk'k's blades sang.

Silence abruptly fell.

The smell of singed fur and flesh rose around them, and Roeglin spoke.

"Marsh, we...can't hold this much...longer."

"Tamlin, Etk'k, Aisha, and Mordan, go through." She forestalled their protests, watching as the lightning swirled around the courtyard, slowly coalescing into a massive energy storm in the center of where the prisoners had been held.

Keeping half an eye on that and half an eye on the children, mantid, and kat, Marsh backed up to where Roeglin and Brigitte stood. "Go!" she urged when Tamlin hesitated. "We can't do this until you're through, okay?"

The boy gave her a doubtful look, but Etk'k laid a clawed hand on his shoulder.

She speaks the truth, the mantid told him. *The sooner we go, the sooner she will follow.*

The boy's reply was full of fear and pending hurt. "What if she doesn't?"

Then we will return for her, the mantid assured him.

Until that point, Marsh hadn't known it was possible to lie in mental speech, but she was pretty sure that Etk'k knew as well as she did that if she did not follow, there would be no point in returning for her. The energy building in the middle of the space the prisoners had occupied would see to that.

Whatever she knew, the mantid's words had the desired effect. The mantid, both children and the kat stepped into the portal, leaving Marsh, Brigitte, and Roeglin alone.

"Are you ready?" Marsh asked, reaching for the

shadows holding the portal, and Roeglin and Brigitte gave her pale-face nods. She focused on the shadow mistress, well aware that she had called the lightning, but Brigitte was the one controlling it now.

"Are you sure?"

"On three," Brigitte replied, her ebon face paling to a very dark gray.

"On three," Marsh agreed.

Roeglin nodded, tightlipped, pale, and sweating as he kept his hands raised toward the portal.

"One, two...*three!*"

She slid her arm through Roeglin's, feeling for the shadows he held and lending him more of her control. At the same time, she reached out and snagged Brigitte by the bicep and yanked her through after them.

The shadow mistress gave a startled yelp, losing control of the energy she'd held in the center of the courtyard as she was hauled through the portal. The three of them hit the ground together.

"Close the portal!" Brigitte shouted. "Close it! Close it! Close it!"

There was a single oath from Master Envermet, then the gate to the prison closed. Shortly afterward, the ground trembled beneath them.

"Go!" Marsh shouted, pointing at the portal leading to the Devastation. "Get out of here!"

Looking back through the red-stained ruins, she was sure she could see dark smoke rising beyond them, but Roeglin didn't give her the chance to make sure. He and Master Envermet looped their arms around her and pulled her through the portal.

"But…" she protested.

"We don't have time!" Roeglin snarled as they raced into the tunnel on the other side. Marsh started running with him.

None of them stopped until they were halfway to the junction.

PREPARATION

"What now?" Marsh asked after they'd stopped running.

The three of them turned to face the still-gleaming portal.

They will be coming. Tok's voice replied out of nowhere. *There is no way they will leave this insult unavenged or the threat you have become unanswered.*

Roeglin groaned. "How much time do we have?"

We need to short-circuit the portal as soon as you are able.

"Like tonight?"

If by that you mean as soon as you reach the surface, then that is correct.

They started down the tunnel, and the mantid joined them as they passed the passage leading to his nest. It wasn't until they'd crossed the junction and reached the stairs that they realized the tunnel was empty.

"What happened to everyone?" Marsh asked.

Fortunately, Tok could see who she meant.

I sent them back to the nest. They will be safer there since the Others will attack the source of the greatest threat.

"The Library," Marsh concluded.

That is correct. Tok hesitated as though unsure of how she would react to what he wanted to say next.

"What is it?" Marsh demanded.

The nest can provide shelter for the people of the Library, the mantid offered. *For those who cannot or do not know how to fight.*

Marsh exchanged glances with Roeglin, taking his arm as his eyes gleamed white. She guided him up the stairs to the guard post and through it into the Library. By the time she reached the front steps, Obasi and Master Envermet were there, the other settlement leaders hurrying to join them.

"What's this about an attack?" Xavier demanded, mounting the steps as the wind gusted around him.

Marsh glanced up at the sky, and Evan followed her gaze. "Druids have been working on calling a storm ever since this morning's meeting. I told them we needed another two days for the crops to be ready. They said we needed the storm sooner."

He glared at Marsh. "Why do I think *you* have something to do with this?"

"Only because you know I'd do anything to *save your asses,*" Marsh snapped back, ignoring Etk'k's worried whistle and clicks.

Be gentle. He is very afraid.

Thunder rumbled overhead and Alain looked up, studying the ripples of light flaring through the clouds. The frown on his face grew deeper, and he scowled as he came to a stop in front of Marsh.

"The lightning in the stones not enough for you?"

Marsh snorted with bitter laughter. "There's a portal leading into the Below that we need to close, and you want to fight about how much lightning your children get to play with?"

Alain's anger turned to alarm, and he glanced at the growing storm again. "You're not expecting them to play with *that*?"

"Not on their own," Marsh told him, all humor disappearing, "but yes. Roeglin will explain why."

She looked around, finding the person she needed and moving away before Alain could stop her. Roeglin moved to block his path as Marsh turned her attention to the leader of the Grotto's warriors and druids.

"Obasi, I need Brin and Sylvie."

Behind her, she heard Roeglin begin telling the leaders about the pending attack from Below. Exclamations of disbelief followed his brief explanation, and she almost turned back.

Trust your mate, Mordan admonished her. *He shows them the images of what you faced.*

He doesn't!

He does. He shows them pictures of the foe and of the lightning your cubs called.

They are not *my cubs!*

They are as much your cubs as they are the cubs of their parents, the kat told her and sent her a mental image of her stalking away, her tail straight up in the air.

"Nice," Marsh muttered. "*Real* nice, kat."

"Anything I should know about?" Obasi asked, breaking into her thoughts. Marsh started.

She hadn't realized he'd come to meet her. "The kat says I should leave Roeglin to do what he does best," she admitted, glancing back to where Roeglin and the town leaders now stood in a huddle that included Etk'k.

The mantid's antennae waved, and his clicks, chitters, and rasps were no doubt accompanied by a mental translation she couldn't hear. She almost wished she could, but was glad to be able to concentrate on the matter at hand.

"What happened?" Obasi asked.

"We started a fight we weren't ready for," Marsh admitted.

"Why?" Obasi looked puzzled. "That doesn't sound like you."

For a moment, Marsh wasn't sure if he was being sarcastic or if he meant that.

Obasi noticed the look on her face, or perhaps he skimmed it from her thoughts, and he laughed.

"I meant that as it came out. You and Roeglin would never do something to deliberately place this settlement in jeopardy. You've worked too hard to make us all safe.' He paused and then asked again, "What happened?"

"The team that went to check the portal was taken," Marsh admitted. "I went to get them back. Now I need to close the portal before the Ookens get through it."

She stopped, her eyes wide with the memory of how many of the tentacled monsters there were. "There are too many for us to defeat any other way."

Obasi stared at her, absorbing the news, then he plucked her sleeve, drawing her after him. "Brin and Sylvie are this way," he explained. "You can tell your story while we walk."

She followed him down the Library stairs and out the front gate.

"We got lucky," he said when he saw the confusion on her face. "They're waiting above the gate, and it's outside the walls."

"What about remnant?" Marsh asked, noticing how much darker the day had become with the gathering storm. It was perfect weather for the once-men to be on the move.

"Any remnant with half a sense of self-preservation will be holed up and hiding," Obasi told her. "I didn't know the druids could call a storm...and neither did they until they tried."

They picked their way around the base of the wall, the rocky ground shifting underfoot.

"How did they manage it?" Marsh asked when Obasi stopped to scan their surroundings, his eyes shading white.

"Well, they couldn't call a storm by itself, if that's what you're asking," Obasi admitted, his eyes returning to normal, "but they did work out they could call the wind, and they figured if they called enough wind, a storm was sure to come."

"But that could have taken days!" Marsh exclaimed.

Obasi shook his head and struck out toward one of the nearby ruins. "You felt the wind this morning?"

Marsh nodded. "It was cold. I thought...I thought there might be rain."

"Exactly," Obasi told her. "There were all the signs of weather coming, so when I came out of that meeting this morning and asked the druids when the next storm might come, they said the signs were for one in the next day or so. I asked them if they could make it come faster."

"And?" Marsh asked when he hesitated.

"They called me crazy, said I was taking your example too seriously, and then decided they'd try to bring the storm, given they knew which direction it would come from. Some called the wind, and some called the sky for moisture the same way they would draw water from the earth to water the crops."

"And that worked?"

He shrugged and gestured toward the sky. "It was a matter of expressing need and desire," he explained. "This is the result."

"How did they know it would stay for me to use it?"

Obasi's teeth flashed white in the semi-dark. "They asked the clouds and the wind to gather above us."

He glanced up as a particularly loud rumble filled the air. 'I don't think that was such a good idea. I think this storm is going to be worse than any we've seen so far."

The storm rumbled again as if to punctuate his words. This time the lightning turned the sky white, and the distinct scent of ozone filled the air.

Obasi looked even more worried. "We cannot hold it here much longer. It will be our destruction if we do."

Marsh agreed, and then she realized she'd come alone. "I need Aisha, Tamlin, and Brigitte," she said.

She started to turn back, but Obasi laid a hand on her arm.

"I will call them. Tok or one of the mantids will bring

them." His teeth flashed as he smiled without mirth. "No doubt the kat will carry the little one."

When he started moving again, Marsh followed. They ducked under an overhanging floor and found Brin and Sylvie already at work.

The woman looked up as their steps crunched over the stone.

"It's a good thing you let us know you were coming," she scolded Obasi, "or you'd have had a hammer to the head."

She frowned, catching sight of Marsh beside him. "Don't you need to be at the portal to direct the lightning into it?"

"*A la putain!*" Marsh cursed, realizing she was right. "*Putain a merde*! Deep's-spawned, shroom-cursed…"

She pivoted on her heel.

"Obasi, send Brigitte and the kids to the portal!" she called, flinging the words over her shoulder as she started to run.

26

THE ENEMY AT THE GATE

Marsh didn't wait for the children. She ran straight back to the library, tearing through the gate and up the Library stairs, aware of the stares as she passed but only vaguely aware of the curses rising in her wake.

"Marsh! Wait!" Tamlin's youthful cry rang out behind her, but she didn't stop.

She felt a terrible foreboding with every step she took, as if a storm was coming—and one that had nothing to do with the clouds boiling outside. If she didn't get back...

An all-too-familiar scream echoed up from the depths as she took the sharp left into the hidden stairwell. Behind her, Tamlin's voice rang out again.

"Roeglin, they're coming!"

Marsh took the stairs as fast as she could. She heard footsteps behind her and the sounds of suckers slapping stone ahead. The screeches had died to quieter keens of inquiry as the Ookens searched the dark, and she was glad she hadn't thought to light the tunnels.

Let the Deeps-spawned shroom-shaggers search.

She hit the bottom of the stairs, racing into the arena and across it. It was a relief to see nothing in the space beneath the grate, and she hoped she could reach the junction before any of the invaders got there.

Almost... Her eyes caught the flash of movement at the edges of the tunnel leading out of the junction as she got there.

Marsh didn't hesitate; she launched a handful of shadow darts at the space ahead of where the movement had disturbed the dark and was rewarded with a scream of outrage and pain. The corridor beyond erupted into a cacophony of fury, and she slammed a shield up in front of her.

She didn't care how many of them were ahead—she had to reach the portal. A large furred form leapt past her: Perdemor. His brother ran alongside him, and his sister, with Scruffknuckle on her flank. A bigger form bounded in front of her and stopped, forcing her to come to a halt also.

"Dan!" Aisha wailed. "They're that way!"

Marsh didn't need the kat's impatient look to know what she wanted. As badly as she didn't want to, she pulled Aisha from the hoshkat's back. Mordan was gone before the child was clear.

Marsh set Aisha down beside her. "Armor!" she snapped, even as stone began flowing up the girl's limbs.

"Well, duh!" Aisha retorted. "Where's yours?"

The kid had a point, and Marsh took the time to pull the shadows around her as Mordan's roar shook the tunnel.

"Dan!" Aisha didn't wait. She jerked a shield from the

floor and charged toward the kat, a spear forming in her hand.

"Aysh!" Tamlin's shadow-clad form followed, and Marsh was relieved to see he'd learned from Brigitte's example and his armor rippled with spikes.

Marsh ran after them, not stopping when she heard Roeglin's call.

"Marsh, wait!"

"Find me the Ookens!" she commanded the threads connecting her to the corridor beyond. "Find me the children and the cubs!"

The shadows obeyed, a dozen images forming in her mind as she raced to join the youngsters. Roeglin caught up but didn't try to stop her.

"What are you doing here?"

"Watching your back while you call the lightning?" he asked, and Marsh didn't need to be told twice.

She called the lightning as she went. "I need you!"

Keeping hold of the threads, she called the lightning to her hand, shaping it as she'd seen Brigitte do and sending it down each thread to the Ookens at the ends.

"Only the Ookens," she whispered. "Keep my children safe."

She reached Tams and Aisha just after the first lightning bolt had reached the Ooken the shadow threads had revealed. The creature was intent on trying to wrap a tentacle around Aisha. It never knew what had hit it, its existence ending without it realizing it was finished.

All around her, the other bolts found their targets and dissipated, but Marsh didn't care. She maneuvered around Aisha so that she faced the door and felt for the kat.

Stay on this side of the portal, she instructed, wincing as Mordan crushed an Ooken skull with one swipe of a shadow-clad forepaw. *Your cubs need you on this side with them, and the other world is too dead to hunt.*

Mordan's rumbled agreement was followed by a distinct impression that the kat was too busy to talk, and the link between them closed. Marsh breathed easier when Mordan and the kits circled close enough to strike at the Ookens from behind their legs.

Watch my back, she ordered Roeglin, and his hand dropped briefly to the kat's shoulder.

"We can do that, can't we, Dan?"

Mordan growled, and her kits echoed her opinion. Scruffknuckle barked happily as he darted out from their protection to seize a tentacle and goad the attached Ooken into claw range. Marsh eyed the portal.

As she considered what she was going to do next, a dozen more Ookens came through. When another set of tentacles began to emerge, she slammed a cap of shadow over it, glad to hear a familiar whistle from the junction.

Can you catch all energy?

I don't know. There is lightning. What other energy is there?

There is the energy from the space between portals.

This really isn't the time for her to be playing with new magic, Roeglin admonished the mantid.

She will need to be able to direct it when they try to blast through the shadow, Tok informed him. *That energy is not lightning, and she must expect it and divert it, or you will all die.*

We'll what?

There is no room here to avoid a plasma blast, and I do not think your shield will be powerful enough to stop it.

The shadows sto... Oh. Marsh had been about to say that the shadows would stop the lightning, but then she realized they might not. After all, shadow monsters were made of shadow, and the lightning went right through them.

So do shadow blades, Roeglin reminded her, *and the shields stop those.*

It's not something I have tested, Marsh told him. Turning her attention to Tok, she asked, *What should we do?*

You will need to let them through and try to stop them here.

That should solve both problems, Marsh replied. *If they are coming through like this, their bodies will block the door anyway.*

You had better hope that does not happen. The weapon they use fires... He hesitated, searching for the right word, *... liquid fire. They would use it to clear any organic debris obstructing their path.*

Wouldn't that damage their doorway? Roeglin wanted to know.

Only if they hit it.

Marsh dropped the shield, aware that others had joined them.

"Excuse us," came an unfamiliar voice. "Brin sent us. He says we have to move the rock from above this frame?"

Marsh stepped back from the door, allowing Roeglin and another fighter to take her place. She wasn't surprised to recognize Henri's armored form moving up to defend the entry. Free to concentrate, she looked at the man.

He was one of Obasi's people, not a rock mage from the Monastery cavern. She was about to ask him what he thought he could do when she remembered that the Grotto druids knew how to manipulate stone as well.

"Say that again," she demanded, and the druid gestured toward the ceiling.

"We need to get rid of the rock overhead so you can call the lightning onto the portal." He looked at the two fighters blocking the tunnel, the two children, Brigitte, and the kats. "We really need some room to work."

"I…" Marsh knew he was right, and she knew there was little she could do until the path was opened. There was no shortcut she could take that would allow her access to the lightning or give her the ability to call it onto the portal until the way above was clear.

She stepped farther into the tunnel, reaching for the children along the mental connections between them.

"I heard," Aisha told her sulkily. "I'm coming."

"*Oui*, me too," Tamlin confirmed. He looked up at the druid. "We'll watch your back."

The man regarded him solemn-faced and gave him a single nod. "I would appreciate that."

Marsh breathed a sigh of relief, glad to have the children by her side, and even more glad when Mordan and the cubs moved back with them.

As if they'd been given an invitation, several guards slipped past to block the corridor closest to the portal. Roeglin fended off another tentacle attack, lengthened his sword into a spear, and skewered the Ooken that had just emerged from the other side of the gate.

"Can you work from there, or do you need to be closer?"

The mage eyed the portal and the tunnel's rise over it. "Here is fine," he replied, then frowned. "Where do you want it?"

"Want what?" Roeglin shot a look toward Marsh.

"The rock," the mage told them. "It's got to go somewhere. Where do you want it?"

Roeglin smirked, and Marsh smiled in response. "How hard can you throw it?" she asked.

"Throw?"

"*Mais oui.* I want you to throw all the rock you remove through that portal."

Henri shield slammed an Ooken that leapt through the portal's ruddy glow and then sliced off several tentacles from the creature following. The druid's face cleared.

"Oh. Well, we can do that."

Marsh stepped back, preparing to protect the druids from any Ookens that might get past Roeglin. The druids stepped forward and started drawing rock from the ceiling, hurling it through the portal as fast as they could get it to obey their commands.

The lead druid talked as he worked. "Brin and Sylvie are clearing the ground above, and our folk are helping there as well. Brin just thought the work might go faster if there were some of us clearing down here too."

"The faster, the better," Marsh agreed, and he gave her a humorless grin.

"That's what the others said, too. That storm was strong when they told the winds to bring it, but it's stronger now and getting worse. If we don't hurry, there won't be a Library left to defend."

Marsh didn't know what to say to that. She'd already seen the power of the storm. For it to have gotten even more powerful was an alarming thought.

"What can I do to help?" she asked.

"Stay out of the way, and don't let those things get me." The mage hadn't stopped working as he'd been talking, but his eyes had been darting nervously from the fighting going on at the portal front to the defenders working on either side of him to make sure none of the ones that got past the defenders reached him.

Mordan and her cubs prowled restlessly between them and the junction, and none of them looked happy that the path to the attacking Ookens was blocked.

Just be ready to get Aisha out of here, Marsh told the kat, and Mordan laid back her ears and hissed at her. Marsh glared at the hosh, then slowly and deliberately pictured the perfect kat's ass in her mind.

Judging by the long unhappy growl that rumbled out of Mordan's throat, her response was not appreciated. Marsh turned away.

Too bad. It was hard enough that she had to wait; she didn't need to deal with the kat's conniptions as well.

"Almost through," the mage murmured.

His words pre-empted a sudden burst of cold air and the crack and rumble of thunder. As the last of the rock vanished through the portal, he stepped back. "There you go."

"*Merci beaucoup,*" Marsh told him, moving under the opening, her eyes on the distant sky above her.

As she looked, there was another rumble and lightning danced through the crowd, lighting the circle of anxious faces peering down at her. She waved, then looked at Roeglin.

"Tell them to stand clear," she requested and gestured for Tamlin, Aisha, and Brigitte to join her.

She wasn't ready for another small figure to slip from the shadows and wrap her hand around Aisha's.

"Sasha!" the little girl hissed. "What are you doing here?"

The child gave her a beatific grin and stretched a hand to the sky. "Pretty!"

Marsh opened her mouth to say that 'yes' it *was* pretty, but what happened next left her speechless. A single line of power stretched down to touch the child's open hand and then earth itself in the stone below.

"Sons of the Deep," Tamlin whispered. "Sasha, can you let the lightning go now?"

"Why?" the child asked, her eyes wide with puzzlement.

"Because we all have to call it together," Tamlin explained. "'Kay?"

"Me too?"

Tamlin cast Marsh a worried look but nodded. "Yes, you, too."

"Okay!" Sasha bounced happily and flicked the lightning back into the clouds.

Where did she... Roeglin began, but Marsh cut him off.

I don't know!

She watched you practice, Tok informed them, *but Etk'k says she hid when you attacked the Ookens and he lost track of her.*

So she didn't *follow us through?"*

No. She was with her father when you returned.

And you know this how?

Because it was in Alain's mind when he answered Roeglin's summons. He was glad he'd found her and hoped she behaved for her mother.

Marsh's mind raced as she tried to fit this latest development into her plans. It was clear the child could call the lightning and direct it, but she wasn't sure if Sasha could do that in conjunction with the rest of them. What she needed was...

"Brigitte, can you combine and direct all the lightning we call?" Marsh asked, remembering what the shadow mistress had managed at the prison."

"I can try."

"I help," Sasha said in tones that reminded Marsh far too much of Aisha.

Before she could think of what to say, Roeglin interrupted, "I'll link them, but you need to hurry."

Looking past him, Marsh saw that Zeb had stepped up to take Roeglin's place in defending the tunnel from the Ookens that kept emerging from the portal.

"We can't hold them much longer," was not what she wanted to hear.

Roeglin came and stood between Sasha and Brigitte, resting a hand on each of their shoulders.

"What..." Sasha began as Roeglin's eyes went white. "Oooh. 'Kay."

"Now, Marsh," Roeglin ordered, his eyes still sheeted in white, his voice tense.

"Yes...Marsh..." Henry gritted out, blocking another attack and slashing through another tentacle. "Now."

Marsh turned her eyes to the sky.

"Stand clear!" she commanded, and the ring of faces above her hastily disappeared. She hoped they'd moved far enough back and was happy to hear Tok's reassurance.

They are moving out of the ruin as we speak.

It was all she needed. As another half-dozen Ookens tried to force their way through a space designed for two humans at most, she raised her hand and spoke to the lightning dancing through the clouds.

"Please," she told it. "I need you."

"Get ready," Master Envermet ordered, but Marsh knew he wasn't speaking to her and kept her attention on the sky.

"Please," she begged, stretching a hand toward the portal. "Help me!"

She was vaguely aware of Tamlin, Sasha, Brigitte, and Aisha repeating her mantra. "Please help."

The clouds above glowed an impossible white, dazzling Marsh and making it hard to see anything. She was glad she was already pointing toward the portal as she lost sight of it. The light descended in a single column of coruscating silver, gold, and white.

"Stand clear!" Master Envermet roared.

"Protect us," she prayed, begging the lightning to understand. "Destroy our enemies. Destroy their path to our home."

Her skin tingled and then burned as the lightning descended.

"Break the gate between worlds," Marsh asked it. "Destroy those beyond. Leave no Ookens alive."

"Only the Ookens," was a plea from Sasha and Brigitte that told her Roeglin was wielding as much influence as he dared.

"Only the Ookens," she repeated in case the lightning didn't get the message.

"Stand by!" Master Envermet ordered, but Marsh was too busy calling the lightning to wonder why.

"Now, Brigitte," Roeglin directed, and the sizzling column of light deflected from the upraised hands of its summoners to pour through the gate.

"That's enough, Marsh!" Roeglin cried as Master Envermet roared again.

"Get them out! Now!"

"Than—" was all Marsh got out before a heavy body slammed into her, jolting the words from her mind and carrying her two steps down the tunnel where it was joined by another.

"Dan! Shadow-step!" Izmay shouted.

The lightning continued to pour down from the heavens until an unearthly roar filled the air and the ground shook around them.

"Thank you," Marsh whispered as Henri catapulted forward and tripped.

"Deeps, girl! You couldn't have picked someplace with a softer landing?" he bellowed, ignoring Marsh and tucking so he hit the cobbles shoulder-first and rolled onto his back, holding Marsh against his chest.

"Quit your bitching," Izmay managed, but her voice grated with pain.

Marsh gasped. Her link to the lightning was lost as the air was driven from her lungs. She lay still for several heartbeats until Henri groaned, then she hastily scrambled off him and onto her feet.

"Roeglin?" That panicked tone couldn't possibly be hers! "Tamlin?"

Her voice wavered and she blinked, trying to regain her sight and keep her balance.

"Aisha?"

She looked around, seeing several figures slowly picking themselves up off the ground. Overhead the storm was gone, although the clouds remained. Marsh glanced up at them, registering darkness and the first fat, wet drops of rain.

"Dan?" she called, pushing her hair out of her eyes.

She scanned the courtyard, her vision slowly clearing so she could identify who was there. Izmay and Henri were getting to their feet and checking each other for injury, and Tamlin was being engulfed in his father's hug. Over to one side, Sasha was being lifted and scolded by her mother.

Marsh also caught sight of Aisha. The little girl tried to sneak behind the nearest building, only to be brought back by Perdemor and Scruffknuckle, while Zeb and Jakob helped Brigitte to her feet and apologized profusely nearby.

Marsh's heart lifted but stayed tense when she failed to see Mordan.

"Dan?" she called just as the kat stalked out of the shadows, her ears flat to her skull. She glared at Marsh as she passed and headed for the gate.

"Dan?" Marsh asked, catching sight of Roeglin deep in conversation with Tok.

The pride leader remained.

"What?" Marsh staggered after her. "Where are the kits?"

With the pack leader, Mordan replied, picturing Adrienne. *Safe.*

Some of the pain around Marsh's heart eased.

The pride leader? She frowned, trying to work out who the kat might mean. She'd seen Roeglin, and he was in the courtyard. *Why are we going this way?*

The tunnel is blocked, but he remains.

Marsh's heart sank. *Who?*

The pride leader, the kat repeated, and this time she showed Master Envermet's face.

But why did he stay?

To keep the lightning from returning.

To stop the what? From where?

And to keep the rocks and fire back.

"The what?" Marsh didn't wait for the kat's reply. She ran toward the area Brin and Sylvie had opened to the sky.

As she feared, it had collapsed, and the hole was gone.

"Master Envermet!" she cried, wading to the center of the pit and trying to lift some of the rubble clear. "Master Envermet!"

The boulder wouldn't budge, but Marsh didn't let that deter her. She moved to another one, a smaller one. This one she could lift. She struggled to drag it to one side, vaguely aware of the others who'd followed her out the gate.

"Marsh!" Aisha's voice penetrated the distance between them. "Marsh!"

It was closer the second time.

Marsh almost dropped the boulder.

"Marsh!" Aisha cried again.

The child's persistence annoyed her, and Marsh looked up, getting ready to scold her. "What?"

Aisha was already picking her way into the hollow. "What are you doing?" she asked, coming toward her.

That simple question stopped Marsh in her tracks. She stared at the child, then lifted her gaze to where Roeglin, Henri, Tok, and the shadow guard stood at the edge of the depression.

"I..." she began, gesturing helplessly at the devastation around her. "We can't leave him!"

"Who?" Aisha asked, and Marsh hesitated, trying to work out how she was going to break the news to the child.

Too late, she tried to block the connection between them.

"Master Ennermet!" the girl shrieked and raced to the center of the dip, reaching for the largest boulder she could find.

Instead of trying to lift it, she scrambled onto it. "Find him!" she commanded, but her order wasn't directed at Marsh.

"No!" Marsh shouted, lunging for her, but the boulder stretched up to encase the child, then sank into the ground.

Marsh went to dive after it, only to be stopped short. She turned, fist raised, and Roeglin pulled her tight against his chest.

"He's okay," he whispered, deflecting the blow and trapping her arm against her side. "He's okay. Kalori..."

Marsh froze. "Kalori?"

"The druid who cleared the stone from Below. He stayed and called the stone to shield them."

"But Aisha?" Marsh pulled away, and Roeglin released her.

"Will be fine," Roeglin reassured her. "She's a rock mage, remember?"

"As well as a mind mage...and a...and a lightning mage?" Marsh gulped, staring at the dimple left by the subsiding boulder. "But she already called the lightning. She'll be exhausted."

"And Master Envermet will speak to her about that."

"He will? When?"

"Right after I do." Brigitte sounded beyond angry, but nowhere near as angry as Alain.

"After I have put her over my knee for scaring a lifetime out of me," he rumbled, coming to stand beside them.

"She's not even supposed to be here," Marsh protested. "I didn't ask her to come."

"Just like you didn't show Sasha how to call the lightning?" Alain challenged, indicating where Calantha stood with the little girl on one hip.

That got to her. Marsh turned to face the man, putting one hand on her hip and tapping him on the center of the chest with the other.

"And you. Were supposed. To keep. Her. At. Home!"

Alain shrugged helplessly. "You *know* what her sister's like."

"Not my responsibility," Marsh scolded. "If you can't keep your children on a tighter leash, they're going to be learning all kinds of things you don't want them to."

"How is that my fault?"

"You're her father! Where do you think they got it from? Thin air? A visiting trader? Why don't you have a word to Calantha about that?"

Calantha gasped, and Sasha glared at her. "Rude!"

The tone and word were an exact duplicate of her sister's, and Marsh figured they were *all* in more trouble than they knew. She was thinking of how to respond to that when another voice drew her attention back to the center of the pit.

"Marchant. Marie. Leclerc! *That* was uncalled for!" Master Envermet's stern tones of rebuke were never more welcome.

Marsh pivoted and saw him standing behind her, the rock mage and Aisha on either side. Throwing all protocol to the wind, she launched herself at the shadow captain and wrapped her arms around him.

"I thought we'd lost you. What were you thinking?" she demanded, drawing back to inspect his face.

Master Envermet winced. "That a shadow shield would be more than enough to stop debris from an explosion of that magnitude?" he suggested and gave her a wry smile. "It was *not* one of my better plans."

"Yuh think?" Marsh asked, letting him go.

Master Envermet gave her a deprecating smile and indicated the Grotto druid standing beside him. "If Kalori had not disobeyed my orders, I might have been more lost than I'd like."

Marsh turned to the druid. "Thank you."

Kalori managed a shaky smile.

"Do not thank *me*," he told her and indicated Aisha. "If the child had not come, we would have died inside the shell. Our air was running out."

"Regardless," Roeglin said, coming forward to shake Master Envermet's hand and pull him into a quick hug, "you have returned to us, and the portal is gone."

He frowned worriedly and looked at Kalori. "It *is* gone, is it not?"

The druid nodded. "Oh, yes, and it will not return. I watched it shatter as the energy rebounded."

"You… The energy rebounded?" Marsh asked.

Kalori nodded enthusiastically. "I've never seen the like."

"And I hope to never see it again," Master Envermet commented quietly.

He clapped the druid on the shoulder. "I think I owe you a drink."

Aisha reached up and took his hand, earning a downward glance.

"And I owe you a…" He frowned at a loss as to what to offer the child who had just saved his life.

"A story!" Aisha beamed, bouncing excitedly beside him. She let go of his hand and clapped excitedly. "A really *long* story."

Master Envermet groaned and rolled his eyes. "Very well," he agreed, offering her his hand. "A story, it is."

"A long story?"

"A *very* long story."

"After dinner," Alain interrupted. "We *all* need to eat first, and Tamlin is hungry."

"Tamlin is always hungry," Aisha grumbled, but she didn't argue.

Alain snorted. "Tamlin's not the only one."

Aisha shot him a dark look. "Is so, too."

27

AFTERMATH

They headed back toward the gates, their steps lighter than when they'd left despite the rain falling heavily around them. Marsh and Roeglin followed Master Envermet, Aisha, and Kalori, and Alain, Calantha, and the rest brought up the rear.

As they neared the gates, Marsh watched Perdemor stalk out of the darkness to shoulder his way under Aisha's free hand, Scruffknuckle bounding alongside and then around them. The pup's gamboling made a lie out of the fight they'd just had.

Marsh looked around for Mordan and was rewarded when the kat strolled over to walk at her side. She said nothing but rested a hand on Mordan's back, enjoying the touch of her fur. The kits joined them, although one dropped back to trot at Henri's side.

Marsh shook her head at the youngster's choice of company, but before she could comment on it, Roeglin slid an arm around her waist.

"Promise me we won't ever have to do that again?"

Marsh leaned into him. "I don't think I can, but I *will* promise that I'll do my best to *not* do it if there's another way."

"And now we have another demi-mage to train." He sounded almost resigned.

Marsh chuckled and slid an arm around his waist, leaning into his warmth. Moments later, she recoiled. "Ugh."

"What?"

"You..." She sniffed the air and corrected herself. "*We* stink."

They'd reached the steps leading into the mess hall, but at her words, everyone paused, then Master Envermet cocked an eyebrow and pushed open the door.

"They'll never let us in," Roeglin muttered, but his words were belied by a loud cheer.

Hurry up, Master Envermet ordered, *before the cooks notice and decide to kick us right back where we came from.*

None of them waited to be told twice. They hurried into the mess hall to the sound of more cheering and mild applause. Silence fell as Roeglin raised his hand. He found a chair and pulled it to the front of the room, climbing onto it to address them.

"We closed the pathway into the Below," he told them, and waited for the applause to die down, "and we brought our people back."

Again, he had to wait until the crowd settled.

"We also brought back more people." His jaw dropped as he said it as if he'd only just remembered the people he'd sent through the gate. He searched the room until he saw Tok standing by the door.

"Tok, those who shelter at your nest…"

The mantid's antennae twitched, and his middle legs scraped gently over his thorax.

They come, he informed them. *Please tell your people not to be afraid of those not like them.*

What he meant by "not like them," he broadcast, and nervous movements rippled through the room.

"There are *others?*" someone asked. "More like *them?*"

Tok shifted carefully, whistling softly and clacking his mandibles.

Not like my people. Similar, but different races…and there are humans, too. All have traveled far and seek refuge. Are you able to provide them sanctuary?

It was the right turn of phrase to use. Most of the settlers at the Library had been in need of sanctuary, and it didn't sit right that they should refuse others the same assistance. Faces turned toward Roeglin as the bell was rung at the gate.

Roeglin exchanged looks with Obasi, Tok, Alain, and Evan. They all nodded, and the hall rippled with anticipation and nerves. As Roeglin started toward the door, the bell's tolling ceased.

Etk'k and K'tch speak with them, Tok explained. *They have been granted access and will arrive shortly.*

"How many, and what do they eat? I will have the kitchens prepare more," one of the cooks called from the back of the room.

"Tok?" Roeglin asked, and waited as the mantid passed along the necessary information.

The cook's jaw dropped.

"Talia's gonna skin you all alive," he told them. "That sort of catering we need some *notice* for!"

Our people have brought sufficient additions for the meal, the mantid assured him. *We do not expect you to carry the burden alone.*

The man straightened. "Oh. That's different, then." He took a few steps toward the mantid, thought better of it, and raised a hand in a request. "Wait there. I need to speak to Talia and see what she needs."

Roeglin nodded to Tok and turned to the rest of the room. "Shall we go and greet our new neighbors?"

This was met with uncertain approval, but everyone rose from their seats and hurried outside. They all hurried back in again when they discovered how hard the rain was falling, but they brought the new arrivals in with them, directing food-bearers to the kitchens and making tentative small talk with the rest.

"This could have gone so much worse," Marsh murmured to Roeglin as she looked out over the dining hall. "If we had not met Tok and his people first…"

"And the wolves," Roeglin added.

"And the kats," Master Envermet added, having moved close enough to listen.

"And the raiders," Obasi chipped in, joining them.

They all sighed and watched as their new citizens were included by the old.

"You know it's not always going to be this smooth, don't you?" Marsh asked, and they all nodded.

Two large shadows fell over them, and Tok's mind voice was limited to just them. *We do, but for tonight, it is working.*

"And we cannot ask much more than that," Alain intoned.

"Yes, we can," Marsh argued. "We can make it known that this is to continue, or I will drop a bolt of lightning on the first troublemaker I lay eyes on."

The mantids shifted in alarm, and Alain and Evan exchanged worried glances.

"We'd rather you didn't," Alain told her, and Marsh gave him a feral grin.

"Then you'd better pass the word," she replied. Her expression softened as she looked at Tok. "Because this isn't over, is it?"

Again, the mantids shifted uneasily, and Tok indicated the smaller room where the leadership usually gathered for their meetings.

This is a thing better discussed in a more private space, he explained, and they sighed, saddened by the news that was to come.

We have only closed one portal, Tok told them when they had shut the door behind them. *The Ooken are capable of opening more.*

"Here?" Alain asked, his voice rising in alarm.

Tok flicked his antennae and rasped a negative. *No, not here. That portal will not be opened again, and its closure will buy us a little time since they will need to reacquire the coordinates.*

"What do you mean, 'reacquire?'" Roeglin asked.

Each portal has its own coordinates. If fortune smiles upon us, the Ookens will not have this gate's coordinates in easy reach. Even if they do, it will take them some time to find safe alternatives via extrapolation.

Marsh's heart sank. "You mean there are more?"

Etk'k cocked his antennae. *There are always more. They never cease.*

Marsh slumped in her seat, exchanging looks with Roeglin and Master Envermet. The mantids waited as if they knew the humans would need time to process their news.

Evan cleared his throat. "How, uh... How *many* more?"

The mantids conferred amongst themselves. *That was a raiding force,* Tok offered when they were done. *The next will be bigger.*

"Bigger?" Xavier didn't try to hide the alarm he felt.

Because you destroyed the portal and slaughtered so many. Their next force will come with the intent to invade. They will want to conquer and control rather than raid.

"But isn't that what they wanted anyway?" Marsh asked. "The thing that pursued me in my dreams. It was... It wanted our world, and it wanted to be the first."

First gives it precedence to resources, Tok explained. *Of course, it wanted to be first.*

"We could move the settlement," Alain offered. "Just not be here when they arrived."

Tok inclined his head at the suggestion. *That would prove a temporary solution. Given that you have destroyed their gate, they will search for you anyway. Moving will offer no advantage.*

Etk'k interrupted him with a soft whistle and some clicks and Tok flipped an antenna.

What Etk'k states is true, he acknowledged. *Remaining gives you the advantage of being in a position of familiarity with your land. Your winter is coming, and time and resources spent relocating could be better used preparing your defenses and making sure your people have escape routes.*

And in training, K'tch added. *You have abilities that will make warfare with you difficult.*

"But with the numbers they have, we cannot win," Alain said, his voice heavy with defeat. "We are not powerful enough to defeat them all. They will eventually win."

Tok started to laugh, his mandibles clattering as small wheezing chitters escaped him.

You will win, the mantid told them, absolute certainty in his voice. *You will win because this is Death's homeworld, and she will not abandon it. She will come, and you will be protected.*

"Don't you mean 'saved?'" Evan asked hopefully, and Tok's mirth stopped.

Saved is exactly what I mean, he said, *but you must prepare and be strong enough to carry the fight until she returns.*

"Will she take long?" Alain asked.

The mantids stilled.

We do not know how long she will take, but it will be before the Ookens have time to corrupt your world in the same way they corrupted ours.

Alain sat back in his chair and exhaled a long, slow breath. Roeglin and Master Envermet exchanged glances and sat in silence. Marsh stared at the ceiling, mulling over what they'd been told. The mantids waited.

How long they would have stayed that way, she didn't know, but one of the cooks knocked on the door. "It's been a full turn," he told them, referring to the hourglass they'd set in the kitchen.

When none of them argued, he pushed the door wider

and ushered three of his staff through. They carried laden trays.

"Even heroes have to eat," he informed them. "No matter how much they need to plan our future."

His words brought a smile to Marsh's lips.

"*We* have a future," she reminded them, "and help is already on the way." She stood, taking some of the meat and greens from the platters in the table's center.

Slowly, the others followed her example. Marsh watched them start to relax as they ate. She let them get halfway through their plates before she asked, "So, what's the plan for tomorrow?"

"Well, I know of three demi-mages who need serious training," Roeglin remarked, and the others chuckled.

"Just no lightning," Alain started, but Roeglin, Marsh, and Master Envermet laughed.

"I think that bird has flown, don't you?" Brigitte asked. She'd sat quietly through the mantids' news. Now she arched an eyebrow and looked at Marsh. "So, you and I are taking on this task?"

"Partly," Marsh replied, "but Tamlin has some training duties of his own. This ability he's developed to step from one point to another *without* using the shadows needs to be learned. They can't follow us into thin air."

That started the discussion in the direction of training schedules, supply needs, and when and how they were going to warn the other settlements.

"The Caverns must be informed," Marsh was adamant, "as must Briar's Ridge and Downslopes."

Sadness and worry rose as she thought of her family,

and Roeglin laid a hand on her knee. "We can return if you need to."

Marsh shook her head and smiled at him. "My home is here, and so are my responsibilities. All we can do is warn them and trust Monsieur Gravine and the Shadow Master and the Rock Mistress to organize the rest."

That drew murmurs of agreement from around the table, and they explored what they would need before they approached the other settlements with the news. It was late, and Alain and Evan had excused themselves to see to the housing of their new citizens before the others decided to meet again the following day.

Marsh and Roeglin made their way to the top of the walls, checking on the guards before settling in their customary spot above the gate. The rain had cleared, having spent itself in the aftermath of the battle in the earlier part of the evening.

Marsh sighed as Roeglin wound his arm around her waist, and she leaned into him. For the first time that day, they relaxed together, looking out over the Devastation.

"Do you think they'll come before spring?" he asked. They both knew he was wondering if they'd have enough time to prepare.

Marsh sighed, glad of his warmth and grateful to have him beside her. She slid her arm around him, happy they were together.

"Perhaps," she replied, "but this is our home, and these are our people. We'll face whatever the future brings. You never know; we might get lucky, and the next portal that opens might bring more friends. We can take whatever comes."

If Roeglin had doubts, he didn't voice them. Instead, he pulled her closer.

"Whatever comes," he murmured, his lips brushing her hair.

"Whatever comes," she agreed, staring over the ruins as the last light vanished from the sky. "Together."

"Oh, Deeps, yes," he said. "*Always* together."

The End

Origins is the first book in C.M. Simpson's Mack 'n' Me 'n' Odyssey series, and it's available now at Amazon.

I ran away from home to find a better life—not be forced into one.

You can call me picky, but a girl likes to be asked if she wants to work for you, not coerced—and Odyssey should know better. Now, I have to find a way to kick free—of Odyssey, and my trainer, Mack—without getting myself killed.

Surviving the mission is just the first step. Getting out from under, that's gonna take some doing.

Available now at Amazon.com

AUTHOR NOTES - CM SIMPSON

APRIL 10, 2020

It's always hard coming to the end of a book – and even harder, when a series says it's done. Thank you, for making this journey with me, and sharing the adventures of Marsh, Roeglin and their friends as they travel the Deeps below Paris, and the Devastation the city has become. I have enjoyed exploring the Age of Magic with all of you.

As I write this, the world outside is dealing with a pandemic that looks like it could last a few months longer, and I hope you are all okay. My family is scattered all over Australia, and I have friends all over the world, so I try to keep an eye on how things are for all of you. It's been a difficult few months.

I started the year grateful that the aircraft I took to return from Adelaide was able to land safely after a bird took out one of its engines on take-off, and happy to reach home only 12 hours later than planned.

I was even more grateful that the fires surrounding Australia's capital did not repeat the bushfire event of 2003, as well – and we are now breathing clean air, again.

I wasn't so grateful for the two weeks of flu we had in early January, though. We traveled to Adelaide as a family and all caught some dreaded lurgy while traveling, but it could have been worse. We're all well, now.

Today, as I write this, I'm looking out at grey skies and rain, with the occasional patch of blazing sunshine – and I couldn't be happier! The cockatoos, lorikeets and king parrots come and visit when I remember to put out seed, and I've discovered that both magpies and currawongs *love* sunflower seeds. Who knew, right?

It's quite the parade out there some days, and sometimes means the words get done a little more slowly. There's nothing like a screeching sulfur-crested cockatoo to pull you right out of a story!

And, speaking of stories... I'm going to have go and work out which project to write next. There are a few peeking over the edge of my folders, and I just can't decide...

I'm going to miss the Devastation...and writing about Aisha and Tamlin's antics, but there are so many more tales waiting to be written – and I hope to see you for some of them, which reminds me...I *still* have to ask Michael what he meant in his last set of notes.

What does *Paris* and the Devastation have to do with the "@#@%! Kurtherian" he keeps talking about?

And why do I get the feeling that there is mischief afoot...

Michael-*Anderle*-type mischief...

I'm also wondering how his menudo challenge is going...and that's something else I forgot to ask.

Hmmm... So, before I go do that, I just wanted to say 'Thank you,' again, for your company on this journey, and that I look forward to seeing you around as I embark on the next, and to let you know that you all make my world a better place to be.

AUTHOR NOTES - MICHAEL ANDERLE

APRIL 29, 2020

THANK YOU for reading our story!

We have a few of these planned, but we don't know if we should continue writing and publishing without your input.

Options include leaving a review, reaching out on Facebook to let us know, and smoke signals.

Frankly, smoke signals might get misconstrued as low hanging clouds, so you might want to nix that idea...

The End.

We really appreciate you continuing to read our stories in the Kurtherian Gambit Universe and here, in Paris. While I live in the United States and my collaborator lives in Australia, it is interesting that the city that is the focal point is basically in the middle of us.

A city where we already showed the Eiffel tower broken in two from a series started way back in 2016.

It just goes to show that Paris might be a bit messed up

in this post-apocalyptic future but not enough that it doesn't draw the imagination of authors along with it.

Thankfully, we put the Menudo Challenge on hold.

Colleen asked me about the menudo challenge in her author notes, and here is an update:

It's on hold.

You see, when Las Vegas shut down, and we had no idea how our company would do going forward, it was a bit unsettling. All sorts of questions move forward through one's brain, and I was getting stressed out.

It wasn't just the questions about making sure our people were safe, or what could we do at a time like this, but larger questions I hadn't asked myself.

Questions that included, what is my job during a pandemic? How do I help those that I can? What about the people here on the Las Vegas Strip, when the Strip is shutting down?

Some of these questions we made it through by answering as best we could, other questions I had to sit and really understand or ask a few people their thoughts about the situation that we found ourselves in.

So, coming back from a grocery run, I called my brother and asked him to put the challenge on hold.

He wasn't too pleased.

He called me back the next morning and explained his concerns. Darryl was (and I am both paraphrasing and it's been a couple of months) worried that we would take this opportunity to just skip off the diet, and our long term health would suffer. Having considered it further, he figured it would be ok, provided we both checked in our weight each week.

Give us a way to encourage each other and have a sense of obligation to keep ourselves healthy. At least that way, we wouldn't gain weight and continue a bad downhill slide in health as we get older.

I respected his justification, and while we don't have a menudo challenge anymore, I still plug my weight into an app one to three times a week.

I am more aware of what I eat and how it affects my weight than before we started, and that is a good thing.

Diary for April 26th- May 2, 2020

So, it's about six weeks into the stay-home phase, and there are mentions that states are going to slowly open up. A few words (well, a bunch) are slung all across the internet with opinions going both one way or the other.

Then I see a video about Anderson Cooper and the Las Vegas mayor. (Full disclosure, I live on the Strip and am not officially in the Las Vegas city limits but in Clark County. This is something I did not realize until this whole kerfuffle came about, and for some reason, I'm standing just a little bit straighter.)

Now, whether you knew this or not, I think it is interesting to note that the present mayor of Las Vegas is Carolyn Goodman (in office 2012 to 2022 (likely term limit)), the wife of the previous mayor Oscar Goodman (in office 1999-2011 term-limited).

Further, she has been very industrious in the Las Vegas area, working for multiple organizations and leadership roles with the tourism industry, child welfare, and education. So, regardless of the state of the discussion on opening Las Vegas back up and using the citizens in this area (me included) as a science experiment (I'm rather against this notion), I find myself shocked to find out she has a lot of qualifications.

Amazing, I know.

Everyone who knows me through these *Author Notes* realizes I am cynical when it comes to government. In fact, before I reviewed more about the present mayor, I figured there had to be some shenanigans going on for the mayorship to go from spouse to spouse.

However, it seems I should have been paying more attention to the life of Mayor Goodman the First. He has a book (by him as author) published by Hachette titled *Being Oscar: From Mob Lawyer to Mayor of Las Vegas.*

I happen to know that there is a steakhouse he owns downtown at the top of the Plaza Hotel named... Guess? *Guess?*.... Oscar's!

He is a brand now.

I have to go.

I might be cynical, but steak covers a lot of cynicism.

I did a good thing...I think.

So my best friend and fellow author Craig Martelle lives in Alaska...inside the North Pole designation, and it costs him an arm and a leg to get decent internet up there in the frozen north.

I happened to ask him how come he loves it up there, and without a beat, he mentioned: "don't have to live near any politicians."

That's hardcore.

So, I received a marketing email from Skyroam about little internet pucks and sent the email to him. I have used Skyroam in the past for internet connectivity while traveling, so I knew how it worked. Apparently, it was working well enough to let him drop a line and save a few hundred bucks a month.

Then, I started looking at shotgunning his internet connections. I'm going to call and see if I can get him on the phone...

Hold on.

.... TALKING ....

I'm back. The short answer is no, it isn't working.

The longer answer is Craig spent an hour and a half playing with his Windows laptop, his Skyroam, and a phone that needed iTunes(??) to make it work. It hasn't so far, and I'm kinda bummed.

He was using some software (of which I can't remember the name), but I think there is just one major reason he is having this trouble.

Windows...He is using *Windows*. (This is complete and utter @#%@@! As it probably has nothing to do with Windows... But, he's on a PC, I'm a Mac guy... We have to carry the ribbing farther, even if I have to do it locked up in my condo thousands of miles away from him. Since Editor Lynne will be checking these author notes, I would not be surprised if she mentions something in here (she's a Windows person as well.)

(*Editor's Note: I shall nobly restrain myself, MacMan*)

I did the Brownstone Fries...

Short update to the Brownstone Fries idea with Jessie Rae's.

So, I had to speak with Mike Ross (Jessie Rae's BBQ) to explain my Brownstone Fries effort to help support their effort to make free lunches for those in the medical field.

Then, I left a message at their answering machine for call-in orders, but I was too late in the evening to get them to answer.

Bummer.

By the next morning, when I got a return call from Mike's mom, she already knew all about the Brownstone Fries, and it didn't confuse her at all.

Damn.

I was looking forward to explaining the "I need you to charge me for fries, but it's really a gift to help pay for people at the hospitals..." schtick I talked about in my last *Author Notes*.

Oh well, the gift went through, regardless.

Ad Aeternitatem,

Michael Anderle

OTHER BOOKS FROM C.M. SIMPSON

The Magic Beneath Paris (with Michael Anderle)

#1 Trading into Shadow

#2 *Trading into Darkness*

#3 *Trading Close to Light*

#4 *Trading by Firelight*

#5 *Trading by Shroomlight*

#6 *Trading into Daylight*

#7 *Trading into Stormlight*

#8 *Trading to the Deeps*

Magic Below Paris Complete Series Boxed Set

Mack 'n' Me 'n' Odyssey

#1 *Mack 'n' Me: Origins*

#2 *Mack 'n' Me: Blaedergil's Host*

#3 *Mack 'n' Me: Arach*

#4 *Mack 'n' Me: The Transporter's Favor*

#5 *Mack 'n' Me: The Wolves of Alpha 9*

#6 *Mack 'n' Me: Diplomacy 101*

Mack 'n' Me: Odyssey Omnibus #1

Mack 'n' Me: Odyssey Omnibus #2

Mack 'n' Me: Odyssey Collection

C.M.'s Collections

#1 *365 Days of Flash Fiction*

#2 *365 Days of Poetry*

#3 *A Collection of Dragons*

#4 *366 Days of Flash Fiction*

#5 *366 Days of Poetry*

#6 *Another 365 Days of Poetry*

#7 *Pixie-Dust Dreaming*

#8 *Tales of Mack 'n' Me*

#9 *Tales of Odyssey and Miss Delight*

Lunar Wolves

#1 *Lunar Wolves: The Unwilling*

#2 *Lunar Wolves: The Unwanted*

#3 *Lunar Wolves: The Undiscovered*

The Ransomeers

#1 *A Planet's Ransom*

Chronicles of a Dark God

#1 *Dark God Emergent*

I also have work in the following publications:

The Expanding Universe: Volume 4

I also write fantasy, urban fantasy and short stories across the genres, all of which can be found on my Amazon author page.

CONNECT WITH THE AUTHORS

Colleen Simpson Social Media Sites

Amazon author page: https://www.amazon.com/C.M.-Simpson/e/B0086QFGFO

Blogspot: http://cmsimpson.blogspot.com.au/

Facebook: https://www.facebook.com/CMSimpsonWriter/

Pinterest: https://www.pinterest.com.au/cmsimpsonauthor/

Twitter: https://twitter.com/simpsoncolleen1

Youtube (Writing): https://www.youtube.com/channel/UCFUNN9PxeSu6DjNPFjoLRjQ

Youtube (Gaming): https://youtube.com/channel/UCjOK2SvOHoT_ru9rlnlVS-g

Linked In: https://au.linkedin.com/public-profile/in/c-m-simpson-8279344a

Patreon: https://patreon.com/cmsimpsonwritergamer

ReamStories: https://reamstories.com/cmsimpsonwriter

Connect with Michael Anderle

Website: http://lmbpn.com

Email List: http://lmbpn.com/email/

https://www.facebook.com/LMBPNPublishing

https://twitter.com/MichaelAnderle

https://www.instagram.com/lmbpn_publishing/

https://www.bookbub.com/authors/michael-anderle